THE FIRST ELIZABETH MacPHERSON NOVEL

"A delightful, spooky romp among the mad and wise of a Southern family."
Dorothy Salisbury Davis

"All mystery fans have a treasure in Sharyn McCrumb. If Evelyn Waugh had written mystery stories set in the American South, he might have produced *Sick of Shadows*."
Fred Chappell

"This witty mystery is a book to read twice—first for the story, then for a chuckle at McCrumb's dry, humorous style."
Lexington Herald-Leader

"Lively...Hilarious...Sharyn McCrumb offers up some zany characters, clever dialogue, and an ingratiating heroine....Lots of fun."
Alfred Hitchcock Magazine

Also by Sharyn McCrumb:

BIMBOS OF THE DEATH SUN
HIGHLAND LADDIE GONE**
LOVELY IN HER BONES*
PAYING THE PIPER*
THE WINDSOR KNOT*

*Published by Ballantine Books
**Forthcoming from Ballantine Books

SICK
OF
SHADOWS

Sharyn McCrumb

BALLANTINE BOOKS • NEW YORK

Library of Congress Catalog Card Number: 84-90802

ISBN 0-345-35653-5

This edition published by arrangement with Avon Books

Manufactured in the United States of America

First Ballantine Books Edition: July 1989
Third Printing: December 1990

For David and Nick with gratitude

"'I am half sick of shadows,'
said The Lady of Shalott."
—Alfred, Lord Tennyson

CHAPTER ONE

Dr. & Mrs. Robert Gray Chandler
request
the honour of your presence
at the marriage of their daughter
Eileen Amanda
to
Mr. Michael Satisky
on Saturday, the nineteenth of June
at one o'clock in the afternoon
at the home of the bride
Long Meadow Farm
Route One
Chandler Grove, Georgia

Dear Bill,

Thank you very much for the graduation present. It was the only I.O.U. I received and I shall treasure it always.

No, I haven't decided what I want to do yet. There isn't much you can do with a liberal arts major these days. Mother's bridge club keeps asking me when I'm going to get married, so they have a pretty firm grasp of the situation at least. It seems careless of me to have broken up with Austin in my senior year. Now I have to think up something to do! I have given myself until the end of the summer to decide.

How are things with you? Is Tax Law 307 still putting you to sleep? Your new roommate Milo sounds interesting. Do archeologists make much money? What does he look like?

You may have noticed the enclosed invitation to Cousin Eileen's wedding. I enclosed it partly at Mother's insistence and partly as proof of martyrdom.

They want me to be a bridesmaid. Well, I don't suppose "want" is exactly the right way to put it. I expect I'm a necessary evil: the poor cousin drafted in lieu of friends, because of course Eileen hasn't got friends—unless she made some at Cherry Hill; and Aunt Amanda would never let this affair degenerate into a reunion of mental patients. Though of course it will be anyway, with all those Chandlers present. I myself will probably have to be taken away after a week of their collective presence. I never saw why they had to send her away, did you? All Chandlers considered, they could have just cordoned off the place and sent in ten nurses. Did you know that Aunt Amanda still refers to Cherry Hill as a "finishing school"?

The real purpose of this letter is to appeal to your better nature (assuming you have one) to persuade you to accompany me to this blessed event. I do not want to suffer alone. In fact, I feel that since you are older than I, you should be the one sacrificed (firstborn son, and all that), but then I can see that you'd make a terrible bridesmaid.

I know already that you are either going to ignore this letter or write back some tripe about your law courses keeping you too busy to go. Well, I will give you forty-eight hours to answer, and then I'm writing Aunt Amanda that *we* will be delighted to come to dear Eileen's wedding.

Your atavistic sister,

Elizabeth

June 2

Dear Bill,

I was kidding about the forty-eight hours. You did not have to send a Mailgram. Anyway, since I am your sister, I am not likely to believe that you have to go to your grandmother's funeral.

Please thank Milo for the description of himself, but tell him I didn't find it very enlightening. I am not thrilled by the fact that he has a "cranial capacity of 1,350 cc, a foramen magnum facing directly down, and a pyramidal-shaped mastoid process." Does he still leave bones scattered on the kitchen table? You two deserve each other.

Mother is worried about your dietary habits. She wanted me to ask if you are eating anything green and leafy. (Dad looked up from the newspaper and said: "Money.")

By the way, I most certainly will *not* give your message to Eileen. I looked up *Hamlet,* Act III—Scene I, lines 63-64: "'Tis a consummation devoutly to be wished." Most unfunny. Aunt Amanda still hasn't forgiven you for referring to Eileen's release from Cherry Hill as her "coming-out party."

I am going alone to the wedding—hereafter to be referred to as The Ordeal. Mother was willing to go, but Dad said he'd rather be staked out on an anthill. So I'm going by bus. If *you* had gone, we could have driven down.

I hope your law books fall on you.

Elizabeth

Dear Aunt Amanda,

We are delighted to hear about Eileen's wedding. Thank you for inviting me to be a bridesmaid. I'll be happy to accept, but I'm afraid I'm the only MacPherson who can come.

Dad and Mother had already arranged to go to a sales convention in Columbia, and Bill is simply prostrate with grief that he can't make it, but he has tests that week in law school.

I'll be arriving on Wednesday afternoon about two-thirty at the bus station in Chandler Grove.

Looking forward to seeing you all again,

Elizabeth

P.S. I think you will have to alter that bridesmaid's dress. I did not, as you predicted, grow up to be a size sixteen.

THE CHANDLER GROVE bus station was a dingy yellow waiting room whose openings and closings were probably dictated by *TV Guide*. Flies hovered lazily about the torn screen door, some drifting over to the faded drink machine, whose dents testified to its dubious honesty. Near the counter was a rack of travel pamphlets that Elizabeth might well have to read if someone did not turn up soon to claim her. She picked up the least dusty brochure (Florida, of course) and sat down in the plastic chair to wait.

She decided that she would be disappointed if the first circle of hell were not a bus station waiting room where you waited forever for people you didn't like who weren't going to come for you anyway.

Her blue suitcase rested within inches of her foot, in case the crazed felon Aunt Amanda always swore inhabited bus stations should dash through the room and snatch it on the run. If he did, she hoped the dress would fit him—and if he would consent to take her place at The Ordeal, he was welcome to it.

She glanced at the suitcase, imagining the permanent wrinkles it was grinding in the yellow bridesmaid's dress. Yellow. Aunt Amanda had either remembered or surmised that Elizabeth looked ghastly in yellow. No, more likely she hadn't given it a thought. The Chandlers would scarcely consider the country cousin in their choice of wedding colors for dear Eileen.

So here I am, thought Elizabeth, the sacrificial lamb of the MacPherson Clan, shunted down to Chandler Grove and decked out in malarial yellow to see Eileen married off to What's-His-Name.

At least it would be a distraction. Anything would be better than the postpartum depression of having received a degree in sociology and no job prospects. Her father wanted her to go to graduate school, but she couldn't face that decision just yet. It felt too much like postponing life. She stared at the rack of travel brochures—there was always the Peace Corps. Reconciling with Austin out of sheer panic suddenly seemed dangerously easy.

After all, Austin was well on his way to becoming an architect. He would soon be so well established that Elizabeth could postpone life-determining decisions indefinitely. Though, of course, marrying Austin would have been a life-determining decision. It would lock her forever into the world of tailgate picnics and country club dances. "You just know there's always an alligator somewhere on his person," Bill had said. But she had been able to overlook his conventionality; much is forgiven of tanned, wiry blonds.

Her disenchantment had been gradual. She began to see the birthday and Christmas gifts of Bermuda bags and add-a-beads as a tacit reproach of her own taste. The feeling culminated on a golden April afternoon as they strolled along the path by the campus duck pond. Austin had gazed tenderly into her eyes and said: "If you lose ten pounds, I'll marry you." Elizabeth pushed him into the pond and walked off without a backward glance.

"I come from haunts of coot and hern," said a solemn voice behind her.

Elizabeth turned around to see what was obviously a Chandler. He was in his early twenties, and he had the look of a faun in country tweeds.

"You must be Geoffrey," she said, after a moment's study.

"I know. I must. I once thought of being Caligula, but when Alban came back from Europe as Ludwig of Bavaria I gave it up."

"Alban? Aunt Louisa's son? I haven't heard of him since she sent him off to William and Mary to become a 'suthen' gentleman."

"My dear, you are quite out of it," Geoffrey assured her. "After he graduated—KA with a B.A.—Aunt Louisa took him on the grand tour. The castles and churches of Ye Olde Worlde. Unfortunately, they visited Ba-

15

varia, and Alban became smitten with that fairy-tale thing that looks like the Disneyland castle. Built by King Ludwig, who was crazy."

"And?"

"You'll know soon." He sighed theatrically. "Far too soon. Is this blue suitcase yours? Shall I carry it for you and further impress you with my good breeding?"

Elizabeth stood up. "I'm so glad to be rescued, I don't care who carries it."

Geoffrey raised one expressive eyebrow. "The prospect of going to Long Meadow strikes you as a rescue?"

There didn't seem to be an answer to this one. After all, Geoffrey was Aunt Amanda's son, so it wouldn't do to tell him the truth—but he seemed to have no illusions about the place. They walked out to the car. Elizabeth decided to change the subject.

"We've been so out of touch for the past couple of years that I'm afraid I don't know what you've been up to," she said brightly.

"People are always afraid they don't know what I've been up to," Geoffrey replied.

"I mean, are you in school?"

"Hardly. I do have a degree. I hear you've just acquired one from the family alma mater."

"Yes. I majored in sociology."

"Of course you did. Are you about to ask me what I do?"

"I guess I was."

"Well...one has one's hobbies—the theater and so forth. But my main function is that of critic."

"Of drama?"

"Of life."

They had passed through Chandler Grove's downtown, a dozen shabby storefronts, several minutes before, and were now speeding along the county blacktop, which curled through rolling hills, dividing Hereford pastures from Holstein. He doesn't know what he's going to do either, Elizabeth thought. But the Chandlers have so much money it doesn't matter. I, on the other hand, will need either a job or a husband by the end of the summer. The only other alternative is to go to graduate school, which will postpone the whole issue for another couple of years.

"Of course, Captain Grandfather keeps insisting that I join the navy. He says it would make a new man of me. 'Not unless you believe in reincarnation,' I told him."

Elizabeth laughed, filing the military away for further consideration.

"You're not by any chance an actress, are you?" asked Geoffrey.

"Me? No. I'm too self-conscious. But Bill played in the Shakespeare Festival on campus last year. Why?"

"We have quite a decent little theater group in Chandler Grove. Our director actually had a bit of Broadway experience ages ago, but he's retired now, and only does this to keep busy. We did *Camelot* last winter, and I was Mordred. I just thought you might be interested."

"What are you doing this summer?"

"Sinclair has got it into his head that we must do a classic, though I assure you it will be wasted on the audience in Chandler Grove, who think that Madame Bovary is a type of dairy cow."

"Are you doing Shakespeare?"

"No. Even more obscure. *The Duchess of Malfi.* I am to play Ferdinand. It's very handy, really. Our *Camelot* costumes can be reworked and used again this time. I am beginning to feel quite at home in a sweeping black cloak."

"I'd love to see your production," said Elizabeth politely. "When will it be?"

"Well, we're not sure. It was going to be in three weeks, but we'll have to postpone it. With all the uproar at home, I haven't been able to learn all my lines. We've had to cancel a few rehearsals, and Mother has commandeered the only local seamstress, so instead of altering costumes, she is turning out unspeakable yellow dresses!" He shuddered.

"I guess things must be pretty hectic with the ceremony so near..."

"Well, they are for Mother, of course," Geoffrey replied. "She's ringmaster of this show. Father confines himself to his study and pretends to be writing his book on colonial medicine; Captain Grandfather affects a masculine disdain for women's matters; and Eileen is mooning about like a *Vogue* Ophelia, working on a painting. I myself am bearing up remarkably well."

"And Charles? Did he come home for the wedding?"

"Yes, dear brother Charles is on exhibit. Fresh from his commune. You know, I used to think that a commune was sort of a twentieth-century version of a monastery, but if Charles is any example, I think it must be a twentieth century version of a leper colony."

"Well, he's always been a changeling, hasn't he?" asked Elizabeth.

"Always," Geoffrey agreed. "When we played Civil War as kids, he always wanted to be Harriet Tubman."

"I know," said Elizabeth. "Bill always says that Charles is either going to be famous or notorious before he's thirty."

"Sorry Bill couldn't come. He would have made a nice change."

"Oh, I know, but he had these tests in law school . . ."

"Spare me," said Geoffrey. "I am not a cretin. I have made enough excuses to know one when I hear it."

"How is Eileen?" Elizabeth blurted out. She had wanted to change the subject, but the subject of Eileen didn't seem safe either.

"Eileen is vague," Geoffrey said thoughtfully. "She moons about, and doesn't say anything significant. She's lucid, of course, but you can have a conversation with her and come away not knowing anything about what she thinks or feels."

Elizabeth considered this. "You know, there's somebody you haven't mentioned."

"Captain Grandfather? I told you—"

"The groom," said Elizabeth.

"Oh."

"Well? Don't you like him?"

Geoffrey was quiet for a few moments. To keep from staring at him, Elizabeth turned to look out her window at the sweep of pine forest and pasture. Wild mustard flashed yellow against the red clay ditches, and dark wooded hills framed the sky.

Finally Geoffrey broke the silence. "What do you want to know? Whether he'll fit in? Doubtful. He doesn't have our particular brand of insanity."

"Could you manage a description?" prompted Elizabeth.

"He is the sort of liberal who affects an Afro. He has a New Jersey accent, and he is a graduate student in English literature—specializing in quotation without analyzation, I think."

"That sounds just like you," Elizabeth said. "You don't dislike him because of Eileen. You dislike him for some obscure literary reason. But does he really care about her?"

"It's hard to tell. Everybody that Eileen ever brought home proposed—we always assumed it was the house. We'd find them wandering down corridors counting the bathrooms."

"I guess you're not looking forward to the ceremony."

" 'Such weddings may more properly be said to be executed than celebrated,' " Geoffrey intoned.

"Is that from your play?"

"Yes. I revel in Ferdinand. He is most apt at times."

The car rounded the last bend in the road.

"Oh, well," sighed Elizabeth, "I'm sure everything will— Good Lord! What is *that?*"

"I knew I should have warned you," said Geoffrey sadly.

CHAPTER TWO

THE CHANDLER MANSION was a blunt-faced structure of Georgian brick, at least a century old, and looking rather like an architect's rendering of a Hereford
bull. It had served both as residence and business establishment for the original owners. While it did not
predate the Civil War, it was considered a showpiece
in the county, and when the Chandler Grove weekly
newspaper published its Christmas issue it always asked
Amanda for recipes to print as examples of the gentry's
holiday food. Amanda always complied, dutifully copy-
ing out a few cake recipes from back issues of *Ladies
Home Journal*. She never tried them herself, but the
paper seemed satisfied.

The house had been built by Amanda's great-grandfather, Jasper Chandler, shortly after the Civil War.
He had financed it with the profits of a lumber mill,
which he had founded, and which was later sold by
Jasper's grandson William Chandler, who had decided
to make a career of the sea. He kept the house, however,

leaving his wife and three small daughters there while he sailed various oceans.

Years after the death of his vague but patient wife, William retired inland to his country home, which was now the residence of his middle daughter Amanda and her husband, Robert Chandler, a scholarly country doctor who was also her second cousin. William's retirement from the navy had been physical, not mental, and his habit of wearing a uniform at all times and running the house like a destroyer quickly earned him the title of "Captain Grandfather" from Amanda's three offspring: Charles, Geoffrey, and Eileen. His daughter Margaret's children, Bill and Elizabeth, also called him that, but Alban, the son of his oldest girl, Louisa, called him "The Governor"—the result, no doubt, of the prep school education Louisa had insisted on giving him.

Except for the addition of bathrooms and other modern conveniences, the house looked much the same as it had when it was built. Amanda's obsession with antiques kept the furniture in the nineteenth-century mode; in fact, much of it was the original furniture. The grandfather clock by the staircase had been brought from England by sailing ship, and the Persian rugs, Benares brass, and Chinese figurines testified to Captain Grandfather's career as a sailor.

Scattered about the house were geometric paintings in a very modern style, representative of Eileen's efforts as a painter rather than a reflection of the inhabitants' taste in art. The paintings might have been more prized by psychologists than by art critics. Indeed, more than one of the consultants in Eileen's case had passed many silent minutes studying the indistinct purple forms that swam in gray backgrounds.

The paintings had all been done before Eileen was sent away to Cherry Hill for treatment. Since her return ten months earlier, she had not resumed her work—not until the painting she was presently working on, a wedding gift for Michael, which she would allow no one to see.

Various other touches of individual personality were visible in the house: a rat's nest study, which was Dr.

Robert Chandler's domain; a chemistry lab in the attic, outfitted for Charles, on the condition that he not blow them all to kingdom come; and a studio for Eileen in the glassed-in porch.

The most formidable example of family eccentricity was not in the Chandler house at all—but it was visible from any of the front windows.

June 9

Dear Bill,

I'm here—by way of the Chandler Grove Bus Station, though I'm sure there's a more direct route—through the looking-glass, perhaps. It's worse than we thought.

Geoffrey picked me up at the bus station. I think he has been possessed by Noël Coward, but even that didn't prepare me for what was to come.

There I was on the drive back to Long Meadow, making polite conversation and mentally casting the Marx Brothers in a movie version of this fiasco (Harpo would play Eileen), when we rounded the last bend and I saw what I hoped was a hallucination (I've been expecting them), but what turned out to be a monument to the rampant insanity in our family. There across the road from the Chandlers' sedate Georgian brick mansion is the Disneyland castle, complete with little spires and turrets and a sentry box.

"An architectural right-to-life group!" flashed through my mind, immediately to be replaced by the real explanation: Alban.

I'm sure you haven't succeeded in repressing the memory of Alban completely. He's years older than we are, of course, so we rarely had anything to do with him; I always thought of him as the target for Aunt Louisa's monomania: "Is Alban anemic? Is Alban adjusting well?" You remember.

23

Well, he has inherited Uncle Walter's business now—and fortunately the people who run it—so he is at large. He came across this castle when he went to Europe with Aunt Louisa, and has duplicated it in the pony meadow. Aunt Louisa is living in the castle, too. (Nobody is quite sure what to call it. Geoffrey calls it Albania.)

I haven't seen either of them yet. As we swung into the driveway, I asked if Alban might be in the tower observing us (with crossbow?). "He's not home," said Geoffrey. "The flag isn't flying."

Other than that, everything is pretty much the same. The backyard stable now houses a Ferrari instead of a barrel-shaped pony, but the orchard and the lake and the mansion are all the same.

So is Aunt Amanda.

When we went in, she was sitting in the back parlor, surrounded by a pile of envelopes, murmuring, "Dessert fork, tray, towels..." She reduced me to servitude at once. "Elizabeth! I'm so glad you're here. There is so much work to be done about the invitations and the gifts and whatall. And of course we can't bother Eileen with all this. She's painting."

I am writing this letter in between addressing invitations. I haven't seen anybody yet, so I can't give a full account of the horrors. I want to slip this out with this afternoon's batch of invitations. I'll write you again soon, because I want to subject you to as much vicarious misery as possible. Tell Milo hello for me.

Chanderella,

Elizabeth

Charles Chandler sat curled up in the middle of his bed with an open chemistry book and an assortment of colored sticks and jackrocks, which he was carefully fitting together. He resembled his brother Geoffrey— as Geoffrey might have been drawn by El Greco: ascetic, emaciated, and rather scraggly. He was totally absorbed in his project, oblivious to the blare from the stereo.

Geoffrey appeared in the doorway.

"Elizabeth's here," he said to the figure in lotus position on the bed. "I would have brought her up, but Mother snared her with wedding work."

Charles nodded, or perhaps undulated to the music; it was hard to tell.

"Anyway, you'll see her at dinner," Geoffrey continued. "We are having swine flesh, as you so colorfully put it, and Mildred seems to be fixing some sort of fodder for you."

"Soybean casserole," said Charles. "Much better for your body."

"On the contrary, cows eat it constantly, and they only live to be twenty-three. On that scale, you may not last out the month."

"Do you want to know what I'm making?" asked Charles, indicating the sticks and jackrocks.

"It looks like a reindeer," snapped Geoffrey. "What I *would* like to know is why you are playing the *1812 Overture* at 45 rpm."

"It helps me to visualize covalent bonding," Charles answered, screwing another white stick into a jackrock. "I am building a molecular structure."

"Fine, as long as you don't put it up across the street!" He scowled in the direction of the window. "Bill didn't come, by the way."

"No? That's unfortunate. I would have liked to discuss my proton theory with him."

"Why don't you discuss it with Satisky?" asked Geoffrey. "You might bore him to death and put an end to this circus."

"What circus? Oh, the wedding! Now *there's* covalent bonding for you. Eileen gets the trust fund when she's married, doesn't she? Do you suppose Michael knows he's marrying an heiress?"

"I doubt if he forgets it for a second," said Geoffrey grimly.

"I'm sure it will work out," murmured Charles, running his finger along the page of the chemistry book.

"Don't be too sure," said Geoffrey softly.

Michael Satisky had sought temporary refuge in the downstairs library, where he sat in blessed solitude in a leather armchair, with a copy of *Sonnets from the Portuguese* hidden behind *Appraising Antiques*. The hearth rug, he decided, was definitely a Bohkara, but the mantlepiece vases might be reproductions. He hadn't risked lifting one to see if there were any inscriptions on the bottom.

Eileen was down by the lake painting, and fortunately she refused to let him come with her, or to see the painting. It was probably to be a wedding gift to himself, he reflected, wondering if there were any tactful way to express a fondness for German handicrafts: Leicas, Mercedes, Porsches... Probably not, he decided, turning a page of Browning. He had promised Eileen an Italian sonnet as a wedding gift, but composing one wasn't as easy as he had expected. He wished he could settle for free verse, since that was his usual style, and he could produce a specimen in a matter of minutes, but somehow he felt that the formality of the occasion required more structured poetry. He wondered if she were thoroughly familiar with Browning... Well, maybe a line—to start himself off...

What was that bit about "a creature loved by you might forget to weep"? How close to true that was, he mused. The frail, waiflike Eileen had almost vanished in a flurry of bridal veils and documents.

He had seen her for the first time at a Milton seminar on campus. She was a small, drab creature who sat alone and listened to the discussion with an expression that suggested she hadn't heard a word of it. So he had befriended her, and offered to slay dragons for her— only to learn that she had enough money to buy a battalion of dragon-slaying mercenaries if she chose.

After a semester of free campus movies and long walks around the duck pond and the arboretum, Eileen had shyly suggested that he come home with her. He had pictured a widowed mother and a mortgaged farm; and now—this! Windsor Castle with ten bathrooms, and a family consisting of Clytemnestra, Walter Mitty, Victor Frankenstein, and Oscar Wilde. He shuddered at his own analogy. He was even beginning to sound like them.

He told himself that he couldn't call off the wedding, because the shock might be too great for her reason, but he caught himself visualizing a honeymoon in Nassau, studies at Oxford, not having to work to support his writing habit...Eileen's money.

"If thou must love me, let it be for naught except love's sake only," he wrote carefully.

Eileen Chandler frowned thoughtfully at the paint-splattered canvas in front of her. The shadowy part of the lake needed more gray, and the trees looked wrong somehow.

Perhaps she should have tried painting Alban's castle, since he had been so insistent that she do its "portrait." "Don't forget the mice and pumpkins!" Geoffrey had quipped, so she decided to do the lake instead. After all, this was going to be a wedding gift for Michael. She hoped he liked landscapes; perhaps she should put a sailboat there in the middle of the lake.

No, better not. She was sure to get something wrong, like a rope out of place, and then Captain Grandfather would go on forever. Once she had painted him a picture of the Titanic, using a book illustration for accuracy, and even then something went wrong. He kept insisting that smoke couldn't come out of all four smokestacks, because one of them was a fake, and even when she had showed him the book, he had waved it away.

Michael wouldn't be so critical, of course. He almost never made her head hurt. She felt very safe with him, and very protected, as though she could finally be "real," somehow. It wasn't that her family didn't understand her. That was just it—they did. Once when she had gone trembling to Charles to tell him she saw demons' faces in her window, he had wanted to know if any of them had purple eyes, because if so, he'd seen it once

27

while he was tripping on yellow sunshine. It was all right if you saw demons when you were stoned, but she saw them anyway. Finally the family had realized how trapped she was and let her go away to get better.

But they didn't seem to mind, really, whether she improved or not. In fact, they hardly noticed any change. Michael would mind, though. He wouldn't want her to hear voices or hurt herself. For him, she must be the fairy-tale princess and live happily ever after.

Suddenly her eye caught a detail of the lake that she hadn't noticed before. With a brief smile, she dipped her brush into a smear of paint and began to shape it into the painting.

While she worked, a corner of her mind wondered if it were really there.

CHAPTER THREE

"How ARE YOU coming with the invitations, Elizabeth?" asked Amanda, setting aside a silver ashtray on the pile of gifts.

"I'm down to the Ss already. Carlsen Shepherd."

"Yes. Dr. Shepherd. Be sure to put 'Doctor' on the invitation. He's Eileen's analyst, and he's coming down before the wedding for a visit."

"Oh," said Elizabeth. "What's he like?"

"We haven't met him," Amanda replied. "I believe he's connected with the university. Eileen consulted him entirely on her own, so naturally we're anxious to meet him. I can't help feeling that his connection with us is just temporary. Eileen's own physician, Nancy Kimble, is spending a year in Vienna. I do wish she could have come for the wedding, but she sent Eileen some lovely linen napkins."

"Kimble..." murmured Elizabeth, looking over the list of addresses. "Aunt Amanda, Dr. Kimble isn't listed here. Did you mean to send her an invitation?"

"Oh, we did, dear. Several weeks ago. Your family

should have gotten one about the same time. I sent out the invitations that mattered first. These are just after-thoughts—Eileen's school friends and some people Michael wanted to ask."

"How many people are you expecting?" asked Elizabeth, deciding to let Amanda's last remark pass without comment.

"Oh, less than a hundred, I think," her aunt replied. "Most of our friends from the country club will be there, of course, but I really don't think anyone from out of town will drive all the way down here. Such a pity that Bill couldn't come."

"I think so, too," said Elizabeth evenly.

"I suppose your father's sales convention couldn't be helped. Although I do think Margaret might have let him go alone just this once. But we'll manage, won't we? And, of course, Louisa will be a great help. I am depending on her to see to the flowers. She is simply the life and soul of the garden club. Have you seen her roses?"

Elizabeth shook her head.

"Well, she's bringing some over tonight to use as a centerpiece at dinner. Louisa and Alban are coming for dinner, by the way. We'll stop in a few minutes so you can go upstairs and change. I need to freshen up myself. Oh, and you'll get to see the lovebirds together. Now, you don't need to hurry for dinner, Elizabeth. Take your time and unpack, because I've asked Mildred not to have it ready before dark. We want Eileen to be able to work on her painting as long as it's light."

"What is she painting?" asked Elizabeth, glancing at a gray and purple canvas on the wall.

"We don't know. She won't let a one of us see it. It's going to be a wedding present for Michael. But I know she sets up her easel down by the lake, so I wouldn't be surprised if it's a landscape."

I would, thought Elizabeth, but she only smiled.

"There seems to be quite an artistic vein in our family," Amanda continued. "What with my interest in interior decorating, Eileen's art, and—"

"Alban's castle," said Elizabeth promptly.

"Er—yes. Alban's new home. Of course, I do think that there were some aspects of the Victorian period which were a bit extreme..."

"Victorian?" said Elizabeth. "It looks medieval to me."

Amanda favored her with a pitying smile. "Oh no, dear. It's a replica of Neuschwanstein in Bavaria, which dates from 1869. It's not quite identical, by the way. Alban didn't copy the interior, I'm happy to say. Have you seen it? All gold leaf and dramatic murals. And, of course, Alban's is smaller, though it's still far too large for just the two of them, as I have told him many times."

"I wonder he doesn't get lost in it," Elizabeth said.

"It would be different if he had a family. Such a shame about Merrileigh. I don't believe he's over it yet."

"Who's Merrileigh?"

"Merrileigh Williams. Didn't you ever hear about it? Well, it was at least six years ago, so perhaps you were too young. She was a secretary in your Uncle Walter's company. You know, he insisted that Alban work there when he first got out of the university. And while he was there, he met this Merrileigh, and decided to marry her. I thought at the time she was out to marry the boss's son. For the money, you know."

"Why didn't she?" asked Elizabeth. "The castle?"

"Oh, no. It wasn't built back then. We're not really sure. Alban doesn't discuss it, and of course we're all too well bred to ask. I hope you won't mention it, Elizabeth."

Before Elizabeth could come up with a suitable reply, her aunt continued: "The wedding was all arranged. Louisa and I had to do the planning and arranging, by the way, because the girl didn't have any close family. Still, I suppose it was good practice for me; but at the time I could have cried to think of all that work we did. And every bit of it for nothing."

"I hadn't heard that Alban was married," said Elizabeth. She would have eloped, too, she thought, before the onslaught of Amanda's social planning.

"Because he isn't," said Amanda. "Three days before the wedding that wretched girl jilted him. Not a one of

31

us liked her, but we didn't think she could be as common as *that*."

"Did they have a fight?"

"Nobody knows. I don't think so. Alban seemed just as puzzled as the rest of us. She was just gone. Alban went to her apartment and found that she had taken one suitcase of clothes and vanished. Not even a note of apology. And, of course, we had no idea of her background—though we feared the worst—so we couldn't trace her. Poor dear Louisa just could not be made to believe that any girl would refuse her precious Alban. She went to the sheriff about it."

"Did they find her?"

"They did not. But they turned up some rumors about a truck driver she had been running around with—which is no more than I expected all along. Louisa even wanted to hire a detective—for a reconciliation or a lawsuit, I don't know which—and that scandalized all of us completely. Alban was too proud to let her, of course. He said people ought to know what they don't want. I think he was well out of that trap, though. Heaven knows where she went. Some hippie commune, I expect."

"Maybe Charles will find her, then," said Elizabeth cheerfully.

After an ominous pause, Amanda said: "Charles and his associates are not hippies. They are simply individualists who feel close ties with nature, and who wish to live an uncluttered, philosophical life, much in the manner of Henry David Thoreau."

Elizabeth was about to ask how this differed from hippie philosophy when Amanda continued: "Charles has always been so spiritual. Eileen is an artist, and Charles is a thinker!"

"And what is Geoffrey? Has anybody figured that out?" asked a voice from the doorway.

"Captain Grandfather!" cried Elizabeth, running to embrace the old man.

"Hello, Elizabeth. Welcome aboard. I see you've already been drafted," he said, nodding toward the pile of invitations.

"You're about to get a commission yourself," Amanda replied. "We need somebody to mail these invitations. Remember to ask for commemorative stamps. They look nice. And while you're in town, you might see if Eileen's engraved stationery is ready. Let's see...is there anything else?"

"Have you talked to that lawyer yet?"

"He'll be here tomorrow. I thought I might ask him to lunch. You will be interested in meeting him, Elizabeth. He is not married. I don't know how long the business will take, though..."

"Depends on if he charges by the hour," snapped Captain Grandfather. "Who's coming to handle it? Bryce or that young fella?"

"Mr. Bryce's partner, Mr. Simmons, is coming. I believe Al Bryce has to be in court."

"Court indeed. Tennis court, maybe," her father retorted. "Don't blame him, wouldn't bother with paper-signing myself, if I had a partner fresh out of law school. Silly business, anyway. Silly will. Just what I'd have expected from my sister. She had a lot of nerve naming me executor, I can tell you that!"

"Well, Dad, you might look in and remind Mr. Simmons about tomorrow, though I'm sure he hasn't forgotten. Dinner's not until eight tonight, by the way, so you'll have plenty of time. Oh, and Alban and Louisa are coming."

Captain Grandfather grunted a reply, and turned to Elizabeth. "Seen the castle?"

"Only the outside," said Elizabeth. "Are there tours?"

"Ought to be!" he snapped. "Well, I'm off. Where are those letters I'm supposed to mail?"

Elizabeth handed him the invitations.

"Thank you, my dear. I'd ask you to ride along, but I'm sure you've had enough riding for one day. I'll see you at dinner."

"Aye, aye, sir," teased Elizabeth, and he tossed her a mock salute as he left.

"Really," sighed Amanda. "He's almost as bad as Alban. I declare, he'd build a battleship if the lake were

33

any bigger. Don't encourage him. You know how old people can be."

"Oh, I think he's the same as ever," said Elizabeth. "He's always been enthusiastic about ships, but I don't think he's out of touch with reality."

"No, of course not!" Amanda agreed. "Just tiresome. We have ships for breakfast, lunch, and dinner in this house. He's trying to work up a project for using sailing vessels for coast guard patrols, or something like that. I'm afraid he'll just bore everybody to death at the wedding. Dad is a very brilliant man, but geniuses tend to forget that the rest of us don't want to hear about their projects at every waking moment. Oh, Elizabeth! Before you go upstairs, let me just show you our display of wedding presents. We've fixed up a table in the library to display them. Some of them are just lovely."

Elizabeth had been given the guest room next to Eileen's bedroom. Its decor of rose and pink marked it as the one reserved for female guests. The dainty satin bedspread and matching canopy and the carved walnut furniture reflected Amanda's view of country elegance.

Elizabeth had put her clothes in the chest of drawers and stashed her suitcase in the closet. The bridesmaid dress would probably need pressing before the rehearsal. Looking at herself in the dresser mirror, she wondered what one wore to have dinner with the king of the castle. Royal blue, she thought, smiling. In the end, she settled for a green print dress and Mexican sandals.

If he comes as a Prussian general, he'll just have to lump it, she thought.

She had hoped to talk again with Geoffrey, to find out what to expect of this dinner, but he hadn't reappeared. Amanda, too, had vanished about five o'clock, saying that she spent the hours before dinner resting.

Elizabeth occasionally tried to picture a Napoleonic Alban, but the image wouldn't come. She couldn't even remember what he looked like. Alban was ten years older than Bill, which made him twelve years her senior, and there certainly hadn't been anything outstanding about him that she could recall from her childhood visits to Chandler Grove. The pony she remembered with perfect clarity, but Alban's face was a vague blur with rather short brown hair and brown or hazel eyes. He had been much too preoccupied with his own concerns to pay any attention to Elizabeth or his other cousins. Then when she was eleven and Bill thirteen, their father had been transferred to a company office six states away, and the visits stopped altogether. Her mother's family became voices calling long distance or gloves and bath powder at Christmas time. She doubted if she would even have been asked to participate in the wedding, except for the fact that Eileen had no close friends—at least, none that her mother was prepared to see in a formal wedding ceremony.

Amanda's seasonal letters to her sister's family had been voluminous on the subjects of tomato plants and carpeting. She lavished great detail on her own occasional indispositions—her every headache was a migraine—but on the subject of Eileen's illness she was consistently reticent. Therefore, Elizabeth knew very few of the details. Amanda mentioned it first as "Eileen's sensitive nature," or "bad dreams and other signs of a delicate temperament." Just what symptoms were masked by these euphemisms the MacPhersons were not told. Finally Amanda announced in a letter that her daughter had been sent away to a "finishing school" that specialized in dealing with sensitive girls. The MacPhersons knew that Cherry Hill was a private and rather expensive mental institution, but they never betrayed this knowledge to Amanda, though Bill was fond of alluding to it in ambiguous jests.

Eileen had been out of Cherry Hill for a year now, during which time she had been enrolled in the university as an art major, though she had produced no works except for small sketches assigned as class projects, which she did not bring home.

Elizabeth wondered what her family felt about her engagement or her present health. Whatever she learned would not come from Amanda.

CHAPTER FOUR

WHEN ELIZABETH REACHED the bottom of the staircase, the only person in sight was a pleasant-looking young man in a tennis outfit who was sitting in the library leafing through a copy of *Sports Illustrated*. He fit the description of Mr. Bryce's new law partner, so Elizabeth concluded that he must have been summoned a day early. Aunt Amanda must be matchmaking in earnest, she thought. Still, he wasn't bad-looking.

"Hi!" she said, peering over the magazine. "Are you here for dinner?"

"So they tell me," he said. "But if Charles chose the menu, I may remember a pressing engagement. He's into soybean casseroles."

"Dinner is destined to be strange no matter *what* we have," Elizabeth retorted, taking the chair across from his. *"He's* coming, too." She nodded in the direction of the castle.

"You mean Alban?" he asked.

"Yes. I can't wait to see what he's like. He'll probably

come clanking in wearing a saber and an iron cross from the Thirty Years War."

"Actually, they didn't start giving out iron crosses until 1813," he replied. "But it sounds like a very interesting sort of evening. What do you do?"

"Well, if you mean 'What do I do' in the sense of: do I worship oak trees or think I'm Peter Pan, the answer is nothing. I'm Elizabeth MacPherson, from a sane branch of the family. I just finished college a few weeks ago, and I haven't started job-hunting yet, so I guess the answer to what I do is still 'nothing.' "

"Enjoy it while you can," he replied. "Because if I know Amanda, you won't be doing nothing for long."

"I've been addressing invitations all afternoon," Elizabeth said.

"But the wedding is next Saturday. Surely it's a little late to be mailing them!"

"They're afterthoughts."

"Friends of the bride," her companion offered. They looked at each other and burst out laughing. "Well, if it gets too grim, you can always sneak off and amuse yourself. Do you play tennis?"

"Yes, after a fashion," Elizabeth answered. "I mean, you haven't seen me at Wimbledon."

"Well, you'll make a nice change anyway. I get tired of beating Tommy Simmons. He's Bryce's new law partner, so he doesn't get much of a chance to practice."

Elizabeth stared at her companion. "But if *he's* Mr. Bryce's new law partner, then who—"

Just then Amanda appeared in the doorway with her best company smile. "Oh, here you are, Elizabeth. Dinner is ready. You and Alban come along."

When Amanda had marched away to assemble the rest of the family, Alban turned back to Elizabeth. "I gather I'm not what you expected."

"Did I tell you I'm considering a career in the diplomatic corps?" asked Elizabeth faintly.

He laughed. "I always got along with you, Cousin Elizabeth. You were my favorite relative."

Elizabeth was puzzled by this remark, because she could scarcely remember Alban speaking to her at all, but she had made enough gaffes for one day, so she made no reply. It was probably an exaggerated form of Southern politeness, she decided.

Charles and Geoffrey were already in the dining room, standing stiffly behind their chairs like sentries. Even Charles had put on a coat and tie for dinner, probably because anyone more casually dressed would feel uncomfortable in the strict formality of Amanda's dining room.

Elizabeth stole a glance at Alban, who was padding to his place in bleached sneakers and sweat socks without a flicker of self-consciousness. Of course, there's no telling what *he's* got, she thought. His dining room may make this look like a Dairy Queen.

It would have been hard to outdo Amanda Chandler in traditional opulence, however. The room was a careful blending of red and silver: crimson carpet and curtains; white linen tablecloth stretched across a William and Mary table with places for twelve; red roses in silver bowls for the centerpiece and on the sideboard, where more silver serving dishes gleamed. Even the huge painting on the long wall conformed to the color scheme: a bloody stag lay collapsed in the snow while wolves approached him, their red tongues lolling.

"So appropriate for our dining room, don't you think?" asked Geoffrey, nodding toward the painting.

Amanda and her sister Louisa appeared in the doorway, their conversation in full swing. "...Though if we don't get some rain soon, heaven knows what's to be done about it..."

"Better notify the florist in case you need him, dear," Louisa replied. "You know they cannot conjure up arrangements at the last moment."

"Yes, but I did want to do the flowers myself from the garden. Those things from Wallers are so trite, they might as well be plastic!"

"Amanda, you don't have any flowers to speak of," her sister reminded her.

"Well, I was thinking of *your* garden, actually, Louisa. You know what a genius you are with growing things.

39

I just know that you could create something perfectly splendid—oh, good evening, everybody!"

"General Patton and Omar Bradley have arrived!" Geoffrey announced.

Amanda ignored this sally. "Elizabeth, you are over there between Alban and Charles; and, Louisa, of course you'll be on Dad's right, across from me. I think we can all sit down; the others are on their way."

Louisa, a smaller, grayer version of Amanda, took her place beside her son. "Well, Alban, you are a sight!" she twittered, frowning at his tennis outfit.

"Sorry, Mother." Alban grinned. "I considered it, and decided that being late would be the greater social crime, so I came as I was. Oh, Aunt Amanda, Simmons sent word that he'll be around tomorrow morning on his legal errand, whatever it is."

"Thank you, Alban, we were expecting him. Oh, Robert, here you are! You remember Elizabeth, of course? Do sit down. Where is everybody else?"

"I'm right here, my girl," said Captain Grandfather, taking his place at the head of the table. "And don't tell me I'm late, because you said twenty hundred hours."

"Never in my life have I said 'twenty hundred hours,'" Amanda assured him. "And it is now eight-seventeen."

"Excuse me," said a voice from the doorway. "Has anybody seen Eileen?"

Elizabeth later wondered whether the family's reaction would have been the same had Eileen been an "ordinary" bride, without her particular history. Certainly they seemed unduly concerned about a grown woman who was late for dinner. When everyone jumped up from the table, apparently intending to rush outside and search for her, this realization seemed to strike them, because they stopped abruptly and began to murmur little disclaimers.

"Probably forgot her watch."

"It's still very light outside. Doesn't look past eight o'clock." This from Louisa.

"She's absorbed in her masterpiece," Amanda an-

40

nounced. "But we can't let it ruin her health, can we now?"

"Or our dinner," murmured Geoffrey, resuming his seat.

"She's down by the lake. Charles, would you—"

"Aunt Amanda," Alban cut in. "I'm dressed for a trek through the weeds. I'll go and find her. Sit down, everybody. I'll be back before you finish your salads."

He was gone before anybody could protest.

Michael Satisky shied past Amanda's benevolent smile with a nervous titter of his own and took his place between his prospective father-in-law and the empty chair reserved for the bride.

Elizabeth, ostensibly listening to Charles's monologue on proton decay, watched Michael nibble forkfuls of salad and wondered if Geoffrey's assessment of him were correct. He looks as though he'd forgotten his lines, she thought.

"...Because although the proton is 1,836.1 times heavier than the positron, they have identical charges, which has been explained by..."

"I've always thought so," Elizabeth assured him.

"Just the slightest nuance of desperation in your voice invites me to interrupt this conversation," said Geoffrey. "Perhaps I should introduce our new dinner guest. Elizabeth, Michael Satisky."

Satisky started at the sound of his name and produced a stricken smile at them from across the table.

"This is my Cousin Elizabeth," Geoffrey told him. "Her brother is in law school at your university. Bill MacPherson. Perhaps you know him?"

"I—er—no," Satisky mumbled. "I'm in the English department. We don't see much of the people in law school. Eileen didn't tell me..."

"It's a big place," said Elizabeth. "Sixteen thousand students, I think. In fact, we didn't even see Eileen all year. You're in graduate school?"

Now that the conversation had become less awkward, Geoffrey lost interest in it and reentered his mother's conversation on the relative merits of various punch recipes. His own favorite, he insisted, was made with grain alcohol and anything.

Michael began to explain about his interest in the Brontës (Branwell was the real genius of the family), and his own modest efforts in what he called "the realm of poetry." He seemed more relaxed as the conversation progressed.

Here at least is a chance to say something, Elizabeth decided, because in a physics conversation it is hard even to come up with a question unless you know a little about the subject. Since Michael looked less miserable when expounding on his own interests, she decided that it would be kind to encourage him.

"What did Branwell write?" she asked.

Satisky pulled up short in mid-sentence. "What?"

"I said: 'What did Branwell write?' Branwell Brontë."

"Well—actually, nothing. I mean, not a novel or stories or anything. Actually, when he was a child he wrote fantasies with the girls, but his potential—"

"Oh, I see!" said Elizabeth eagerly. "He died while he was still young, and the others grew up to become writers."

"Well...no." Satisky rearranged a few stray peas on his plate. "Emily and Anne only outlived him by a few months."

"But—I don't understand. How is he the real genius of the family when he didn't do anything?"

Geoffrey, whose attention had been recaptured by the scent of conversational blood, had followed this last exchange with lively interest. "What Michael is trying to say is that Branwell must be the genius of the family by sheer potential, Elizabeth. Because his sisters were mere girls, and look what they accomplished. Since he was the male of the family, think what a wonder he'd have been if he'd tried. Right, Michael?"

Satisky flushed and stammered that he hadn't meant that at all, but by then Elizabeth had begun to talk to Geoffrey about something else, so he lapsed into silent contemplation of his baked ham. He professed to be something of a vegetarian himself at the university, but he told himself that there was no sense in letting all this good food go to waste—a thought which he hastily amended to: a change of diet will be good for my system, and anyway I can't save the creature's life by not eating him now that he's already here on the plate. I might as well eat, since conversing with these people is impossible.

He wished Eileen would hurry up. At least she was so besotted with him—committed to their cherishing relationship, he corrected himself—that she would listen to all his opinions in respectful silence. Eileen had thought the master's thesis on Branwell was a good idea. Thank goodness she wasn't a little schemer like that catty cousin of hers sitting over there talking and laughing with the Cobra-Fairy.

Oh, well, thought Satisky, he could put up with it. He had a million reasons to put up with it.

Eileen Chandler always braced herself before she entered a room. She envisioned herself walking in to a hail of laughter and catcalls, and she cringed in anticipation of the ordeal. Never had it happened in real life, but years of dread had forged the possibility into a tenuous reality in her mind.

"Well, Eileen, you haven't got time to change, so we'll have to take you as you are. Whatever kept you?" her mother demanded.

"She was on her way, really she was," said Alban, who stood smiling in the doorway. "She was just packing up the painting when I got to the lake." He patted Eileen's shoulder reassuringly. "Go and eat, kiddo."

Eileen took her place beside Michael, giving him a quick smile and then staring absently at her plate.

"Is the painting finished?" asked Charles.

Eileen shook her head.

"How much longer will you be, dear?" asked Amanda. "I expect you want it framed before the wedding. It would look so nice on display at the reception, wouldn't it, Lou?"

"I should be finished by tomorrow night," said Eileen to no one in particular.

"What are you painting?" asked Elizabeth.

43

Eileen stared at her for a moment, and then slowly shook her head.

"That's the bride's little secret!" said Amanda gaily. "She won't breathe a word 'til it's finished."

Thinking back on it later, Elizabeth realized that this moment was the turning point. If Eileen had answered her question, then the rest would not have happened.

CHAPTER FIVE

ELIZABETH SPENT MOST of dinner dreading the inevitable after-dinner wedding conference, which she was sure Amanda would inflict on her captive audience, but to her surprise Amanda was the first to leave the dining room. She bade everyone a brisk good night, with a few reminders of tomorrow's tasks, and hurried upstairs.

"Isn't she feeling well?" Elizabeth asked Charles.

"Oh, she always does that. We never see her after dinner. The rest of us go into the family room and drink coffee until we can think of something better to do, which for me will be at ten o'clock. They're showing a special on television: Enrico Fermi and the Chicago Pile."

"A horror movie about hemorrhoids, no doubt," snapped Geoffrey. "Come along, Elizabeth. How do you take your coffee?"

Michael and Eileen announced that they were going outside for a walk and strolled off down the hallway, holding hands.

"Well, Elizabeth, it's nice to see you again," said Dr.

Chandler, seeming to notice her for the first time. "How are Doug and Margaret?"

"Just fine, Uncle Robert. Mother wanted me to ask if the package they sent arrived."

"Lord, *I* wouldn't know, Elizabeth. I doubt if Eileen even does. You ask your Aunt Amanda in the morning. Did you see that pile of stuff on the card table?"

Elizabeth nodded.

"I just try to stay out of the way. How's that wrist of yours doing?"

"My wrist, Uncle Robert?"

"Yes, wasn't it you? I seem to recall one of you kids taking a tumble off that pony..."

"Oh, my wrist! It's fine, Uncle Robert. Just fine." And has been since I was twelve, Elizabeth thought. She barely remembered falling off the gray pony one summer and spraining her wrist. She had run to the house crying, and Dr. Chandler had wrapped it for her. Odd that he would remember. Either his memory ran strictly to medical incidents or her tumble had been the most memorable thing she had done at Chandler Grove. The doctor had bandaged her wrist skillfully, she recalled, showing considerable patience. He had been calm and in command of the situation, very much the figure of authority. Elizabeth had not seen him that way before or since.

Robert Chandler poured his coffee from Amanda's silver coffee urn. "I hope you'll excuse me," he said pleasantly. "I have some paperwork waiting for me in the study." He hurried out.

"Elizabeth, would you like the leather chair?" asked Geoffrey. "I'll bring you your coffee. Oh, Mother's plaid blanket is draped across the back of it. Shall I move it out of your way?"

Elizabeth smiled at the red and green cloth. "Plaid blanket! That's the royal Stuart tartan. Leave it right where it is!"

"What ho, Cousin Elizabeth! Do I hear the bagpipes of the Clan MacPherson?"

Elizabeth blushed. "Well, there is a Clan Mac-

46

Pherson, you know. They were a branch of the Clan Chattan confederation."

"What's this?" laughed Alban. "Another history buff in the family?"

"Something far more sinister, I suspect," said Geoffrey lightly. "I'd say that our cousin is a victim of that hereditary Southern disease, ancestor worship."

"I am not!" Elizabeth retorted. "Dad is interested in it. And I wanted to get him a scarf for Christmas one year in the clan tartan, so I read up on the subject. It was very interesting."

"Elizabeth! You mean you actually researched your family origins? Why didn't you just claim to be descended from Bonnie Prince Charlie like all the other MacSnobs?"

"Because he never married!" snapped Elizabeth. "The MacPhersons fought with him, though, in the Rising of 1745, and helped him to escape after Culloden."

"I congratulate you on your originality," purred Geoffrey. "It seems you have been unable to escape the Southern weakness for lost causes, but at least you managed to avoid the conventional one. I would rather hear you go on about the Scottish Alamo than to hear about the Confederacy. I'll scream if I hear one more person tell me that if we had just marched on to Washington after the first Battle of Manassas, we could have won the war in 1861."

"Well, we could have," said Elizabeth. "Everybody knows that!"

Alban started to laugh.

"What's so funny?" demanded Elizabeth.

"I'm sorry, Elizabeth," Alban managed to say. "I'm not laughing at you. You just don't know how refreshing it is to hear somebody else get raked over the coals for being a history buff!"

"What made you interested in Ludwig? You're not related to him, are you?" asked Elizabeth.

"Oh, no. English on both sides," Alban replied. "I think it was the style of the man that attracted me. He was such an idealist, yearning for medieval beauty in

47

a world that was quickly plunging into the plastic twentieth century."

"I'll scream if I hear that speech again, too," Geoffrey remarked.

"We hear rather a lot of one another's hobbies around here," said Louisa, smiling at Elizabeth. "Why, Charles, is that the *1812 Overture* you're humming? Have you taken up classical music?"

Geoffrey snickered. "Tell her about covalent bonding!"

Captain Grandfather looked up from *The Sailor's Journal*. "Can't a man read in peace around here?"

"Probably not," said Charles cheerfully. "I'm turning on the television in five minutes. They're having a special on physics."

"Nuclear subs?" asked the old man hopefully.

"No. Sorry. Atomic reactors."

Captain Grandfather sighed. "I think I'll say good night, then. Getting on for ten o'clock, anyway. Louisa, shall I have one of these young scoundrels walk you across the street?"

"No, Dad. Just come and turn the porch light on for me. I'll be fine." She stood up to leave. "Elizabeth, so good to see you again! You must come over and see us while you're here, and tell us how Doug and Margaret are doing."

"They're fine, Aunt Louisa. They would have come, only Dad had a sales convention—"

"Yes, dear. We quite understand. Good night."

Elizabeth sighed. She supposed that she would have to go on explaining why her parents hadn't come until the day she left, although no one seemed convinced by the explanation. There really was a sales convention, although its importance had been greatly exaggerated in the excuses to the Chandlers. The fact was that neither of her parents cared to spend any length of time in Chandler Grove. Margaret Chandler MacPherson, the youngest of Captain Grandfather's three daughters, was not very much like her sisters. She had passed up her debutante season to marry Douglas MacPherson, and had been content in a suburban existence that did not include the country club or the Junior League. Most of her spare time was taken up with courses at the community college, where she had learned calligraphy, macramé, and conversational Spanish. Because of her parents' lack of interest in social matters, Elizabeth had had no chance of becoming a debutante, and even though she was sure she would have hated it, she wished she had been given the option anyway. Part of the reason Elizabeth had agreed to come to the wedding was because she felt a flicker of gratitude that Eileen had chosen not to be a debutante by marrying Michael Satisky instead.

Charles, Geoffrey and Alban were crowded around the television set, fiddling with the dials. Listening to Geoffrey's sardonic commentary on the program might have been fun, but she decided that she was too tired to stay up. If nobody was going to talk to her, she might as well go to bed.

"Well, I'm going upstairs!" she said loudly. "I'll see you in the morning."

The only response was an absent wave from Geoffrey.

She went upstairs, thinking what a perfect house this was for a wedding. The red-carpeted stairway was a proper setting for the wedding pictures: Eileen on the landing with her train draped in a circular pattern beside her, with the other members of the wedding party on descending stairsteps.

I'm getting as bad as Aunt Amanda! she thought wryly.

She made a face at the yellow bridesmaid dress hanging in the closet. How corny can you get—yellow chiffon! She would want a winter wedding, and maybe— yes, maybe the bridesmaids could all wear black velvet bodices and long skirts of the MacPherson clan tartan! Now that would be stylish!

She caught herself in this daydream and laughed. It's the house. I may have to be deprogrammed when I leave here.

The elegance of the Chandler house had impressed her more than she cared to admit. At times it was a conscious effort to keep from showing it (Geoffrey would have a good laugh over that one). Apparently it was bad form to be impressed by anything, even if you did live in a brick ranch house with a carport, and were visiting people who lived on an estate. She should be used to it. After all, she and Bill had spent summers here as children. But that had been a long time ago, and children seemed to take any environment for granted. Now, after a span of years, it was different.

Someone tapped on the door.

"Come in!" called Elizabeth, wondering what Aunt Amanda had forgotten to tell her.

When the door opened, however, it was not Aunt Amanda who came in, but Eileen.

"Am I—I'm not disturbing you, Elizabeth?" she faltered, hesitating at the threshold.

"Well, of course not, Eileen," said Elizabeth. "Come in."

Eileen, who was still dressed in her painting khakis, brushed off imaginary dust and perched on the edge of Elizabeth's bed with a tentative smile. "I wanted to thank you for coming," she said.

"Oh," said Elizabeth, deliberating between "Thank *you* for asking me" or a more honest "You're welcome." In the end she said neither.

"I see you brought the dress," murmured Eileen, nodding toward the open closet.

"Yes, of course."

"Mother picked it out."

Elizabeth sighed.

"But I'm sure you'll look lovely in it!" Eileen hastened to add. "You have such nice dark hair, and you're taller than I am. You do like it, don't you?"

"It's fine, Eileen. We had to have it altered, but it's okay now." Except that I loathe it, she finished silently.

Eileen relaxed a little. "Well, that's good. I hope everything goes all right."

"I'm sure it will, Eileen. Just try not to be nervous."

"Oh, no! I'm too happy to be nervous. Have you had a chance to talk to Michael?" Her voice softened as she said his name.

"Oh—only at dinner," said Elizabeth.

"Isn't he wonderful!"

Elizabeth smiled nervously.

"I knew you'd like him. Everybody does," Eileen went on, twisting her engagement ring. "I want you to read some of his poetry, too, Elizabeth. It is so beautiful. He says I inspire him."

Elizabeth wondered how long she could go on smiling.

"Maybe I can get him to give a poetry reading after dinner tomorrow night. He's had three published in the campus literary magazine. Though, of course, he won't be able to read the one he's working on right now. It's a wedding gift for me." Eileen smiled complacently.

She went on talking about how she had met Michael and about the wedding plans, while Elizabeth asked herself why women became so smug when they were in love. They all behaved as if no one were important except Mr. Wonderful. ("Michael was in the library working on a poem, so I thought I'd come and see you.")

"I feel like a fairy princess," sighed Eileen. "I don't suppose you'd understand, but I feel as if I'd been shut up in a tower all my life—just *looking* at life. And now that Michael has come along, I can finally begin to live."

"Well, then, I hope you live happily ever after," said Elizabeth. She did hope that. Eileen had been through enough unhappiness as it was, and Elizabeth wished that things would work out. And the farther from Aunt Amanda, the better, she thought.

"Thank you," murmured Eileen. "I have to go in a minute and see if Michael is finished, but I am glad I got to talk to you. Things are so rushed these days. I guess Mother will arrange a rehearsal for us in a couple of days."

"I expect so."

"And I just found out that I can't paint tomorrow because Mr. Simmons is coming over."

"So I heard," said Elizabeth grimly, remembering her mistake before dinner.

"It's been so long since I've seen you, Elizabeth! You just graduated, didn't you?"

51

Elizabeth nodded.

"And I'm getting married before you! Just imagine! I was sure you'd be the first one of us to do it, so I never even counted on the inheritance—"

Elizabeth, who had been mentally rehearsing an edited version of the story of Austin, interrupted her. "What inheritance? What are you talking about?"

"Oh, haven't you heard about it? It's a family joke, really."

"Well, I heard Captain Grandfather mention something about a 'silly will' being just what he had expected of his sister, so I assumed that it had something to do with Great-Aunt Augusta, but she's been dead for ages. What about her?"

"Back in the twenties, her parents wanted her to go off to a finishing school, but she wanted to get married to a country singer. Of course, Great-Grandfather disowned her when she finally did elope with him. But it was *very* romantic," sighed Eileen.

"Well, if she left you an inheritance, she must have been rich. Who did she marry? Hank Williams?"

"Oh, no. Nobody famous. He was killed in a bus accident a year after they were married."

"Killed? Then where did the money come from?"

"Great-Aunt Augusta invested his insurance money in California real estate and made a fortune," said Eileen.

"Why does the money come to you, Eileen?"

"Didn't you know? Everyone else has been teasing me night and day. According to the terms of her will, the money comes to the first of her grandnieces or grandnephews to get married," said Eileen. "And next Saturday, that will be me."

"I wish someone had told me," said Elizabeth. "I would have tried harder."

Eileen giggled. "Oh, Elizabeth. You're as bad as Geoffrey! Always joking! Anyway, it isn't that much, really. Just about two hundred thousand after taxes."

"Is that all?" murmured Elizabeth.

Eileen stood up. "Well, I've intruded on you long

enough. Let me go and see if Michael has finished in the library. Good night, Elizabeth."

"What? Oh! Good night, Eileen."

When Eileen opened the door, Geoffrey, who was coming up the stairs, called out, "Don't shut it! I have a message for Elizabeth! Is she decent?"

Elizabeth peered out into the hall. "What is it?"

"Alban has gone home. It is my belief that he turns into a pumpkin on the stroke of midnight, but—"

"What is the message?" Elizabeth demanded.

"I am coming to that, my dear. It's from Alban. He said to tell you that you are to go over at ten o'clock tomorrow to be shown around the Albantross. Not his exact words, of course. Got that? Good. Then I shall say good night 'til it be morrow." He sauntered off toward his room.

"Thank you, Geoffrey!" called Elizabeth, closing the door rather more loudly than necessary.

Eileen Chandler did not go downstairs immediately. She flipped off the hall light and sat down on the top step. The drone of the television drifted up from the family room; she sighed and settled back into the companionable darkness. Behind her something moved, and she turned sharply to look. The pier mirror at the top of the stairs had caught her reflection as she moved. Nothing to be afraid of, she told herself; it was her own face she had seen. Eileen closed her eyes and thought back over her conversation with Elizabeth. Had she been convincing? Was that how a bride was supposed to talk? No one must suspect the fear that was growing inside her. She must sound normal. She must!

With a careful smile, Eileen stood up and started down the stairs.

CHAPTER SIX

THE CHANDLERS TOOK BREAKFAST on a glass-topped table in the morning room adjoining the kitchen. When Elizabeth came downstairs at eight-thirty, only Charles and Captain Grandfather were present.

"Good morning," murmured Elizabeth, taking a chair next to Charles. "Where is everybody?"

"All over the place," said Charles between bites of toast. "Dad had an emergency case at the county hospital; Mother and Aunt Louisa left for town a few minutes ago; Eileen went out to paint, since she has that meeting later this morning; and What's-His-Name's asleep."

Elizabeth looked at the two clean place settings in a shaft of sunlight across from her. "I don't see Geoffrey."

"Geoffrey says that breakfast before ten o'clock is uncivilized. He's still asleep."

Captain Grandfather looked up from his plate of eggs and bacon. "That boy is a perfect candidate for impressment," he grunted.

"Well, I have an interesting morning ahead," Elizabeth announced. "Alban is giving me a tour of his house."

Charles yawned and stretched. "It's too pretty to stay cooped up inside," he remarked. "I'm going down to the orchard to get a little ultraviolet on my epidermis. I will see you later."

He picked up a thick book on quantum physics that had been lying next to his plate, and ambled off in the direction of the back door. Elizabeth sighed and shook her head.

"What does he do?" she asked.

"Who, Charles?"

"Yes. If he's so interested in physics, shouldn't he be in grad school somewhere?"

"Oh, it'll come to that, I expect. Right now, Charles and his friends are fed up with academia. They claim it's too restrictive. You can't do research without a lot of rigamarole, and they don't want to be bothered with policy. Think they can do it on their own. Like Isaac Newton, Charles always says. Course, apples are cheaper than cyclotrons, as Geoffrey is fond of pointing out."

"Apples? Oh! The law of gravity!"

"Right. They've started sending off grant applications trying to get funding to do their own work without having to hook up with some university or existing company. I don't hold out much hope, though. Nobody's going to give hundreds of thousands of dollars to that bunch. But you can't tell Charles that. I give them six months."

Elizabeth smiled, thinking how odd it was to find a Chandler with money problems.

Captain Grandfather began to chuckle. "I know what you're thinking, young lady. You think they've all got their sea cocks open, don't you?"

"If that means they're strange, you're absolutely right."

"What they are is independent," he said, pouring himself a cup of tea from the Victorian silver teapot.

"Independent and smart. So they find their interests in life and stick to them. They can afford to."

"What about Charles?"

"Well, his income doesn't run to nuclear reactors, but he won't miss a meal. As I was saying, with the Chandler money, we don't have to impress prospective employers or try to win friends with conformity. We do as we damn well please. You ought to try it sometime— not caring what anybody thinks. You'd find out who you are."

"I wouldn't be another Charles, that's for sure."

"I don't know. Charles is very like your mother."

Elizabeth stared. "My mother? Are you kidding? Suburbia's macramé lady—like Charles?"

Captain Grandfather nodded. "Exactly. Margaret was the rebel of my three girls. I used to get letters from your grandmother in those days: 'What are we going to do with Margaret?' Your mother went off to Columbia with that friend of hers—Rhonda or Doris or some such name. They went to a dance at Fort Jackson, and Margaret met Lieutenant MacPherson. You know the rest."

"Well, don't make it sound like we live in the back of a station wagon!" laughed Elizabeth. "There were two cars in the driveway when I left home, and Dad's business is doing pretty well."

"I know," said Captain Grandfather. "And your parents are very happy, which is all that matters. I was only trying to explain to you that your cousins are people who can do just as they please. Don't set such a store by what you call normality. Sometimes I think the strain of trying to keep up that pose could make a person crazy. Better let them be themselves, so the pressure doesn't build up."

"Have it your way," sighed Elizabeth, getting up from the table. "At least it's never dull."

The mellow tone of Amanda's "cathedral-chimes" doorbell echoed down the hall.

"I expect that's Alban now," said Captain Grandfather. "Weren't you supposed to meet him at ten?"

"I'm just going."

"Don't answer it, Mildred!" Captain Grandfather bellowed toward the kitchen. "Elizabeth will get it!"

"Do I look all right, Captain Grandfather? Should I have worn my bridesmaid's dress?"

"No. But perhaps your dress tartan." He chuckled and settled back into his newspaper. "Normal, indeed!"

Alban's replica of the Bavarian castle had caused a substantial amount of comment during its construction. The general attitude of the town was one of pride overlaying the fact that no one had any idea of what it actually represented. Because it had been built by a member of the county gentry, and because it provided jobs for the local contractors, Chandler Grove was determined to take the castle seriously. Facetious titles like "Albania" or "The Disneyland Castle" were used only in private or by tourists, who often asked in town whether there were tours of the place. These queries were always answered politely in the negative, although in fact Alban did give one tour a year. Each spring the eleventh grade class of Chandler Grove High went out for a field trip, coinciding with their study of *Macbeth*. Alban had agreed to the tour after trying—and failing—to explain to Miss Laura Bruce Brunson that his Bavarian castle had nothing whatever to do with *Macbeth*.

The community considered Alban to be a nice enough fellow. He kept to himself, but that was what they expected of someone who lived in a castle. Mrs. Murphy, the cleaning woman, was able to report that there were no drugs, women, or wild goings-on at the castle, so the community "reckoned as how it was all right for the boy to build any kind of mansion he'd a mind to." The novelty had long since worn off, and county and castle-dweller had settled back into peaceful coexistence.

"What do you call this place?" asked Elizabeth, squinting up at four stories of white stone, capped by a pointed, gray-roofed tower.

"Home," said Alban. "Shall we go in?"

The main building had a pointed roof, flanked by two small towers. Windows like archways, each with a column in mid-arch, studded the white stone front in symmetrical rows. Like a computer card, Elizabeth thought. A wide stone staircase led to the entrance: two elaborately carved wooden doors situated on the second story. The castle's overall appearance was that of a large *E* without the middle stroke, an effect caused by a pair of two-story wings that met the main building at right angles. The wings were not symmetrical, however; the right wing, much larger than the left, ended in a square tower, capped by a white cupola with slit windows.

"And is there an attic where your insane first wife prowls at night?"

"No, Miss Eyre," said Alban gravely. "But people have been known to knock on a Sunday morning, thinking I was a Baptist Church."

"What do you do with all that space, Alban?"

"Well, the rooms are pretty big, and there are a number of hallways. But why don't you see for yourself? Come on!"

"You don't have a dungeon, do you?"

"If I did, would Geoffrey still be walking around?"

Elizabeth followed him up the steps to the golden oak doors. She leaned against one of the columns framing the doorway, trying unobtrusively to catch her breath as she watched Alban push down the brass latch. The door swung inward.

"After you, my dear," he said, with a mock-gallant bow.

Elizabeth stepped into the well-lit foyer and looked about. "Just don't tell me I'm here to do the floors," she said at last.

The foyer, two stories high, was tiled in blue and white squares of marble; it stretched away to an archway at the far end of the room. Two staircases branched to the right and left. Above the staircases, gold-leaf columns separated murals of nymphs and shepherds from marble niches containing life-sized statues of the

Greek gods. Above it all sparkled a pair of crystal chandeliers.

"It's my hobby," Alban was saying. "I started out to be a medievalist and because I got so fascinated with Ludwig I ended up building this. Actually, it wasn't as exorbitant as it looks. I was able to pick up a lot of this stuff in Greece and Italy for much less than it would cost to duplicate today. What do you think?"

Elizabeth nodded slowly.

"Well, the original was built in 1869 by King Ludwig II—"

"Who was crazy. Yes, I know. Geoffrey told me."

"Who was *not* crazy!" snapped Alban. "Ludwig was a genius. I'd back him against your precious Bonnie Prince Charlie any day!"

"Then why do people say that?"

"Oh, because his people thought he spent too much money on castles. But I'll tell you something about *that:* his personal debt for all three of his castles was less than eight million marks, and Bavaria paid four times that much to Prussia when they lost the Seven Weeks' War—"

"They lost a war in seven *weeks?*" interrupted Elizabeth. "Bonnie Prince Charlie certainly lasted longer than that. In fact, his army got within 130 miles of London; if they had kept going—"

"Well, they didn't. As I was saying, the people thought he was crazy then, but today Bavaria makes millions of marks a year using Ludwig's castles as tourist attractions. Verlaine called Ludwig 'the only king of the century.' "

"Well...maybe I'll read up on him sometime," said Elizabeth, who was still smarting from Alban's remark about Charles Stuart.

"Yes, do. He was quite an idealist. Do you believe in reincarnation?"

Elizabeth stopped walking and stared up at him. "Now, Alban," she said. "Don't flip out on me. There are enough eccentrics around here!"

He laughed. "Aren't you ever serious, Cousin Elizabeth?"

"Not to strangers," said Elizabeth promptly. She blushed. "I mean...I know we're first cousins, but...I didn't really know you very well back then..."

"The age difference." He nodded, considering this. "Children tend to regard anyone much older than themselves as part of the woodwork." He looked thoughtful. "You've changed a lot in the last six years. You used to be almost as shy as Eileen. No more ponytails over the ears and Girl Scout tee shirts?"

"Only when I wash the car."

"Am I the way you remember me?"

"No, Alban. Much less blurry."

"Well, that eight-year age difference is a big gap when you're kids."

"Oh, sure. To us you were just another grown-up. And before that you were off at school so we didn't hear much about you. I didn't even know you had been engaged until Aunt Amanda mentioned it yesterday."

Alban frowned. "It—it all worked out for the best, I think. But I don't like to dwell on it, if that's okay."

Elizabeth felt a twinge of sympathy. She was impressed that anyone would be upset over a broken romance that was over years ago! Why, Austin had only been gone a matter of months, and already she was beginning to forget he had ever existed. She looked at Alban with more than polite interest. He was talking about the paneling in the hallway. The architect had bought it from the owners of a French château that had been damaged in World War II. The murals, depicting scenes from Wagnerian operas, were painted by an art student who copied them from photos of the originals.

Finally they sat down on a black velvet sofa in front of a marble fireplace.

"Well, Cousin Elizabeth, what do you think of it?"

Elizabeth sighed. "Well...oh, Alban! It's beautiful and—and opulent and everything, but I keep thinking: 'Oh, shit! Alban's built a castle in the pony meadow.' A mansion, okay—but a *castle?*"

"I say be gaudy and to hell with it," he said lightly. "Would I be less crazy if I had sliding glass doors, Plexiglas coffee tables, and macramé plant holders? Because if I am hearing you correctly, you are not objecting to my spending money on a large house; you are merely complaining that I am being showy in an unfashionable way. But if I had a swimming pool and a television with an eight-foot screen, I'd be a sensible fellow, right?"

"I am losing this argument," said Elizabeth sadly.

"I am winning this argument because of practice." Alban smiled reassuringly. "Don't you think I've had this argument with my relatives, my architect, and the lady at the grocery store? I ought to be good at it by now! But it's true. I like antiques; I like medieval history. I studied it at William and Mary, when I wasn't having to take business courses to satisfy my father. Why shouldn't I have the house the way I want it?"

She nodded. "Captain Grandfather was telling me that just before I came over here."

"He's a wonderful old man, the Governor is. Very easy to explain things to."

"But, Alban, if everybody around here is so tolerant, why did they send Eileen away to Cherry Hill?"

Alban looked thoughtful, but he made no attempt to answer her question. He's trying to decide how much he can tell me, Elizabeth thought.

"I have heard one side of it," she said quickly. "I just wanted your opinion." That ought to do it. People never mind discussing secrets if they think you already know them.

"Eileen was really sick," Alban said at last. "I don't mean eccentric or nonconformist. Really sick. Nobody ever tried harder than Eileen to conform. She wanted to be just like everybody else, when none of the rest of us gave a damn for it.

"She *worked* at things that you do without even thinking—like wearing the right clothes, making the proper small talk, laughing at the current jokes. But she never managed to pull it off. Her clothes are always just a little bit wrong, and her hair is either too long or too short. But she's not an eccentric like the rest of us. Just a failure at conformity."

"Couldn't Aunt Amanda have set her straight on clothes?"

"Oh, I think she tried for a while, but it didn't seem to work. Making a social success of Eileen would have taken more time than Aunt Amanda was willing to devote."

Elizabeth traced the pattern on the Oriental rug with her foot. "I didn't realize you were so close to Eileen," she murmured uneasily.

"We're not at all close emotionally," Alban replied. "But I am not unobservant. An unhappiness of that magnitude would be hard to miss."

"Isn't she happy about getting married?"

"I hope so," sighed Alban. "She's certainly trying hard enough to be."

"I know what you mean. The groom is not exactly an unmixed blessing, is he? But you still haven't told me what her symptoms were. I mean, they would hardly have sent her away for being unfashionable and gauche."

"Okay. If you must have details...About six years ago, Eileen began to get very depressed. Wouldn't talk; wouldn't eat. Finally she started to 'see things,' and Uncle Robert took her to Nancy Kimble. I think there were a few violent episodes when I was in Europe. Anyway, I know that she was put in Cherry Hill shortly after that, and since then she has improved greatly, enough to get her high school diploma and to get accepted at the university. And now she's back—with a fiancé."

"You said 'episodes of violence.' Is Eileen—dangerous?"

"I think she could be extremely dangerous," said Alban softly.

He wouldn't say anthing else about Eileen after that, but insisted that they go on with the tour. The rooms became a blur of silver and velvet and polished wood. Elizabeth's thoughts were elsewhere.

"—and this is the last one," Alban was saying, as he opened double doors at the end of a hallway. "My study. I wanted you to see these murals."

The paintings, turbulent with colors, filled three walls

of the small study, which otherwise contained a claw-footed oak desk and a casement window curtained in damask.

"How can you possibly concentrate in here?" asked Elizabeth.

"I don't. I relax here. Listen." He pushed a button on the wall, and heavy strains of music issued forth from unseen speakers. "Recognize it?"

Elizabeth shook her head.

"It's from *Das Rheingold*."

She looked blank.

"I like Wagner very much," said Alban. "Not only the music, but the stories in the operas. Are you familiar with him?"

Elizabeth sighed. "No, Alban. Am I about to be?"

He smiled. "Ludwig virtually discovered Wagner, you know. He had the foresight to appreciate his music and to finance his work. He even built Wagner an opera house—Bayreuth. An architectural marvel. For Wagner alone the world should be eternally grateful to Ludwig!"

Elizabeth was thinking: I am going to have to read up on King Ludwig. There must be something he's not telling me—something unpleasant, I hope. Elizabeth wasn't sure that she would argue with Alban about his hero, but his lectures would be easier to bear if she could hug some secret knowledge to herself.

Alban, at first puzzled by her silence, suddenly began to chuckle. "Poor Lillibet! You've had lectures on proton decay from Charles and English literature from Satisky, and now I'm boring you with my hobbyhorse. Do forgive me. I'll shut up about Ludwig at once."

"Oh, I'm used to it," said Elizabeth sweetly. "When you go out with a man, first he asks you where you're from and what you're majoring in, and then for the rest of the evening he talks about his job, his hobby, or the story of his life. I stopped listening ages ago, but no one has ever noticed."

Alban grinned. "Would you like to stay for lunch? I could go in and tell Mrs. Murphy—"

"No, thank you, Alban. They're expecting me back at the Chandlers'. Are you coming over?"

"No. I have some errands to do in town."

When they were back in the sunlight outside the front door, Elizabeth thanked him gravely. "It really is very impressive," she said. "Very individualistic."

"Yes, I'm very happy with it," said Alban. "Except, of course, for the fact that it's haunted."

"Haunted?" echoed Elizabeth. "But—who haunts it?"

Alban bowed. "Why, madam—you do," he said, and gently closed the door.

CHAPTER SEVEN

June 10

Dear Bill,

Please note the return address printed carefully on the outside of this envelope. It is an indication that I expect a reply to this. You owe me several letters. Anyway, I need to hear from someone sane so that I can keep my sense of perspective. I have developed an alarming tendency to ramble on about Clan MacPherson and the Rising of 1745. The prospect of that habit continuing after my return home should frighten you into writing. Or would you like another tartan tie for Christmas? I thought not.

I have news. You'd better sit down for this one.

Did you know that Captain Grandfather's sister (Great-Aunt Augusta) made a will leaving two hundred thousand dollars to whichever one of us gets married first? *Now* they tell us—when I've pushed Austin into the duck pond and Eileen is inches away from the altar! I'll bet Mother knew about this, don't you? She probably didn't want to tempt us into being rash, which was certainly prudent of her in *your* case. You would have married Lassie for two hundred thousand dollars. Well, maybe not Lassie, but at least Peggy Lynn Bateman, which is just as bad. (I never liked her.)

Actually, the contest was almost over five years ago. Alban was supposed to marry some girl who was a secretary in Uncle Walter's company, which is another piece of family gossip we either ignored or were left out of. Aunt Amanda told me the whole story "now that I'm old enough to hear it." There's not much to it, though. Apparently, the girl just changed her mind a few days before the wedding and left town. Now, I know you're expecting me to say something snide about that girl taking a good look at Alban and coming to her senses, but I'm not. More likely it was the rest of the family she couldn't take. In fact, I wouldn't put it past them to have paid her off to keep her out of the family tree. Anyway, Alban is not so bad after all. Around here he seems positively wholesome and normal. He wears tennis outfits instead of lederhosen, and he's quite nice. (He says I'm his favorite cousin, which just proves how sensible he is.)

I went on a tour of his house today, and it really is beautiful. Of course I asked him why he built a castle, and he says because he likes them. "If I had a swimming pool and an 8 ft. TV screen, would that make me an acceptable person?" He has a point. Captain Grandfather was telling me pretty much the same thing—that our batty cousins are eccentric because they can afford to do as they please. If we had tons of money, do you think we'd become strange? I'd be willing to risk it.

Anyway, Alban is at least interesting, if strange. He puts up with a lot of sniping from Geoffrey about the house, but he seems to take it all good-naturedly. He does drone on about King Ludwig, though. Along with the tour, I got the full lecture of what a genius Ludwig was, and how he was the patron of Richard Wagner, the composer. He even asked me if I believed in reincarnation—which is not a joke I appreciated with so many eccentrics around.

Plans for the wedding occupy Aunt Amanda's every waking moment. It's like watching Eisenhower plan D-Day. I hope everything goes off all right. I am worried about Eileen. I mean, she seems normal enough to me—the typical bridal airhead, in fact—but Alban seems to think she might be dangerous. He says there were "episodes of violence"—he won't say what—and that Uncle Robert took her to Dr. Nancy Kimble for treatment. Dr. Kimble won't be coming to the wedding, because she's in Vienna right now, but Eileen did invite the therapist she's been seeing at school. Do you think that means anything?

Now, do not worry Mother and Daddy with this, but I am getting nervous. I feel like a heroine in a Gothic novel. The organ will play "Here Comes the Bride," and Eileen will come running down the aisle with an ax. Everybody is being peculiar about this wedding. Of course, with the Chandlers it's hard to tell. With them, peculiar may be normal.

Would you like to hear about the groom?

He seems like a rabbity sort of intellectual, if you ask me. About what you'd expect Eileen to end up with, poor girl. I haven't talked to him very much, except to listen to him expound on English literature at the table last night. Geoffrey tossed and gored him, which was rather fun. He does seem pompous, but that may be because he's nervous. Do you suppose he knows about the inheritance? I wonder why he's so jumpy—probably the prospect of Aunt Amanda as a mother-in-law.

On the off-chance that he disappears at the last minute like What's-Her Name, Alban's fiancée, look around the apartment complex for a suitable husband for me. I might even settle for Milo for that amount of money. I promise to give you an allowance.

The wedding is now nine days away. I'll probably write you again then and let you know how it went. I've decided that Michael looks too timid to run away from it. Aunt Amanda would probably track him through the swamps, baying.

I wish you would get a telephone in your apartment. Surely you and Milo could divert some of your beer money toward acquiring a telephone. Writing is tiring and takes up more of my time than you deserve. It is now nearly time for lunch, so I will close. I expect an answer to this, Bill!

Love,

Elizabeth

Someone tapped on the door of the library.

Elizabeth slid the letter to Bill into its envelope, and sealed it. "Come in!" she called.

Eileen peeped around the door. "Elizabeth? I thought you must be in here. Are you ready for lunch?"

"I guess so. Let me just put this letter out for the postman. Am I late?"

"Oh, no! Not for lunch or anything. I just came to see if you wanted any. I mean, we're the only ones home."

"Really?"

"Yes. Michael wanted to go to the library in town and Captain Grandfather offered to go with him, because he wanted to look up something about sailing ships."

In the kitchen, Elizabeth sat while Eileen rummaged about in the refrigerator, occasionally singing out "Tomatoes!" or "Olives!" and setting a container on the countertop. Elizabeth tried to think of cheerful lunchtime conversation.

"How is your painting coming along?" she said.

"Oh, all right, I guess. I did a lot of work on the shadowing this morning. I wish I could paint this afternoon, but I have that appointment. What kind of dressing do you want?"

"French." Elizabeth took the cutting board from the counter and began to chop vegetables while they talked.

"I suppose we should be having a wedding rehearsal in a day or two," Eileen murmured.

"Fine!" said Elizabeth, much more cheerfully than she felt. "Are you nervous about the wedding?"

Eileen looked wary. "What do you mean?"

"Oh, stage fright, I guess. Most girls get the jitters a few days before the ceremony."

"Stage fright," Eileen repeated. "That's a good word for it. I guess that is what I feel. I'm not afraid of marrying Michael, of course, but the idea of walking down the aisle in front of all those people, and afterwards, talking to strangers—"

"But, Eileen! They won't be strangers! They'll be your friends—people that you invited to the wedding!"

Eileen looked at her steadily. "Will they?"

For a minute they devoted their full attention to the salads. Elizabeth dabbed her fork at stray bits of tomato and considered the implications of Eileen's reply. "Will they?" Of course they would not be her friends. Aunt Amanda had sent out all the invitations. Who even knew if Eileen had any friends? But, if she did, they certainly ought to be asked.

"Eileen, listen!" she began quickly. "I've been addressing invitations for your mother, and I know where the extra ones are—in that desk in the library. If there's anybody you want to invite, just tell me, and I'll send them an invitation sneaked in with the others. It'll be no problem at all!"

"There's only one person I want to come to my wedding," said Eileen softly.

"Who is that?"

"Michael."

Elizabeth's eyes widened. "Eileen! You're not going to elope, are you? Because if you go off to South Carolina

71

after all this work and planning, Aunt Amanda is going to have a French fit!"

"Don't worry, Elizabeth. Everything will be all right. If I have to wear that battleship of a white dress and shake hands with every old lady in the county, I'll do it. It will be worth it. Giving Mother her own way is always worth it."

Having had some experience with Aunt Amanda's temper, Elizabeth silently agreed with Eileen's assessment. Amanda Chandler could be a terror when not given her own way. Her family had learned not to argue with her, if only for the sake of peace and quiet. Robert Chandler had obviously been taking the path of least resistance for years, with the result that he scarcely had any opinions left. Willfulness was an interesting trait, Elizabeth thought. Usually when people insist on a thing, and no one else cares much either way, the person who insists carries the day. Elizabeth had noticed, though, that some people nearly always cared a great deal about everything—such as what to have for dinner and when—so that indifferent people were seldom able to choose. A phrase she had once seen on a tee shirt summed up Amanda Chandler perfectly: What's your opinion against millions of mine?

"Oh, for heaven's sake, Eileen!" she blurted out. "It's your wedding, not your mother's! Just put your foot down."

The cathedral chimes of the front door echoed down the hall.

Eileen stood, casting a nervous glance toward the door. "Elizabeth did you ever try to tell my mother something she didn't want to hear?"

"Uh...no."

She smiled bitterly. "Well, I did. Six years ago."

"Six years—you mean, when you..."

"That was the door bell. I think we had better let Mr. Simmons in." Eileen left the kitchen with as much dignity as she had ever mustered. After a few seconds' paralysis, Elizabeth followed.

• • •

If she had to paint him, she would depict him as a medieval friar. That pudgy body would look like a wine cask under a brown cassock, and the blond ringlets curling around his bald spot made a natural tonsure. The wire-rimmed glasses sliding down his nose gave him a look of foolish benevolence. Did they have glasses back then?

"I'm sorry," Eileen murmured. "What were you saying?"

"I just need you to sign here," he repeated, holding out another typed page. "Would you like me to run through that explanation again? I'd be happy to."

"No, that's all right," Eileen assured him. She scrawled her name hurriedly on the line he had marked.

"Do you have any questions about all this?" Simmons persisted. "About the money?"

"How will I get it?"

Tommy Simmons coughed nervously. He had just finished explaining that. "Er—well, Miss Chandler, in a manner of speaking you already have it. It's in the bank, of course. Would you like to discuss possible investments or savings programs?"

"No. Not today, please."

Simmons began sliding papers into his briefcase. "Well, then, I guess that's all..."

"Mr. Simmons?"

"Yes? Is there anything else?"

"I'd like to make a will."

He blinked at her. Whatever put that idea into her head?

"Could I?" she asked. "With the wedding coming up, I thought I ought to."

Simmons peered into his briefcase. "Well...I suppose we could draft it now, and I could get it typed up for you to sign after—"

"It's just a simple one," said Eileen. "I've already written it. I just need you to put it in legal terms, or whatever it is you do to make it official. Excuse me, I'll go and get it." She hurried out of the room.

Tommy Simmons leaned back on the sofa with a weary sigh. He wondered if the family knew about this.

It shouldn't matter, of course; it was her money, and she was of age, but it made him uneasy to do anything without the family's approval. A simple will, she'd said. That probably meant that the fiancé was going to get it. He'd better postpone the formal drafting until after the wedding, just to be on the safe side.

He came to himself with a start, remembering that he was not alone in the room. The cousin, or whatever she was, sitting on the sofa, had put down her magazine and was watching him thoughtfully. Simmons produced a weak smile.

"Are you here for the wedding?"

"Yes."

"Nice girl, Eileen. Should make a lovely bride." Because, Simmons finished silently, if you threw enough satin and white lace on a scarecrow, it would look presentable. He wondered about the groom, though. The brief announcement in the local paper had been very restrained on that point. He looked again at the cousin, wondering if he ought to include a gallant remark about how nice she'd look as a bridesmaid, but before he could frame this pleasantry into complimentary but unflirtatious terms, she embarked on a topic of her own.

"How do you like practicing law?"

"Uh...fine, just fine. Sure beats studying it. The hours are better."

"It doesn't require much math, does it?"

"I'm sorry. Math?"

"Calculus or trig or anything like that."

"I—no." Idly, he began to wonder if he had been mistaken about her being a cousin. Visions of Cherry Hill began to flip through his mind.

"And what did you major in as an undergrad?"

"History."

"Oh. So did my brother. He's in law school, too. I majored in sociology."

"Ah." Simmons kept trying to pick up the thread of the discussion.

"Know any lawyers who majored in sociology?"

"No."

"I didn't think so. Mostly they major in history or

74

political science. Still, it seems like an interesting sort of career. Do you get many good cases practicing in a small town?"

"Mostly we do deeds and wills, things like that."

"I think criminal law would be more interesting. You know, cases where you could really make a difference—like murder cases!"

Simmons smiled. He heard that speech at every social function he attended. People were always pushing cups of warm punch at him and telling him how much more interesting they thought it would be to practice criminal law in Atlanta. He usually just stood there smiling and nodding, because it took too much effort to explain that rich murder defendants hired famous and experienced attorneys—he was neither—and poor ones got court-appointed lawyers who needed the work and got paid peanuts for their efforts. Deeds and wills weren't exactly pulse-quickening, but it was a comfortable life, with plenty of time for tennis, and an occasional out-of-the-ordinary case for the social anecdote.

"Are you interested in law?" he asked politely.

Elizabeth frowned. "I don't know. I majored in sociology, but I haven't decided what I'm going to do yet. I took a course in criminology in my junior year, but it wasn't what I expected. Mostly statistics."

Eileen reappeared just then, with Mildred in tow. "This will only take a few minutes, I promise. Then you can put the groceries away. I just need you to sign something."

"Sign?" echoed Simmons, struggling to his feet. He had the uneasy feeling that the interview was getting away from him.

"Here it is," said Eileen, handing him a piece of stationery covered with round, childishly precise handwriting. "I've asked Mildred to witness it so that it will be legal until you can get the other one drawn up. And Elizabeth, you can be the other witness."

Simmons frowned. "Well, really, Miss Chandler, I don't thnk it would be proper—"

"They don't have to read what I've written, do they?"

The procedural question sidetracked him. "What?

No. They are only attesting to the fact that your signature on the document is genuine, but—"

"Okay then. Watch, everybody!" Eileen held her pen aloft as a magician might wave his wand before performing the next trick. When they dutifully turned to look at her, she bent and signed her name at the bottom of the pink page, carefully dotting the *i* in Eileen with a small circle.

Oh, God, thought Simmons, an *i* circler. I haven't seen that since ninth grade. I'll bet this will is a real beauty; she probably included her stamp collection! He consoled his professional sensitivity by reminding himself that he would be getting twenty-five dollars an hour for drafting the document.

"Okay," he said. "Now that you've signed it, they need to sign it. You can cover up the text with a piece of paper if you like. Some people do that." He handed her a sheet of paper. "That's right, cover up everything except where you want them to sign at the bottom. But I really do recommend that you wait for an official draft. Really!"

Eileen shook her head. "No. I want to do this as— as sort of a gesture that I'm really getting married. Like a preliminary ceremony." That ought to satisfy him, she thought. And it ought to make Michael realize about the money. How real it is; how close it is to being ours. He couldn't change his mind after that. Not that he'd want to, of course, because he really loved her. He said so over and over.

"Oh, please don't worry, Mr. Simmons," she said. "It's only for a few days—until the other one is ready. It will be all right. I mean, nothing's going to happen to me."

Simmons looked shocked. "Certainly not!" he said hastily. "That goes without saying. But you must understand that it is a bit irregular. The litigation possibilities in the event—"

But Eileen was carefully aligning the blank cover sheet over her piece of stationery. She motioned for Elizabeth and Mildred to witness it. After a moment's hesitation, they bent down and scribbled their names on the bottom of the page. Eileen then handed the paper to the lawyer.

"Thank you very much for your time," she said, walking with him toward the door.

"Just let me wish you much happiness. You just think about that lovely wedding coming up, and put all thoughts about wills and legal matters right out of your mind."

Eileen nodded solemnly and showed him out. When the door had finally closed behind him, she leaned against it with a sigh of relief. "Now I can go and paint."

Elizabeth had the house to herself for most of the afternoon. Amanda and Louisa had not returned from their shopping expedition; Dr. Chandler called to say that he wouldn't be home until dinnertime; and there was still no sign of Captain Grandfather and Michael. She wondered what they found to talk about on the drive to the county library. Geoffrey had stopped in about two o'clock to announce that he was going to a rehearsal for his play, and she had politely declined his invitation to go along. Charles and Eileen were still somewhere between the house and the lake, she supposed.

She finished reading the book she had brought with her, and was in the library trying to do a sketch of Alban's castle for Bill.

She wondered where Alban was. He had driven off an hour or so before without a tennis racket. She held up her drawing and inspected it. The lines were a little crooked and the proportions weren't quite right, but Bill would get the general idea. Alban ought to provide postcards, she thought, smiling to herself. After all their laughter at Alban's expense, it seemed strange to think of him as an ordinary, likable person. The castle looked less bizarre to her than it had at first—probably in the light of his explanation. She decided to leave off the dragon she had originally planned to put in the foreground. But she was still going to put the little flag on the top of the tower, with her version of a suitable motto: "A man's home is his castle." Elizabeth walked over to the window to count the tower windows again—maybe his car would be back in the driveway.

It wasn't, but another car was pulling up in the Chandlers' drive: a little green Volkswagen she hadn't seen before. She watched as the driver stopped the car and headed for the front door. He was a stocky, dark-haired man of about thirty, wearing a yellow tee shirt that read "Jung At Heart." He looked up at the house, then over at Alban's and shook his head. When Elizabeth saw that he was indeed coming to the Chandlers' front porch, she hurried to the front door and waited for the bell to ring.

I wonder who this is, she thought. Not the minister, surely! Maybe he's somebody from Cherry Hill who has come for the wedding. Aunt Amanda would love that. He must be new around here if he hasn't gotten used to Albania. Who else is supposed to come?

A few seconds later, when he introduced himself, she remembered.

"Come in, Dr. Shepherd. I'm Elizabeth MacPherson, Eileen's cousin."

"Thank you very much. I wasn't sure I had the right house." He glanced uncertainly over his shoulder. "What is that facility across the road?"

"Oh, that's my Cousin Alban's castle," said Elizabeth sweetly. "Would you like to come into the library? I can get us some coffee. I'm afraid I'm the only one here right now, but the family should be back soon."

He followed her into the library, pausing only to register a glance of recognition at the gray and black painting in the hall.

"Aunt Amanda just sent you a wedding invitation," said Elizabeth, settling down in the wing chair. "Yesterday! You couldn't have received it yet!"

"No, that's right, I haven't. Eileen presented me with a handwritten invitation and a map before she left school. Actually, I know I'm a few days early, but—circumstances changed." He shifted uncomfortably.

Elizabeth's eyes widened. Circumstances had changed! She thought of Alban's description of Eileen: "extremely dangerous." Her uneasiness about the situation had been right! "Who—who called you?" she asked faintly.

"Called me? Nobody called me. It's so idiotic." He looked at her carefully for a moment. "I think I'll take you up on that offer of coffee, if you don't mind. And then if you want, I'll tell you about it. It's really been a trip for me."

He followed her into the kitchen and watched as she filled the copper kettle, and rummaged around the cabinets for cups and instant coffee.

"Did you have car trouble on the way down?"

"No," he said, settling down on the kitchen stool. "Y'see, I'm on vacation from the clinic. I have to be back for summer session, but right now I'm off. So instead of going home to New York I figured I'd play tourist and take my time driving down here for the wedding. Eileen's a nice kid, you know. Did you say you're her cousin?"

"Yes. Our mothers are sisters."

"Anyway, she didn't seem to have many friends, and I know it's been an adjustment for her, so I promised her I'd come to the wedding. I've always wanted to see this part of the country anyway—ever since I saw *Gone With the Wind* as a kid."

Elizabeth nodded, suppressing an urge to giggle.

"Well, anyway, I drove up to that big national park in the mountains, and I rented a cabin. That was day before yesterday. Commune with nature, you know. I'm from the city myself, but some of my colleagues have been Sierra Clubbing me to death, and I decided what-the-hell, I'd give it a try. So, anyway, I got this cabin, and night before last I'm lying on my bed reading a book when this *thing* flew over my bed. I just saw it out of the corner of my eye, you know? But I threw down my book, and he made another pass. That time I saw it clearly. It was a bat! Ugly little sonuvabitch. Just cruising around my room. I let out a yell and ran for the bathroom, and he followed me. Sat right there in the doorway and peered at me so I couldn't come out."

"Why couldn't you just leave the cabin?"

"I didn't have too much on, you see. It was a hot night. So I went to the bathroom window and I yelled, 'Help! Somebody! He's got me trapped!' hoping somebody would hear me."

He was telling all this in a perfectly serious tone of voice, but Elizabeth decided that he knew how absurd it was. Her laughter nearly drowned out the rest of the story. Every time she tried to picture the pudgy Shepherd nude and trapped in the bathroom by a bat, she laughed even harder.

"Did it look like Bela Lugosi?" she managed to say.

Shepherd frowned. "Well, it might have been rabid. Anyway, a couple of minutes later—I'm still in the john in a staring contest with Beady Eyes—somebody kicks in the door to my cabin. This guy had been out tinkering with his car and heard me yell. So I look up and he's standing in the doorway with a .30/.30, saying 'Where is he?'"

"And you showed him the bat."

"Well, yeah. I can't say he was impressed."

"Did he shoot the poor little—I mean, the monster?" Elizabeth asked.

"No. He put the gun down, sneered, and then shooed it away, so I could get my pants and get out. Luckily I hadn't unpacked."

"What happened to the bat?"

Shepherd sighed. "I left right then. I don't know what happened to the bat. But his rent is paid up through Sunday."

"Dr. Shepherd," said Elizabeth, "you're going to feel right at home here."

Amanda Chandler's reaction to the new arrival was impossible to determine from her behavior. When she came back from her expedition at four, laden with packages and demanding to know where everybody was, Elizabeth appeared in the hallway and whispered to her that Dr. Shepherd had arrived and was having coffee in the library.

80

Immediately her face froze into a chilling smile that did not reach her eyes. She strode briskly into the library with cordial noises and outstretched hands that did not waver even after she had seen the yellow Jung tee shirt.

"Such a privilege to have you!"

Dr. Shepherd apologized for his early arrival, attributing it to an "unforeseen accident in a national park," and Amanda was all sympathy. She refused to hear of his plans to stay at the Chandler Grove Motel.

"Why, we have more room than they do!" she assured him with an arch smile. "And please don't think I'm being kind! Why, I'm just as selfish as I can be. I want to have you right here where we can get to know you. And, anyway, some of our out-of-town wedding guests just may need those motel rooms, so there! It's all settled. You'll stay here."

Shepherd, unused to the blitzkrieg form of Southern hospitality, succumbed in a puzzled voice, and shambled off to his car to collect his belongings. When he had gone, Amanda's smile vanished.

"What can Eileen have been thinking of?" she murmured, glancing at him through the window. "He can't possibly understand the problems of—of—"

"Of what, Aunt Amanda?" asked Elizabeth.

Remembering that her niece was present, Amanda summoned the wraith of her previous smile. "Why, Elizabeth!" she purred. "You're going to think I have a silly old thing against Yankees after all these years, but really! —Oh, dear, could you just run out to the kitchen and tell Mildred that there'll be another guest for dinner? I'm afraid she'll be cross, but tell her that we are simply martyrs to the unexpected!"

"Martyrs..." murmured Elizabeth, shaking her head as she left. Bill would never believe that line!

She was on her way back from the kitchen when Shepherd appeared again at the front door with a brown suitcase and an armful of books.

"Would you like me to carry something?" she offered.

He shook his head. "I bet I have to go upstairs, right? Upstairs?"

"That's right. Third bedroom on the left."

He deposited his belongings in the hall chair. "It can wait. Boy, this is interesting. Seeing people in a social context that I've been hearing about for months!"

Elizabeth gasped. "She didn't! I mean— I wasn't mentioned, was I?"

Shepherd grinned. "People always ask me that. And I really can't tell you. Honest. I'll bet I hear that question ten more times while I'm here."

"I'll bet you do."

"Where's Eileen?"

"Down by the lake, I guess. She's working on a painting to give to the groom. Don't ask me what it's like, because none of us have seen it." She leaned forward with a conspiratorial whisper. "Do you think that's normal?"

"Sure," said Shepherd cheerfully. "It would take the drama out of the gift if everybody saw it beforehand. That's a common reaction. Is the groom around?"

"He's at the library. Do you know him well?"

"Oh, no. Met him once. He came to pick up Eileen after a session."

"Well, you'll meet everybody at dinner."

"Including *him?*" he asked, gesturing toward Albania.

"Very possibly," said Elizabeth, "but don't be surprised if he turns out to be sane."

"Listen," said Shepherd, "when you've got that much money, you're not crazy. Just eccentric."

At the other end of the house a door opened.

"Eileen!" called Amanda. "Come in, dear! One of your guests has arrived! Go right out to the front hall and see for yourself!"

A few moments later, Eileen Chandler, in a paint-smeared smock, turned the corner of the hallway. Her face looked tired and strained. When she saw Shepherd smiling at her, she stiffened and stared at him open-mouthed.

"Hello, Eileen. I just—".

"No! I don't want you here! I don't want you! Go away!"

Sobbing wildly, she plunged up the stairs to her room.

Elizabeth and Dr. Shepherd exchanged puzzled looks. Amanda, who had been following Eileen down the hall and had witnessed the scene, hurried up to him. "Dr. Shepherd! Really, I must apologize for my daughter's behavior! Even for a nervous bride, such manners are inexcusable! And I'm going to go right up and tell her so."

"No, please don't. You don't need to apologize, Mrs. Chandler. Eileen is naturally very tense at this time. It's much more important to understand the underlying—"

He was interrupted by a crash from the upstairs hall, followed by renewed sobbing.

"Was there by any chance a mirror in the upstairs hall?"

Amanda nodded grimly. "There was."

CHAPTER EIGHT

EILEEN'S FAILURE to appear at dinner was attributed to her fatigue from painting. The family ate at six, which Elizabeth considered unusually early, but no one else seemed to think it was strange.

Amanda, apparently under the impression that two doctors would be ideal dinner companions, had placed Carlsen Shepherd next to her husband, but Dr. Chandler's monologue on colonial medicine seemed less than successful as a conversational gambit.

"What do you think is really the matter?" Elizabeth whispered to Geoffrey, who was sitting next to her.

"I don't know. I tapped on her door, but she howled at me to go away. I expect she'd let Satisky in, but he seems to have an aversion to hysterical females, even if he's engaged to one."

Across the table, Satisky was cutting his meat with studied concentration. His movements were slow and cautious, as though he were trying to remain as inconspicuous as possible.

"He seems like a nice guy. Dr. Shepherd, I mean."

Geoffrey continued to stare at Satisky.

"And, Geoffrey, she did invite him herself."

"Maybe Mother's right about wedding nerves," said Geoffrey.

Alban had not been asked to dinner, but had phoned to say that he would be over later. Elizabeth hoped she would have a chance to talk to him; maybe things would make sense to him.

Amanda had abandoned her role of effusive Southern hostess, and spent most of the meal conversing with Captain Grandfather in a quiet undertone. She ate very little and excused herself early, pleading that she had a headache.

Elizabeth found the tension annoying, so she left the table soon after Amanda did, and went upstairs to Eileen's room. The door was locked.

"Eileen?" she called, knocking gently. "It's Elizabeth."

There was no sound from within. With a sigh, Elizabeth gave up and started to her own room. The empty frame of the mirror stood crookedly against the wall; the glass shards on the floor had already been cleared away by the unobtrusive Mildred. Elizabeth wondered why Eileen chose to hit the mirror: was it deliberate or did she simply lash out at the first thing she saw?

"Elizabeth?"

She turned. Eileen had opened her door partway and stood looking at Elizabeth with a pitiful expression.

"I came up to see if you were all right," said Elizabeth.

Eileen's eyes welled with tears. She peered anxiously toward the stairs as if she were afraid that someone else would see her. Impatiently she motioned to Elizabeth. When the door was safely shut behind them, Eileen sat on her bed and hugged a yellow stuffed bear, resting her chin on the top of its head. Elizabeth sat in a chair beside the dresser.

"Everybody is very worried about you," she said in what she hoped was a sympathetic tone.

"I'll bet they are! I know what they're thinking!" Her voice quavered.

86

Oh, God, thought Elizabeth. If I set off another attack of hysterics, Aunt Amanda will tar and feather me. Soothingly, she said, "You're just nervous because you're getting married next week. You have all these plans to cope with, and you've been trying to finish that painting. I know what a strain it can be to have to finish something by a certain time. You're wearing yourself out, aren't you?"

Eileen looked thoughtful. "The painting. Yes, it has been quite a strain."

"Of course it has!" said Elizabeth heartily. Eileen looked calmer now. She had put down the stuffed animal and was looking at Elizabeth with an expression of relief. I should have been a psych major, Elizabeth thought with a twinge of satisfaction. "You know, Eileen, I'm sure Michael would understand if you wanted to stop working on the painting until after the wedding."

"No. It's almost finished. I'll be fine. Really. You're right; I was just tired."

"There's no reason you wouldn't want Dr. Shepherd here, is there?" asked Elizabeth doubtfully. Despite her success in calming Eileen, she still felt that hysterics and mirror-breaking were excessive reactions, even for a nervous bride.

"No, of course not. Dr. Shepherd is very kind. I'll apologize to him tomorrow."

"Look, Eileen. You're worried about something. Why don't you tell me what it is?"

"You wouldn't understand."

"About what? Worrying? Oh yes I would! Do you realize that I've just graduated from college and haven't the slightest idea what I'm going to do next?"

"Oh," said Eileen faintly.

"I know I should have thought of that earlier, but I was sort-of-engaged to an architecture major named Austin. Did I tell you about Austin?"

Eileen shook her head. Good, thought Elizabeth, I've got her attention. She explained about Austin and the duck pond incident. Eileen actually began to smile when she heard that story, so Elizabeth went into great detail, describing Austin clambering out of the pond, dripping weeds.

"And I told him if he stayed in there long enough, he might have a *real* alligator on his chest!"

They began to laugh. "He was such a sight!" Elizabeth giggled. "I wish I had a picture of him coming out of that pond!"

Eileen's smile faded. "Elizabeth, I'm not feeling well. I really think I need to be alone."

"Well—sure, Eileen..." I wonder what I did to upset her this time? Elizabeth wondered as she closed the door behind her. Curiouser and curiouser.

It was too early for bed, so she went back downstairs to see if Alban had come over as he'd promised, or if Geoffrey were doing anything amusing. She heard voices coming from the library. Hoping that it might be one of them, she opened the door and peeked in.

Alban and Carlsen Shepherd were hunched over the table amidst a pile of papers. Shepherd was scribbling furiously on a small note pad, and Alban was saying, "I've been Ludwig of Bavaria for about four years now, and on the whole—"

"Oh, excuse me!" she blurted out. "I'll go."

Shepherd looked up and smiled. "No, it's all right. Come on in. Nothing important. You're welcome to sit in."

Elizabeth tried to sort things out in her mind. Alban had "been" Ludwig of Bavaria—should she stay and hear the whole story or run? And why should she be permitted to sit in on a medical consultation?

"But—what about your psychiatrists' rule about patient confidentiality?" she stammered. Surely they weren't really going to allow her to listen to a description of Alban's reincarnation delusions.

They stared at her, letting the question sink in. Shepherd's face lit up in sudden comprehension, and he roared with laughter. "Patient confidentiality! Well, now you know what your family thinks of you, Cobb!"

Alban grinned. "I think I worried Elizabeth a bit this morning by mentioning reincarnation."

Elizabeth wished they would stop laughing at her

88

and start making sense. "Will you please tell me what is going on here?"

They exchanged smirks. "We're discussing a war game, Cousin," said Alban. "It's called Diplomacy. Ever heard of it?"

"Only in connection with Camp David," she sighed. "A game? You're playing a game? You just met!" She might have known it would turn out to be another batty family hobby. The fact that Shepherd was familiar with it did not surprise her in the least, once she considered the matter.

"Well, we've been playing in separate games—separate wars, even, because Alban's game is a Prussian variant, but we still have a lot to talk about," said Shepherd cheerfully. "It's a very challenging game. See? These little short blocks are armies—"

Elizabeth shook her head. "Thanks, I'll take a deferment."

"Perhaps we can come up with a Jacobite variant," suggested Alban with a trace of a smile. Catching Shepherd's puzzled look, he explained. "The only war that interests Elizabeth is the Rising of 1745 in Scotland."

They turned back to the technical matters of the game, and Elizabeth went off in search of Geoffrey. She found him in Amanda's den, reading a newspaper.

"Hullo," she said, curling up beside him on the sofa. "I'm bored. Anything interesting in the news?"

"Certainly not!" he answered in shocked tones. "This is the *local* newspaper, so it contains no news. Anyway, we only read it to find out who has been caught."

"Then I won't ask to borrow it."

He nodded, absently turning a page.

Elizabeth tried again. "Chandler Grove isn't a very exciting place, is it?"

"You can dial a wrong number and still talk," said Geoffrey, without looking up.

"There's absolutely nothing to do. Alban and Dr. Shepherd are in the library—playing with blocks!"

Geoffrey looked up, raising an eyebrow. "Oh?"

"Have you talked to Eileen?"

He tossed the newspaper on the pine coffee table.

"As a matter of fact, I did knock on her door after dinner. Still no response. So I asked Mildred to take a tray up to her. If she's not hungry, she can throw it, which may help her nerves enormously."

Elizabeth looked at him thoughtfully. "You know, you may be a very nice person," she said, as if the idea had not occurred to her before.

"How dare you think such a thing!" He huffed. "No, Cousin. I think it only counts as being nice if you do it to someone you don't like, if I remember my catechism correctly."

"Are you very worried about her?" asked Elizabeth, wondering if she should confide in him.

"Impertinent of you to ask, since *you* are not," Geoffrey replied.

"I am so! I went up to see her right after dinner. And," she added triumphantly, "she let me in!"

"Is she all right?"

"I think so. She says she's tired and that doing the painting has been a strain for her. I asked her to quit, and she says she won't."

"Of course she won't. That was an excuse. Eileen loves to paint. If she didn't have that damned painting to work on, she'd never get out of the house and away from Mother."

Elizabeth nodded sympathetically. "Well, it's only for another week. If she can just keep telling herself that through the rehearsal and the fittings, and all the rest of it..."

"She'll be all right. Satisky should be all right for her. He's too much of a sponge to hurt her. With, of course, one possible exception."

"What's that?"

"Oh...just that frightened sponges can be deadly."

"Oh, Geoffrey! Don't talk doom and gloom! We're being silly!" Elizabeth shivered, wanting very much to be talked out of her own apprehension. "The wedding is going to go off just fine, in spite of all our collective nerve storms, and after that, it will be up to Eileen and Michael, and that's all there is to it."

"I suppose you're right," Geoffrey said grudgingly. "We are a nervy family. It's probably the money."

"You mean Great-Aunt Augusta's legacy?"

"No, just money in general. Having it, I mean. People with money have to find other things to fret about. Haven't you ever noticed that people on soap operas never worry about car payments or unemployment? They all have their minds on higher planes—like adultery and drug addiction."

Elizabeth laughed. "And what does this family worry about?"

Geoffrey considered. "Well, I myself live in constant fear of boredom, but thus far I've managed to stave it off. Yes, Elizabeth, I know you find it dull here, but I don't—perhaps because I enjoy my own company so much."

"You're never serious," sighed Elizabeth.

"On the contrary, I am always serious," said Geoffrey. "I learned long ago that if you tell the truth as matter-of-factly as possible, no one ever believes you."

"Bill does that, too, sometimes," said Elizabeth thoughtfully.

"Yes, but with him it's a hobby. With me, it is an art."

"He is certainly less arty than you are, if that's what you mean," said Elizabeth, with a suspicious hint of irony in her voice.

"Yes, but he is not nearly so interesting. Law school, indeed!"

"Oh, Bill can be very interesting. You should hear about his new roommate! He's an archeology major and he brings *bones* home to study and leaves them lying around. I'm looking forward to meeting him."

Geoffrey looked at her solemnly. "Why?"

"Because—well, because—oh, you know what I mean! Anyway, just because Bill isn't one of the family eccentrics doesn't mean he's dull." She sighed. "At least he knows what he wants to be, which is more than I can say."

"Don't you know?" asked Geoffrey. "Since you told

me that you were majoring in sociology, I naturally assumed that you were in the marriage market."

Elizabeth laughed. "There doesn't seem to be much demand for the product. Anyway, I guess I was in the marriage market, as you put it, but my campus romance broke up this spring, and—"

Geoffrey held up a restraining hand. "Spare me!" he pleaded. "Spare me all heartrending details! I beg you to carry the sword in your heart, and be brave!"

Elizabeth was struggling to think of a sufficiently witty reply when Satisky blundered into the room, with a ready frown of apology.

"The library is occupied, and I just thought—"

Geoffrey stood up. "They'll be leaving soon, I expect," he said casually. "I think I'll go with them. They may need a referee. You never can tell with barbarians. Would you like to come along, Elizabeth? You could be a cheerleader. Scream for blood and that sort of thing."

"No, thank you, Geoffrey."

"Then I'm off."

"You certainly are," muttered Satisky, when his tormentor was safely out of earshot. He sank down in the armchair with a weary sigh.

"How was your trip to the library?" asked Elizabeth politely.

"Oh, pleasant enough, I suppose. It gave me something to do while Eileen was painting."

"Have you seen Eileen this evening?" asked Elizabeth in a carefully neutral tone.

"No. I don't even know what's wrong. It isn't anything *I* did. I mean, I heard that she took one look at Dr. Shepherd and went cra— I mean...Oh, you know!"

"Yes. She seems nervous. I think she may be pushing herself too hard to finish that painting. How much does she have left to do?"

"I don't know! She won't let me see it either, not that I—" He stopped short of saying "care." If this cousin of hers went tale-bearing, he would really be in trouble. Elizabeth seemed nice enough, he grudgingly admitted, but he suspected her of having a sarcastic wit. Satisky

92

didn't care for sarcastic women; they tended to use ridicule as a weapon in disagreements. He much preferred tears, which he could dry manfully, and forgive, while still getting his own way in the argument. There was a slight family resemblance in looks between Elizabeth and Eileen, but the dispositions were altogether different. Eileen was a sweeter, softer girl. She looked like a picture of Elizabeth taken with an out-of-focus camera. When Eileen was not actually present, he found it difficult to picture her features, but he remembered her as a pleasant beige blur. This Elizabeth person was too positive by half. Vaguely he wondered if he were being interrogated.

"I was thinking that you might tell her not to work so hard on it," Elizabeth was saying. "I think the pressure of trying to finish is upsetting her. Could you tell her that you don't care if it's not ready in time?"

"Oh, sure. Sure."

"You're probably nervous, too, around all these strangers. Will your family be coming down for the wedding?"

"No." Satisky never wanted to say anything more than no to questions about his family, but in the silence that always followed, he found himself explaining that his parents had divorced when he was eight and that he had been raised by his grandmother, who had died two years ago. He had lost touch with his father, and his mother, who had remarried and was living on the West Coast, would not be coming to the wedding. He rattled off this explanation to Elizabeth, hoping that she wouldn't become cloyingly sympathetic and ask him about his childhood. He didn't like to talk about it, but he had survived it, and things were going well for him now. The only effect that he could determine was a distance between himself and other people, which had come from his years of solitary childhood. He had spent much of his time reading, and that was good; his literary background had served him well as a student of English, but it had made him unsure of how real people wanted to be treated. He never knew what to say to people whose next line he could not anticipate. He was uneasy with anyone who was not confined to the pages of a book, preferably a nineteenth-century edition. Perhaps that was why he had been able to love Eileen; she was not quite real.

Elizabeth was looking at him with interest, but not, he had to admit, with any particular sympathy. "How did you meet Eileen?" she asked.

He told her about the Milton seminar, and Eileen looking as vague and lost as—as Lycidas. She had been so shy and frightened that he had forgotten his own uneasiness around people. Eileen made him confident by comparison, so much so that he no longer worried about mispronouncing a name when he talked of literary matters. Like all people who read more than they conversed, Satisky had had his own way of pronouncing things before he had met anyone to discuss them with. This had led to embarrassing moments as an undergrad when he had spoken of "Frood" or "Go-Eth," much to the amusement of his classmates. He did not explain all this to Elizabeth, of course. He had not even confided his insecurities to Eileen. How could Eileen depend on him if she knew how uncertain he was?

Satisky began to hit the arm of the chair gently with his fist. "Maybe I rushed her," he said. "Maybe she isn't ready—isn't sure. Maybe she told Dr. Shepherd how she really feels about this marriage, and she's afraid he'll say something."

He told Elizabeth about the sweet clinging girl he had fallen for, and his fantasy of rescuing her from dragons. Then she had turned out to be a very wealthy and complicated article. More than he'd bargained for.

"And even though I *do* want to marry her—I think—I'm afraid to ask myself why. Afraid it might turn out to be the money. It's so much money! I don't like what it's doing to me! I don't like what I'm becoming."

"Have you tried to explain this to Eileen?"

Satisky looked shocked. "Of course not! She would be terribly hurt that I could even think of money instead of just of her. You know her—uh—background.

94

What if she killed herself because of me? Do you expect me to live with that?"

One of the problems of listening to other people's troubles is the difficulty in finding soothing noises to make. Elizabeth considered saying that everything would be all right, but the chance of that seemed remote. If Satisky really was so unsure of his feelings, he probably shouldn't go through with the marriage, but she shared his apprehension. Eileen's nerves were not yet strong enough to see her through a shock of that magnitude. Elizabeth had no intention of offering any advice on the subject, because she wanted no part of the guilt that Satisky seemed to be stuck with either way. She wished he hadn't chosen to confide in her. One thing was certain: she had better get him off that subject before whoever-it-was-that-just-walked-by-the-door decided to stop and listen. God help her if anyone thought she was encouraging Satisky to have doubts! She would be accused of trying to steal her cousin's fiancé, or trying to improve her chances for the inheritance, or both. She could imagine Aunt Amanda's reaction to the situation.

"We shouldn't be talking about this!" she whispered to Satisky. "Don't even think about it anymore! Just— don't!"

CHAPTER NINE

AMANDA CHANDLER SURVEYED the breakfast table with the air of a general conducting an inspection. In honor of the houseguests and the forthcoming wedding, this breakfast would be a family occasion, like those on weekends, when she would set aside time for getting together to discuss the plans for the day—usually *her* plans for *their* day. Despite the protests of Captain Grandfather and Dr. Chandler, who had to juggle early appointments, the meal was served at exactly ten o'clock—the shocking lateness being a concession to Geoffrey, who maintained that nothing short of Armageddon would arouse him earlier.

"And where is Eileen?" Amanda asked crisply, her eyes on Michael.

He looked away, murmuring something unintelligible.

"Elizabeth, would you please go upstairs and knock on her door? Tell her that we are waiting."

Elizabeth hurried from the dining room, hoping that Eileen had just overslept. If she had decided to prolong her hysterics for another day, everyone's nerves would start to go. She reached the upstairs hall. Eileen's door was closed. Elizabeth tapped gently. "Eileen! Are you awake? It's breakfast time!"

There was no sound from within.

Elizabeth tried the door. The handle turned easily, and she peeped inside. The bed was neatly made, and its occupant was not in the room. Elizabeth went back to the dining room and reported this to Amanda, who received the news in tight-lipped silence.

"I expect she's out painting," said Captain Grandfather. "When I got up at the sensible hour of seven"— he paused to glare at Geoffrey's rumpled dressing gown— "I found a box of cereal and a used bowl on the table here. I expect she got an early start today."

"She needs time to work on it," mumbled Geoffrey sleepily. "Why not just leave her alone?"

"I wouldn't dream of it!" snapped Amanda. "This is one of my little girl's last family breakfasts as a—as a—"

"Chandler," suggested her husband softly.

"Thank you, Robert. As a Chandler." She turned to Dr. Shepherd with a careful smile. "Dr. Shepherd, you must think we have shocking manners! But I'm sure you know what a special time like this can do to the nerves of a sensitive girl like Eileen. But I do apologize for her."

Shepherd murmured that he quite understood and went on eating his eggs.

"Charles," Amanda continued, "go and fetch your sister, please. Or, perhaps Michael would like to have a few moments—"

Charles stood up quickly. "Now, Mother, you know she especially doesn't want him to see the painting before it's finished. I'll go get her. Save me some toast."

"Have you talked to her since last night?" Elizabeth whispered to Michael.

He shook his head. "I thought I'd just leave her alone," he muttered.

Amanda interrupted them at this point to deliver a monologue on wedding rehearsal plans, and Carlsen

Shepherd began to talk quietly to Captain Grandfather, moving the silverware around in positions suspiciously resembling the armada of the previous evening's game.

"Who won?" asked Dr. Chandler, indicating his coffee spoon, which had just been turned into a Turkish fleet.

"Well, I did," said Shepherd, "but it was probably luck."

Elizabeth wondered if Eileen had intentionally skipped the family gathering. She found herself staring at the dying stag in the painting, and wondering whose eyes they reminded her of.

"Dad! Captain Grandfather!" Charles appeared in the doorway, panting for breath. "Could you come down to the lake, please?"

The last thing Wesley Rountree wanted in his county was a murder. County sheriffs do not keep their elected positions by brilliantly solving cases the way cops do on TV. They keep them by staying on good terms with the majority of the voting populace; and if there was one thing that Wesley Rountree knew about murders, it was that they caused hard feelings, no matter what. A conviction cost you the votes of the killer's family; an acquittal alienated the victim's family. It was a no-win situation.

Whenever there was a murder in Rountree's district, he always hoped that a migrant worker had gone berserk and committed the crime, but that was never the case. Marauding tramps were incredibly rare; jealous husbands and drunken good-old-boys were fatally common.

It wasn't that Rountree condoned murder or wanted to see the perpetrator go unpunished. He faithfully brought to justice the local killers, regardless of personal consequences, but whenever a murder was reported to his office, his first reaction was invariably indignation that someone would be so inconsiderate of his feelings as to commit homicide in his county.

Aside from that, the job of sheriff suited Rountree just fine. He had lived all his life in the county, except

99

for college and a four-year stint as an M.P. with the air force in Thailand. After his discharge, he had spent a couple of years with the highway patrol, and then when old Sheriff Miller had a heart attack and died, Rountree went back home to Chandler Grove and was elected sheriff in an uncontested election.

Now, five years later, in his second term as sheriff, Rountree was beginning to think of the job as a permanent thing. At thirty-six, he was a stocky blond who fought his cowlick with a crew cut and his beer belly with diet cola. Outdoor work and pale skin had kept him perpetually red-faced and freckled. The consensus of opinion around Chandler Grove was that Wesley Rountree was "doing okay." As a home-boy, he suited the community down to the ground; they wouldn't have traded him for Sherlock Holmes.

In a small rural county, where everybody knows everybody else, law enforcement is a personal matter. The voters wanted a father image, and one of the cleverest moves of Rountree's life had been perceiving that need and filling it.

He remembered the time that Floyd Rogers had been shot in the parking lot of Brenner's Cafe. There wasn't much of a mystery about it. Half a dozen people had seen Wayne Smith's red pickup leaving the scene of the crime.

It was pretty common knowledge that Smith had been fooling around with Pearl Rogers. "The boyfriend shot the husband?" asked Rountree when they called him. "It's supposed to be the other way around. Don't he watch television?"

Rogers was in critical condition in the county hospital, and Smith had to be brought in before some of the Rogers kinfolk decided to handle it themselves. Wyatt Earp might have organized a posse; Wesley Rountree preferred to use the telephone. He picked up the phone and dialed the number of Wayne Smith's farm.

After six rings, the fugitive himself answered.

"Hello, Wayne? This is Wesley Rountree. How you doing? That calf of yours going to make it? Glad to hear it. Listen, Wayne...we have a little problem here. I understand you shot Floyd Rogers a little while ago. What? Well, he told me himself, as a matter of fact. He was still conscious when the rescue squad got there. Say what? Dead? No, but he's laid up pretty bad in county hospital. I think he'll pull through, though. And Pearl, she's about to run us all crazy. Seems to think there's gonna be a shoot-out or some such foolishness. What, Wayne? Well, you've sobered up some now, haven't you? I thought you had. Listen, we need to have a talk about all this, Wayne. You need to come on down here so we can get this straightened out. No, you don't have to do that. I'll come out and get you in the county car. You just wait there, okay? Maybe you could put a few things in a canvas bag; we might have to keep you here. Your razor, change of underwear, things like that. Then you just go out on the porch and wait, okay? Right. I'll be there in twenty minutes. Stay calm, Wayne. Bye, now."

Case closed. Floyd Rogers had pulled through all right, and Bryce had got Wayne Smith off with two years' probation. Rountree hadn't lost either of their votes.

When the call came in about the death at the Chandler place, Rountree took down the particulars with a heavy heart. "Please, Lord," he muttered. "Let it be an accident, or all hell's going to break loose!"

"What's that, Wes?" asked his deputy.

Rountree looked sourly at Clay Taylor, with the law enforcement degree from the community college, and the rimless glasses, and the peculiar idea that a cop was a social worker.

"I think we got us a homicide," he grunted. "Chandler place."

Clay Taylor whistled softly. Cases involving the county gentry were rare. Occasional reports of trespassers or petty larcenies, that was about it. "The old man?" he asked.

"No. The daughter. They found her in a boat on the lake. Cause of death undetermined. We better get out there."

"Right, Wes. Want me to call the coroner?"

"Oh, Taylor, you asshole! Dr. Chandler *is* the coroner! What the hell you think I'm worried about? The damned coroner is a damned *suspect!*"

In a time of crisis, did people really never suspect what had happened, or did they show surprise because it was expected of them? When Charles appeared in the doorway asking them to come down to the lake, Elizabeth's mind framed the thought that Eileen was dead. Drowned in the lake, perhaps—images of Geoffrey's description of Eileen as a *Vogue* Ophelia flashed in her mind—or slumped down before her easel dead from heart failure. Still, if anyone had asked her later, she would have insisted that she had no idea what had happened to upset Charles. Perhaps she would even have believed it herself, because when people appeared upset, she always did imagine the worst, and she was almost always wrong. Almost always—but not this time.

Orders from Dr. Chandler and Captain Grandfather for the rest of the family to remain in the house were ignored. Indeed, Amanda led the group, while the others trailed at a respectful distance, murmuring among themselves.

Charles was talking in quiet, worried tones to his father. "I don't *know.* I can't find her," Elizabeth heard him say. "But I'm pretty sure something is wrong."

Elizabeth relaxed. False alarm, she thought. Another Chandler dramatization. Eileen will come wandering out of the woods with a handful of daisies and profess to wonder what all the fuss is about. And everyone will make a fuss over her, and call it "wedding nerves." It was becoming very annoying.

When they reached the lake, there was still no sign of Eileen.

As if echoing Elizabeth's thoughts, Geoffrey walked into the woods, calling for Eileen to come out. Amanda strode purposefully toward the easel, which was set up a few feet from the water's edge. There was no canvas on it.

"Robert!" she called. "The painting is gone!"

"Maybe she took it to show to someone," Elizabeth suggested.

Amanda ignored her.

If the painting is gone, Eileen must be all right, Elizabeth decided. She knew we'd come looking for her, and she wanted to make sure that we didn't see it.

Captain Grandfather caught Charles by the arm and pointed to the lake. "What's that doing out there?"

In the middle of the lake, barely afloat, was a half-rotted rowboat. Abandoned years ago, it had stayed pushed up into the reeds at the edge of the lake. A blue fiberglass speedboat had taken its place at the old boathouse on the western shore of the lake; but now the old punt had left its mooring in the marsh and had somehow managed to stay afloat long enough to reach mid-lake.

"We'll get the other boat," said Robert Chandler quietly.

He and Charles walked toward the boathouse, ignoring Amanda's demands to know the meaning of all this and the murmured offers of assistance from Shepherd and Satisky.

"But if she's in the boat, she's all right," Elizabeth said aloud. "You can't drown in a boat."

"Why are they wasting their time?" Satisky demanded. "You can see that there's nobody in it."

Dr. Shepherd gave a slight cough. "Nobody in it—sitting up."

The implications of this remark left them all speechless. They watched in silence as Dr. Chandler and Charles untied the speedboat, and pulled the rope to start the motor. Minutes later they had maneuvered their craft within reach of the old rowboat. They pulled the derelict alongside their own boat, and Dr. Chandler leaned over to look inside.

"They've found her," said Captain Grandfather.

They began to walk slowly toward the boathouse, arriving at the small pier at the same time the boats did. Dr. Chandler waved them away as if he were warding off a blow, but they had only to look down into the sodden rowboat to see what had been found.

"Shall I get your medical bag, sir?" asked Shepherd.

Chandler hesitated, and then nodded. He had nearly said that it was useless, but the formality must be upheld, as it was in every case. Shepherd ran for the house.

Geoffrey had come out of the woods when the speedboat motor had started up, and he joined them on the pier, elbowing his way past Elizabeth and Satisky to look into the boat.

Eileen Chandler lay sprawled at the bottom of the boat as if she had fallen on her back, with her legs apart and one arm flung back over her head. An inch of water in the bottom of the boat lapped at the edges of her painting smock and turned her hair into limp dark weeds floating gently around her shoulders. Her face was calm. Except for the pallor and the plastic look of her skin, she might have been asleep. Her eyes were closed, and her lips slightly parted, as if she might at any moment yawn and stretch. But she was very still— too still to be breathing.

No one had spoken. Amanda Chandler was clinging to Captain Grandfather as though she were afraid of falling into the water. Dr. Chandler and Charles had turned away and were securing the boats, tying one to each of the end pilings. Without wanting to, Elizabeth turned to look at Michael Satisky. He was staring openmouthed at the lifeless form below them, oblivious to the others beside him. Finally he knelt jerkily on the pier, and leaning toward Eileen's still body, he croaked: "She has a lovely face; God in his mercy lend her grace."

And Geoffrey started to laugh.

Wesley Rountree swung his white Datsun around the curve, and glared at the two houses just coming into view.

"That's a doozy, isn't it?" he remarked with a snort.

Clay Taylor grunted without glancing up from his well-worn copy of *Anatomy of a Revolution*. The castle was a familiar sight to everyone in the county by now; hardly worth getting upset over anymore. Even in a khaki uniform Clay managed to look counter-establishment. His brown curly hair was a briar patch, and his face, behind small wire-rimmed glasses, wore a perpetually mild expression. His friends, who ran pottery shops or worked in social services programs with low-income people, always expressed surprise upon learning Taylor's occupation. He himself considered it just another way of working with the poor, and he did what he could to keep peace all the way around. When he spent his own money to buy groceries for migrant workers between jobs, he always said that he was "preventing shoplifting," and he joked that he was really trying to save himself some work. He had little sympathy for speeding tourists or middle-class teenage vandals, but the crimes of the real poor always struck him as symptoms of an even larger crime, of which they were only victims. He wouldn't knowingly permit an offender to get away, but he did his best in "preventive measures," such as keeping in close touch with the migrant workers or arranging for his friends in social services to help the needy before they became truly desperate. Apparently, his efforts to deter crime were appreciated by those who had been determined to commit them: in the last two years the county burglary rate had decreased by 5 percent, while that of the neighboring county had risen accordingly. He considered it a tribute, of sorts; although if anyone had asked, he would have insisted that it was pure coincidence, which it might have been.

In theory, Deputy Taylor and Sheriff Rountree were ideological enemies, each one representing all the things the other held most in contempt; but actually, they got along well enough. Rountree still sneered at leftist demonstrators on the six o'clock news, but he allowed as how his deputy was all right. Couldn't fault a man for being nice to people, he'd grumble. Taylor still saw the establishment personified by a fat and drawling old man in a white suit (though he had never seen one), but he generously classified his boss as a well-meaning but unenlightened tool of the system. He made efforts from time to time to make Rountree see the error of his ways—so far, without notable success.

"Bet that house cost quite a bit," remarked Rountree with a hint of a smile.

Clay sighed. "And I'm supposed to say that it isn't fair, one person having so much money, while the sharecroppers sleep five in a room."

Rountree frowned at having his conversational bait so easily spotted. "Just making chitchat," he said hastily. "Did you tell Doris to call the state boys?"

"Yeah, but you never did say why. We haven't even seen the body yet, Wes. Might just be a drowning."

"Well, we got to be sure, whatever happened. They said they found her in a boat. That sound like a drowning to you? Anyway, when the victim is the coroner's own daughter, I don't see what else we can do but go for outside help," growled Rountree. "Not that I don't trust the doctor, mind you. He's a mighty fine man, but it'll look better at the inquest to have somebody else stating the particulars."

Taylor nodded. "Anyway, I don't think doctors work on their own relatives. I know I couldn't. What will they do?"

"Who? The state boys? We'll do the routine lab work here, like we always do, and then we'll send the body to the state medical lab for an autopsy. You brought the kit, didn't you?"

"Yeah. In the trunk."

Rountree swung the car into the driveway of the red brick mansion. "I'll just stop in at the house and tell them we're here. You go on out to the lake."

Wesley Rountree straightened his holster, adjusted his tan Stetson, and headed for the front door. He had worked with Dr. Chandler before, on the inevitable county death cases: summer drownings, wrecks, and hunting accidents; but never on a murder case. The doctor had always been quietly competent, easy to work with. He wondered what to expect this time, with the case so much more personal.

The Chandler family had assembled in the library, where Captain Grandfather had herded them, and where he now stood guard over them, dispensing coffee and sternly discouraging any attempts at hysteria.

Charles and Dr. Chandler had remained by the lake to wait for the sheriff, leaving the old man in charge of the family.

"Someone should call Louisa," Amanda kept saying, making ineffectual gestures toward the telephone.

"Not yet you won't," growled Captain Grandfather. "You're quite enough to contend with as it is. I won't have two caterwauling women on my hands. Or do you want her questioned, too?"

Amanda sniffled that she couldn't be expected to think of things like that, but surely someone ought to realize that arrangements must be made.

"I'll call her myself later, Amanda; and Margaret, too, if you want me to. Now you get hold of yourself!"

Amanda dabbed her eyes, and looked around the room. "Dr. Shepherd! I should like you to prescribe a sedative for me, please!"

Shepherd, who had been sitting in a corner talking quietly to Elizabeth, looked up at the sound of his name. "I beg your pardon, Mrs. Chandler?"

Amanda repeated her request in the crisp tones of a command.

Shepherd shook his head. "I'm sorry," he said. "You are not under my care. Professional ethics, you know."

Amanda bristled. "Young man, I should think that in a crisis such as this, your physician's instinct would compel you to—"

"Aunt Amanda!" Elizabeth interrupted. "There's some brandy in the dining room. Shall I get you some?"

"Yes, thank you, Elizabeth."

"Oh, I don't think so," said Geoffrey quickly. "Let's all just be brave, shall we? More coffee, Mother?"

"I wish I knew what to do," Elizabeth whispered to Shepherd.

"It's perfectly normal to feel inadequate in a crisis," he whispered back. "Just don't create any more problems than there already are."

"Well, at least I wish I could do something about *him*." She nodded toward the bereaved groom, curled

107

up in the wing chair and leafing methodically through the *Oxford Book of Verse*.

Dr. Shepherd frowned. "I know; but if you try to talk to him, you'll only force him to try to think up things to say. It can be a great strain for some people—trying to act bereaved. It would be much kinder to leave him alone."

"Trying to act?" Elizabeth echoed. "Don't you think he really is?"

Wesley Rountree opened the door, hat in hand. "Afternoon, everybody. Captain, sir. Sure am sorry to be here under these circumstances." He looked around, embarrassed at his own calm in a room that radiated strain, perhaps grief. "Is Dr. Robert down with the—er, down at the lake?"

Captain Grandfather set down his coffee and went over to shake hands with the sheriff. "I'll walk you down there, sir, while I tell you what we know. This way." He turned back to his daughter, who sat on the sofa twisting her handkerchief. "Amanda, you're to stay here. Don't do anything until we get back." Without waiting for an answer, he turned to go.

Wesley Rountree edged past him and said to the others, "Y'all please stay close at hand, if you don't mind. I'll be back directly to take statements." He closed the door behind him.

"It couldn't be called ungentle, but how thoroughly departmental," Geoffrey remarked.

"Robert Frost," said Satisky, without looking up from his book.

Amanda Chandler rose majestically. "I am going to my room," she announced, glaring in the direction of the wing chair. "When Mr. Rountree returns, tell him that I may be up to seeing him tomorrow." She swept out of the room.

"I guess I'd better try to reach my folks," murmured Elizabeth.

"Better wait until we know more," Shepherd suggested. "You'll only worry them without being able to tell them anything for sure. And, remember, you won't be able to leave yet."

Elizabeth sighed. "Is there some stationery in that desk?"

Wesley Rountree stared down at the small figure crumpled in the bottom of the boat. After a respectful silence of several minutes, he said softly, "You don't know the cause of death, do you, Doctor?"

Robert Chandler shook his head. "We didn't touch anything—except that I touched her to confirm that—" He turned away.

"You did right," Rountree assured him. "And just as soon as Clay takes some pictures, we'll get her out of there. You want to go on back to the house now?"

"No. No. I'll stay here," the doctor replied. "She was going to be married, you know. Next Saturday."

"Pretty girl," said Rountree politely. "It's a pitiful shame. Now, you don't have to talk about it right now, if you'd rather not, Dr. Robert. Clay and me have to do some routine stuff right now; taping, measuring—you know, the same stuff we always do. I understand she was painting down here. Is that the easel over there?"

"Yes. We haven't disturbed it either." He straightened up to look at the easel and shook his head. "I just don't understand how this could have happened. This boat is never used. Eileen didn't even care for boats."

"You say she was painting," said Rountree quickly. "Painting what? I don't see a picture on that easel."

"That's just it," Charles put in. "It's gone."

"You're the one that found her?"

"This is my son Charles, Wesley," said Dr. Chandler.

Wesley nodded. "Uh-huh. And you found her, did you?"

"Well, when she didn't come down for breakfast, Mother sent me to look for her. I got here and she was gone. So I went back to the house and got Dad, we took the boat out and—and we found her."

"But the painting was not there when you first came looking for her?"

"Right."

Clay Taylor lowered his camera and stared at

109

Charles. "Are you saying that somebody stole the painting?"

Charles shrugged.

"Get over to that easel, Clay," said Rountree impatiently. "I want a shot of it, and also one of the ground around it. Look sharp for footprints. If you see any, give a holler."

Taylor nodded, and left the dock.

"Now, Dr. Chandler, do you mind if I just start filling out this report? I know you want it done as quick as possible."

"Go ahead, Wes," sighed Robert Chandler.

"Name of the deceased?"

"Eileen Amanda Chandler."

When he had filled in the preliminary data—age, date of birth, and so forth—Rountree asked, "Now, Dr. Chandler, did your daughter have any medical problems that might explain this? Heart or something?"

"No. Nothing."

"You wanna speculate on the cause of death? Can we rule out drowning?"

Chandler waved him away. "Please...I'd rather have the state lab do it."

"They're on the case," said Rountree. "Called 'em before we left the office. They said for us to bring them the body in the station wagon, and they'll do the autopsy there. I thought I'd have Clay do it when I finish here."

"Fine."

"Oh—I'll have to schedule an inquest. Would Tuesday be all right for that? You'll need to be making arrangements with Mr. Todd down at the funeral home, I reckon."

"Yes, of course," whispered Dr. Chandler. "Excuse me. My wife will be needing me." He turned away from the lake and hurried up the path toward the house.

"She would have been married next week," Charles explained. "Now, instead of a wedding, we have to plan a funeral."

Wesley Rountree heaved a sigh of discomfort. This case was going to be a sticky one! What a case! Hys-

110

terical women, grief-stricken relatives, and not a hope in hell of getting any straight answers. He gazed at the blank white face below him. What had she really been like? Crazy, according to the local gossip. Suicide, maybe? If so, you'd never catch the family admitting it. If there had been a note, it sure wouldn't have been left for him to find. A lot of spiteful things were said in suicide notes; a person getting the last word wanted to make it worthwhile. People were funny about suicides, anyhow. Took it as a criticism of the family; well, maybe it *was* a lot of times. Still, a girl a week away from getting married wasn't a likely candidate for suicide. He'd known a few grooms that might have considered it, but brides were different. Unless there was something about this couple that hadn't come to light. He made a mental note to ask the medical examiner about the possibility of pregnancy.

Turning to Captain Grandfather and Charles, Rountree said, "Y'all go back to the house now. Clay and I will finish up here and get the body loaded in the car, and we'll take it on out to the lab. I'll be back later this evening. I want to get preliminary statements while it's still fresh in everybody's mind."

"I assure you, Sheriff, we are not likely to forget," said Captain Grandfather. He turned and followed Charles up the path.

Clay Taylor set the camera down carefully in the grass, and began to examine the ground around the easel. The family had pretty much trampled the place looking for the girl, so he couldn't really tell if there had been an intruder or not. Still, he guessed he'd better do his stuff while the evidence was still there—just in case it turned out to be a homicide.

"What do you know about these people, Clay?" asked Wesley Rountree when they were alone. "Aren't you about the same age as the Chandler boys?"

"Yeah, but I never knew them," said Clay. "They went off to private school. I've seen 'em around."

"What about the daughter? Didn't I hear some story about her being crazy?"

"I think they'd prefer to call it a nervous breakdown," said Clay impassively.

"Whatever. You ever hear anything about suicidal tendencies?"

"No. But you'd do better to ask the family," said Clay.

Wesley Rountree gave his deputy a pitying look. "Oh, son, if you believe that, you got a lot to learn about police work."

When they had finished the crime-scene work, Clay drove the car into the Chandlers' backyard, parking it as close to the path and as far from the house as he could. He took the body bag from the trunk and carried it down to the lake, where Wesley was waiting beside the body. Together they lifted Eileen's body out of the boat and fitted it into the canvas carrier.

"Let's get this loaded and get on out of here," said Wesley. "I don't think the family needs to see this. You want some help?"

"Not really," said Clay. "She's real light."

They walked in silence up the path. Rountree occasionally went ahead to clear branches out of the deputy's way. When they reached the car, Clay said, "You want me to transfer her to the station wagon at the office and take it on up to the lab?"

Rountree shook his head. "What the hell," he said. "Let's go from here. I'd like to have a word or two with Mitch Cambridge on this one. Seeing as how it's Dr. Robert's daughter, and all."

"Okay."

"That ought to put us back here late this afternoon to talk to these people. I hope they've calmed down some by then."

The Chandler house was silent for most of the afternoon. The family and guests had followed Amanda's example and retired to their rooms, except for Captain Grandfather, who had remained in the study. He had tried to call Elizabeth's parents, but there was no answer; they were still away at the sales convention. When he telephoned Louisa, Mrs. Murphy had answered the phone and informed him that Alban had driven his mother to a garden show in Milton's Forge. They were not expected back until early evening. He spent the remainder of the afternoon sketching designs for a sailing vessel, with the name "Eileen" carefully pencilled on the prow.

When Rountree and Taylor returned late that afternoon, the Captain answered the door himself and ushered them into the library.

"Now, we don't know a thing yet," Rountree cautioned him, interrupting a spate of questions. "I've asked Dr. Cambridge to get on it right away and to call me as soon as he knows anything. I promise you, I'll let y'all know just as soon as I hear. Now, would you be good enough to get everybody together for me? Right here in this room would be fine."

A few minutes later, Rountree addressed the small group assembled in the library. "This is going to be a purely preliminary investigation," he announced. "We don't know the cause of death yet, but I can tell you that there will be an inquest, so I'm going to need a few facts from y'all: information about that little girl's state of mind; when she was last seen; that kind of thing. Clay, do you have everybody's name, and so forth?"

Taylor handed him the list of persons present, and Rountree glanced over it. "Mrs. Chandler?" he inquired, looking around the room.

"My daughter is upstairs," said Captain Grandfather with a trace of disapproval. "Her husband is attending her."

Rountree nodded and went back to the list. "Miss MacPherson? That must be you. Only lady present." He smiled reassuringly at Elizabeth, and then returned to the names. His finger stopped at the next name. "Dr. Carlsen Shepherd. Doctor? There's another doctor here! Why didn't somebody—"

Carlsen Shepherd half rose from his seat. "I am a psychiatrist, Sheriff, and if you were referring to an examination of the body just now, I assure you that you did the wisest thing by consulting your state pathology department. It's been a long time since I did anatomy."

"Not too long, from the look of you," Rountree grumbled. "Psychiatrist, huh? Was the deceased, by any chance, your patient?"

"Well, yes, she was, but—"

"Now we're getting somewhere!"

"But, Sheriff—"

"In a minute, doctor. Excuse me, could I just get everybody to clear out of here for a little bit and let me talk to this fellow? I'll call you back if I need to talk to you. Go on now, please." He shooed them with reassuring noises and comments about the routine nature of the proceedings, but with the oak doors firmly shut behind the last of them, the genial county lawman was transformed into an unsmiling, efficient investigator.

"Now, Doctor, you were about to tell me about your patient."

"Well...it depends," said Shepherd, shifting uneasily in his chair. "I've never had to discuss a patient with the police before. What do you want to know?"

"Pertinent facts, Doctor, that's all," said Rountree. Catching Shepherd's look of surprise, he grinned. "Were you surprised at that five-dollar word? Don't be. My accent may slip a little now that we're alone. When I was in the air force, I discovered that folks just naturally relax around a country accent. They seem to think a fellow can't know much if he talks so funny, and that little discovery proved to be such an asset to my chosen profession that I have done my durndest ever since to see that I keep one."

"That's an interesting psychological phenomenon, Sheriff. I wonder if it has ever been studied."

"Oh, I don't know if you fellas are on to it, but politicians have known it for years. Now, to get back to what we were talking about before, I just want to have a little unofficial talk. And don't be afraid of using any of your big words on me. I expect I'll tag right along."

"He has a degree from Georgia Tech," Clay murmured.

"Dr. Shepherd, this is my deputy, Clay Taylor. Clay,

will you take notes during this session, please? Doctor, would you like to lie down on the couch while you talk?"

"People always think we do that," sighed Shepherd. "Mostly, people just sit in chairs, you know."

"I understand," said Rountree, with a trace of a smile. "Now—about Eileen Chandler..."

"Well, I'm connected with the university clinic, and when Eileen enrolled at the university this fall, she came to the clinic. She had been referred by her previous physician, Dr. Nancy Kimble."

"Why was that?"

"Oh, for several reasons, I think. Eileen had just been released from Cherry Hill, and Dr. Kimble was going on sabbatical to Europe this year, so she would have been unable to follow up on Eileen personally."

"Uh-huh. And what were you treating her for?"

"Well, she was recovering from schizophrenia, but I dealt mostly with her adjustment problems. Dr. Kimble had already worked through everything major. I mean, Eileen was well enough to attend school and to lead a normal life. Seeing me was more of a safeguard than anything else. So she wouldn't feel completely alone in her new surroundings."

"Were you treating her for depression?"

"No. I wouldn't call her adjustment problems depression..."

"Well, would you say she was depressed? Capable of suicide?"

Shepherd hesitated. "It is possible, of course. But I can't say that I foresaw it. Not depression."

"All right then, Doctor, why are you here?" asked Rountree gently.

"I was invited to the wedding. I'm not here professionally."

"And who invited you?"

"Eileen Chandler. She didn't have too many friends, poor kid. She was extremely shy. And from what I heard about this whole setup, I thought it might be a nice thing to do."

"I see. Well, anyway, you can tell me something about

115

her state of mind as you've observed it since you've been here."

"Er—no. I really can't. I saw Eileen for less than a minute." He shifted uncomfortably in his chair.

Rountree leaned forward with quickened interest. "Now, why is that?"

Dr. Shepherd was silent for a moment, framing his answer. Finally he said, "Sheriff, it beats the hell outta me. I had been here less than an hour, and I was out in the hall talking to her Cousin Elizabeth, when Eileen walked in, screamed that she didn't want me here, and went charging off upstairs."

"And why did she do that?"

Shepherd shrugged. "I'm a psychiatrist, not a mind reader. All I know is, she fled when she saw me, then broke a mirror in the upstairs hall. Her family said it was just wedding nerves, and that may be as true as anything. She wasn't a stable girl."

"Should she have been getting married?"

Shepherd grinned. "That, Sheriff, is one form of insanity I don't deal with. I told you: she was no longer a mental patient. We would have classified her as neurotic. And surely you know that neurotics get married all the time."

Rountree grunted. "Did she have any reason to resent you being here?"

"I wouldn't think so, Sheriff. Remember, she invited me herself. Handwritten invitation."

Rountree sighed. "Well, I'll have to look into it. You got all that down, Clay?"

The deputy, hunched over his notepad, nodded briefly, and went back to writing.

"So, we've established that she was upset, but we don't know why. Of course, I reckon there's the obvious. You want to tell me what you thought of the groom?"

"I didn't know him. I mean, I'd met him, of course, but only once. He came by to pick her up one afternoon after our session, that's all."

"But she'd have talked about him, wouldn't she? Must have been pretty important to her."

Shepherd grimaced. "Did she talk about him? Con-

116

stantly! But you see, Sheriff, her viewpoint was hardly objective. According to Eileen, Michael Satisky was a knight in shining armor. She talked like a bride, in fact."

"Which she was—or almost was. Well, if this turns out to be a suicide, we may have to check the shining armor for rust spots. Reckon I'll have a talk with the young man. All right, Dr. Shepherd, that's all I can think of. Is there anything else you want to tell us?"

"Well, let me remind you that I knew Eileen when she was away at school. Away from her family, I mean. That change of environment could make a big difference in her state of mind."

"How's that?" asked Rountree.

"Well, Eileen seemed anxious about coming home. As if she were dreading something."

"You want to take a guess at what that was?"

"Well...offhand..." Shepherd glanced up at the ceiling. "Have you ever met her mother?"

CHAPTER TEN

"HE WASN'T MUCH HELP, was he?"

Clay shrugged. "Well, if she was suicidal, and he didn't know it, it won't look so good for him professionally."

"Oh, hogwash!" sneered Rountree. "Her state of mind could have changed something awful since she got home. That's what we got to figure out: what's been going on around here—and could it have made her want to kill herself?"

Michael Satisky, who had been sent in by Shepherd, halted in the doorway. "Kill herself?" he echoed, forgetting his nervousness. "Is that what happened? Are you sure?"

"Will you sit down," moaned Rountree. "And don't jump to so dad-burned many conclusions. You probably know more than we do right now. So, what do you think? Did she kill herself?"

"How—how could I know?" Satisky stammered. The sheriff's genial drawl did not make him feel at ease. It reminded him of the easy, philistine confidence of the high school athletes who had made his life miserable as a teenager. He felt that he was being baited, and he became even more tense.

"Well, since you were going to marry her, we thought you'd be able to tell us a little something about her state of mind," said Rountree with heavy sarcasm.

Satisky winced. "She was upset about something," he admitted. "But I don't know why. It wasn't about our engagement, because she didn't know—"

Rountree pounced. "Didn't know what?"

"Oh...well...nothing important. I mean, she didn't know, so it couldn't very well be relevant, could it?"

"I think I'd better hear this," said Rountree. "You'd be surprised at what people know. They got the darndest ways of finding out—listening at doors and I don't know what-all."

Satisky blushed, remembering his opening words of the interview.

Rountree pretended not to notice that his shot had hit home. "Anyway, you never can tell what's going to be important, so I think you'd better tell us what this is all about."

"It's nothing really," Satisky insisted. "I was just ...you know...getting nervous. About the wedding and all—uh, this is hard to discuss with police officers..."

Rountree snorted. "You think this is hard? You should have tried explaining to the bride that you'd changed your mind."

"Well, I hadn't actually made any decision..."

Too spineless to go through with it, Rountree's look suggested; but he merely asked: "Are you sure Eileen Chandler couldn't have figured this out?"

Satisky hesitated. "Well...I did mention something about it to her cousin last night."

"Her cousin. Who would that be?"

"Elizabeth MacPherson."

"Oh, that pretty little gal with the dark hair. I see!" Rountree beamed at him with understanding.

"No! I'm sure you don't see at all. I merely mentioned to Elizabeth that I was somewhat apprehensive. I certainly did *not* make any advances of the kind that you suggest!"

"Talks just like a book, don't he?" Rountree beamed happily at Clay.

Clay nodded. He had seen Rountree's clown act pay off too many times to question it, but he couldn't join in on the spirit of it. He contented himself with playing straight man.

"So, we know you had a little confidential talk with 'Cousin Elizabeth,' right here in the house of your intended. Is that right?"

"Uh—yes," said Satisky miserably.

"Now, are you sure you couldn't have been overheard?"

"Oh, I don't think so! I mean, no one has mentioned it!" Rountree and Taylor exchanged glances of exasperation. "Anyway," Satisky continued shrilly, "I don't think that had anything to do with it! And I don't think she killed herself! I think she was murdered for money. Have you heard about the will? Well, find out about *that!* If you ask me, she was murdered!"

"Yes, I witnessed the will," Elizabeth told them a few moments later. "She had her lawyer come out to talk to her about the inheritance, and she asked him to draw one up. But she had a handwritten one already done, and he told us it was legal—though he didn't seem to like the idea much."

"A will," mused Rountree. "Did she have a lot to leave?" He wondered what the Chandlers would consider "a lot."

Elizabeth explained the terms of Great-Aunt Augusta's will, leaving her fortune to the first of the cousins to marry. "But I think Eileen left it all to Michael, anyway," she concluded.

"Well," drawled Rountree, "if I understand you right, she didn't accomplish much there. She only got the trust fund when she was married—which she never was. So she had nothing to leave, did she?"

Elizabeth stared at him. "I never thought of that," she said slowly.

"So there's an inheritance up for grabs. This gets more interesting all the time. Is anybody else engaged? How about yourself?"

"Well, no, I'm not."

"How about the others?"

"Not that I know of. My Cousin Alban was engaged once, about four years ago, but the girl broke it off, and he hasn't seen her since. I haven't heard of Charles or Geoffrey being interested in anybody, and my brother— oh, but he's not even here! So—no, I don't think any of us is considering getting married."

"Bet you will now," said Rountree.

When Elizabeth did not reply, Rountree tried another approach. "Now, Miss MacPherson, we need to get an idea about your cousin's state of mind. I'd be obliged if you'd tell me when you saw her last."

"Umm...last night after dinner. I went up to her room to see how she was."

"Any reason why you might be worrying about her?"

Elizabeth recounted Eileen's reaction to Dr. Shepherd's arrival.

"Didn't she want Dr. Shepherd here?"

"She didn't seem to," Elizabeth admitted. "But that doesn't make sense. She invited him here herself."

"Who told you that?" asked the sheriff.

"Well—he did. Dr. Shepherd."

Rountree glanced over at Clay Taylor, who was still scribbling furiously.

"So you went up after dinner—to see if Miss Chandler was feeling better."

"Yes. We talked for a little while, and she said she was nervous about the wedding—"

"Why do you suppose that was?"

Elizabeth sighed. "Probably because my Aunt Amanda is turning it into a three-ring circus. Poor Eileen was feeling like an exhibit. I'd have been nervous, too."

"Could be. Anything else you can think of?"

"Well, I thought she might be overtiring herself trying to finish the oil painting she was working on.

122

She'd work on it for hours every day."

"Why was she painting pictures at a time like this? What's it of, anyway?"

"It was to be her wedding gift to Michael. And she wouldn't show it to anybody. But we think it must have been a view of the lake, because she always went there to work."

"Did Miss Chandler seem depressed to you in your talk with her last evening?"

She considered this. "No. Not if you mean suicidal. I think she was impatient to have the whole thing over with, but she really wanted to marry Michael."

"Michael," Rountree repeated. "Let's talk about him awhile. I understand you had an interesting conversation with the prospective groom. What did he have to say?"

Elizabeth sighed in exasperation. "I guess he must have told you already, or you wouldn't be asking. He said that he didn't really want to go through with the wedding. I think he was terrified of feeling like that, but also very much afraid of hurting my cousin."

"Did he tell her how he felt?"

"I don't think so. He wasn't planning to."

"Then why did he tell you?"

Elizabeth thought for a moment. "I think because I was an outsider, too. Maybe he felt that I might understand."

"And did anybody else listen in on this conversation?"

"No. At least, I don't think so."

"But if by some chance the bride had slipped downstairs and overheard all this, that might change her state of mind, don't you reckon?"

"I guess it could have. I told him to be quiet about it, because he was certainly making me nervous by talking about it."

"What was making you nervous? That he was transferring his affections to you?" asked Rountree casually.

"Of course not!" snapped Elizabeth. "I certainly didn't want him!"

"Even for all that money?"

123

"Well, Clay, what do you think?" asked Rountree when they were alone. "Suicide, or accident—or something else?"

Clay Taylor shook his head. "This one's too close to call," he said, leafing through his notes. "I'll believe anything the lab tells us this time. There's evidence for almost anything. Suicide—she was a psychiatric patient, and her fiancé would have been glad to ditch her; murder—she was an heiress, or she would have been. Accident? Well, they do happen, even to people whose death would be convenient. I wouldn't even bet you a Coke on this one, Wes."

"Well, I would," Rountree grumbled. "I'd bet a whole raft of Cokes on a nice little old homicide because her death was mighty damn convenient for a bunch of folks, and I didn't see anybody genuinely grieved at losing her. Did you?"

The deputy looked startled. "Well..." he faltered. "Her mother?"

"Clay, we haven't even seen Amanda Chandler yet," Rountree reminded him. "And when we do, you look real carefully at her. And ask yourself if you're seeing a mother grieving over a lost child or a property owner mad as fire because something belonging to her got taken."

"I still think it might have been suicide," said the deputy. "We still have a lot of people left to talk to, and we haven't found anybody who saw her since last night."

"Nobody admitting it, anyway. That's the trouble with you, Clay. You always go around believing everything."

"What do you believe, Wes?"

"I believe I need more to go on." Rountree grinned. "And I believe I'll have a cheeseburger at Brenner's while I wait for the lab report. Let's go tell all these people we'll be back tomorrow, when we know something definite."

Robert Chandler closed the door to his wife's bedroom and went down the stairs to the library. Captain

Grandfather and Charles were sitting at the gate-leg table, dispiritedly pushing little fleets and armies around a map of the eastern hemisphere.

Captain Grandfather glanced up from the board. "How is she, Robert?"

Chandler sighed. "Asleep. Finally. I don't want her disturbed."

"It's all right. Sheriff Rountree left a little while ago. Said they'd be back in the morning, and that they should have the lab report by then. I expect they'll want to talk to us then—and to Amanda as well."

"Where are Geoffrey and Elizabeth?"

"In the kitchen making sandwiches," Charles replied.

"And our other—guests?"

"In their own rooms, I believe," declared Captain Grandfather. "They didn't seem to know what to say. Bit awkward all around. I for one am glad they're not underfoot."

"What do you think, Dad?" asked Charles.

The doctor shook his head. "I don't know, Charles. I want to believe it was an accident, but I can't think what she would have been doing in that boat."

"Maybe she wanted another perspective for the painting," Charles suggested.

"The painting! That's another thing. I keep asking myself what's become of the painting."

"So do I," said Captain Grandfather quietly. "So do I."

"Charles, did you by any chance see the painting she was working on? When you went to the lake at dinner?"

"No, Dad. I didn't go get her for dinner. That was Alban. You'll have to ask him if he saw what she was working on, but I doubt it. She wouldn't let any of us see it. You know how secretive she was."

"But she kept on painting by the lake," mused Dr. Chandler. "So it must have been a lake scene. Now, why is the painting missing?"

"How can it be important?" asked Charles. "If she painted the lake, there's no point in stealing the painting. Anybody could look at the lake and see what Eileen saw."

The telephone rang insistently. Dr. Chandler hurried from the room to answer it. Charles and Captain Grandfather turned their attention back to their game.

"Fleet: St. Petersburg to Norway," Charles murmured. "Have you told Alban and Aunt Louisa yet?"

"Still not home last time I checked," grunted Captain Grandfather.

Charles got up and peered through the curtains. "I see some more lights on. I think they must be back." He settled back in his chair and studied the board. "You know, it seems strange that they don't know yet. It's as if Eileen is still alive in their minds, because they haven't been told. I believe Hegel deals with that concept—"

"Well, Elizabeth or Geoffrey can tell them," snapped the old man. "I'm not going to relive it in the telling. She was a sweet little girl, Eileen was. But she grew up so troubled. You couldn't reach her. When you'd ask her anything, she'd shy away, as if it were an intrusion. Guess we should have insisted. Should have intruded. Maybe things would have been different. This family sets too damn much store on peace and quiet!"

"Sir?" Charles blinked.

"What's wrong with making a few waves? Good storm clears the air, dammit!"

"Uh—it's your move, Captain Grandfather."

"Oh, put it away. I don't want to play anymore."

Charles stood up. "Well, then, if you'll excuse me, I think I'll go upstairs and do some reading."

Captain Grandfather waved him away impatiently. "You go on. I'll put this away myself."

He was still arranging the wooden blocks in the proper compartments when Dr. Chandler returned, closing the door behind him. "That was Wesley Rountree," he said. "He's got the lab results." He sank down wearily on the sofa.

"So it was murder," said Captain Grandfather.

"It was murder."

* * *

Wesley Rountree rolled up his napkin and pitched it at the wastebasket beside Clay's desk. "Bingo! You know, if I keep eating cheeseburgers from Brenner's for dinner, pretty soon Mitch Cambridge'll be doing an autopsy on me."

Clay Taylor stopped typing, his two index fingers poised in midair. "If I were you, Wes, I'd worry about those diet drinks you've been having. No telling what's in those artificial sweeteners."

Rountree grunted. "Nobody lives forever, Clay. Sometimes I think I'm lucky to have made it this long. My mama was always after me to quit the highway patrol 'cause she was afraid I'd get killed in a high-speed chase, and now you're trying to take my diet sodas away from me." He shook his head. "Ain't nothing safe."

"Not even getting married," said Clay.

"Lord, who ever told you that was safe? Oh! You mean the Chandler girl?"

"Is Cambridge sure about the results?"

"Now, you know Mitch Cambridge. If he wasn't positive, you couldn't get an answer out of him with a stick! The official cause of death, to which he will testify at the inquest, was the bite of a poisonous snake—"

"Water moccasin?"

"Yep, which bit her four times on her neck and upper back. He thinks she fell on the snake in the boat."

"And it wasn't an accident?"

"No indeed. See, there's also a subdural hematoma, which is what Mitch likes to call a bruise, on the back of her head. Skull was fractured due to a sharp blow to the"—he consulted a piece of paper on the desk in front of him—"to the occipital bone."

"So somebody hit her on the head and threw her in the boat."

"That's about the size of it, Clay."

Rountree scooted forward in his swivel chair, and began to root in the papers that littered the top of his desk. He had what Clay liked to call an archeological filing system: the papers nearest the top were the most recent. He generally managed to find what he was looking for, though. Eventually. Really important items, such as warrants, were kept under the bronze sphinx paperweight at the top center of his desk. Rountree had inherited the desk along with his job from the late Sheriff Miller, who had kept both for thirty years. "I don't want to change nothing except the calendar," Rountree had vowed when the office became his. It gave him a sense of continuity with the past, as though Nelse Miller were still around somehow, backing him up.

"Have you seen the mail today?" Rountree asked, momentarily giving up the search.

"Doris always puts it on your desk," said Clay, between taps at the typewriter.

"I was afraid of that," sighed Rountree.

He pawed through another stack of papers and pulled out a small bundle of letters bound by a red rubber band. "This must be it," he muttered, flipping through them. "Hardware store sale, light bill, something from the community college." He opened the yellow circular and scanned it briefly. "Seems they're advertising their courses for this fall."

"Yeah, I got one at home," said Clay. "They must've put me on their mailing list, since I took their scuba diving course."

"How would you like to take another one?" asked Rountree. "I see one in here that would be mighty useful for a deputy."

"Oh, the judo course? I've been thinking about it."

"No. That isn't the one I had in mind," said Rountree, running his finger down the page. "It's this one, B-14: Beginning Shorthand."

Taylor gave him a sour look and went back to typing.

"Well, admit it. You do more note-taking than fighting," Rountree persisted.

"Doesn't mean I have to like it," said Clay.

"It's useful, all the same. Is that what you're typing up now?"

"The notes on the Chandler case, yeah. I thought you might want to see them."

"That's the honest truth," sighed Wesley. "These people not being what I'm used to is sure throwing me off my stride. You take our average cases now. When Vance

128

Wainwright gets drunk and disorderly, where's he gonna go?"

"To his ex-wife's trailer," said Taylor promptly.

"Right. And when the statue of the pioneer is missing from the high school lawn, where do we look?"

"All over the grounds of Milton's Forge High."

"Right." Rountree chuckled. "Remember the time we found him on the fifty-yard line? But this case is in a class by itself."

"Looks like it's going to take a while," mused Clay.

"That reminds me," said Wesley, lifting the telephone and extracting the phone book, which he kept underneath it for quick location. "You and I are going to be tied up and out of the office for most of the day tomorrow, so I'd better call Doris and tell her we need her here to keep the office open."

"On Saturday?" Clay whistled. "Don't hold the phone too close to your ear."

"And I'll call Hill-Bear Melkerson, while I'm at it," said Rountree, ignoring Taylor's last remark. "He can take the car out on patrol while you and I are conducting this investigation." He was dialing the number as he talked. "Hello, let me speak to Hill-Bear. This is Sheriff Rountree calling," he said into the phone.

When people heard the name Hill-Bear Melkerson, they usually expected to meet an American Indian, but this was not the case. Hill-Bear, a squat and solid Anglo-Saxon, had picked up the name in his French class at Chandler Grove High. He had previously been known by his given name, which was Hilbert. For seventeen years he had endured life as Hilbert, occasionally squashing adolescent comedians who teased him about it, but in high school French all that changed. On the first day, the teacher had assigned everyone French names: John became Jean and Mary, Marie. When she came to Hilbert, the teacher informed him that his name was already French, but that in class it would be pronounced "Hill-Bear." Hilbert Melkerson had been so delighted with the sound of this sobriquet that he had insisted on being called that ever since. By that time, he was a 230-pound tackle on the Chandler Grove varsity squad, so he got his way. Hill-Bear he became.

"Hill-Bear, is that you?" Rountree cradled the phone between his ear and shoulder, while he scribbled on a notepad in front of him. "I'm fine; how 'bout yourself? That's good. Listen, Hill-Bear, we're gonna need you to work tomorrow if that don't interfere with your plans too much. Oh, just regular patrol in the squad car. Doris will be here in the office, keeping an eye on things. No, I won't be off. Fishing? I wish I was. No, I'm afraid something pretty serious has happened out at the Chandler place and Clay and I will be investigating. No, it wasn't a break-in. Listen, Hill-Bear, I don't want to be talking about this on the phone. When I see you tomorrow morning, I'll fill you in. Okay. Around eight. All right. 'Bye now."

"He's coming in?" asked Clay.

"Oh, yeah. He'll be here at eight." Rountree flipped through the card file on a metal stand beside the phone. "Hill-Bear's a good old boy. You can always count on him."

Hill-Bear Melkerson was not a full-time employee of the sheriff's department as Taylor was. He worked for Rountree part-time on an as-needed basis, when he wasn't on his regular job at the paper mill in Milton's Forge. He usually handled the parking at Chandler High football games or at the county fair, and filled in for Rountree or Taylor on their days off. He was good for New Year's Eve road patrols, too. No one was ever drunk enough to argue with Hill-Bear.

"Guess I better call Doris," Rountree groaned. "I sure do hate to ask her to come in tomorrow."

"You can't be that concerned about spoiling her weekend, Wes," said Clay.

"No, the fact is I'm not," Rountree admitted. "But if I ask her to come in, she'll want to know why, and if I tell her, it'll be all over the county by morning."

Geoffrey had been cutting tuna fish sandwiches in resolute silence for several minutes. Elizabeth had not talked to him, partly because she was preoccupied and partly because she didn't know what to say. Any expression of sympathy might provoke either tears or an outburst of mordant wit, neither of which she was prepared to deal with. She had confined her utterances to basics: pass the mayonnaise, is there more bread? The rest of her mind retraced the sequence of the day's events and tried to make sense of them.

She stole a glance at Geoffrey, still working like an automaton on the pile of sandwiches. "Do you think this will be enough, Geoffrey?"

"What? Oh. I suppose so. I won't be eating any. Are you hungry?"

"Just a little," Elizabeth admitted. She was starving.

Geoffrey set the last sandwich precariously on the heap. "I guess we're finished. I seem to have run out of things to do."

"Geoffrey, listen, about Eileen—"

"I'll just carry the tray into the library," he said quickly. "Then I'm going to my room."

Elizabeth put away the bread and mayonnaise, lingering over her self-appointed task of cleaning the kitchen. Mildred would take care of it tomorrow when she arrived. To hell with Mildred, Elizabeth thought, she needed something to do right then. She tried to decide why she was so reluctant to join the family in the study. Because I feel like an outsider, she thought. Geoffrey's grief and the fierce restraint of the others made her awkward. She couldn't pretend, but to exhibit a lack of bereavement within the family seemed unnecessarily rude. The best course would be to go to her room, but she needed to talk. She felt that if she could hear herself talk, things would sort themselves out. She rinsed the tuna fish bowl and washed the knives while she considered the matter further.

A few minutes later, Elizabeth picked up the yellow wall phone by the refrigerator. "Long distance, please." Soon she was connected with the proper city.

"Hello, Brookwood Apartments? Are you the manager? I'm calling long distance. My brother is a tenant of yours. In Apartment 208, and he doesn't have a phone,

131

but there has been an emergency in the family. A death, in fact, and I must speak to him."

Elizabeth paced the length of the phone cord while she waited for Bill to be fetched from his lair. If he didn't feel like listening to her in the manager's apartment, which was probable, maybe he could call her back from a pay phone. She decided that it would be very comforting to talk to Bill, as long as they got it straight right from the beginning that he was to listen to her as a brother, and not as a student of criminal law. I know I have the right to remain silent, she quipped to herself; I waive that right just now. She heard the phone being picked up.

"Hello?"

"Bill! I have to talk to you. It's urgent. Don't interrupt. Can you talk or shall I give you the number here? You can call me back collect, just—"

"Uh—Elizabeth? I'm sorry, but Bill isn't here right now."

"He isn't? Who is this?"

"Milo."

"Milo! Oh, I've heard a lot about you. I'm looking forward to meeting you." Even in an emergency, we don't forget our manners, Elizabeth thought grimly. "But listen, we have a sort of family emergency, and I really need to talk to Bill. Where is he?"

"What's the matter? Where are you?"

He sounded quite concerned, as though he were ready to throw down the phone and come to her rescue. Elizabeth felt slightly better. "I'm all right," she assured him. "I'm at Chandler Grove for my cousin's wedding. At least, there was supposed to be a wedding, but she's dead. The sheriff has been called in, and they're investigating. They seem to think it was murder, but—" She was about to launch into the whole story, when she pictured Milo standing uncomfortably in a strange apartment, with the manager glaring at him. "I'm so sorry to be going on like this, Milo. I've never even met you."

"It's okay. Bill told me about your relatives. He was

132

expecting melodrama, but I don't think he would have predicted this. Are you all right?"

"Yes, of course. I just wanted to talk to somebody. Where's Bill?" Much as she needed to talk, she didn't feel like beginning at the beginning with even as kind a stranger as this. With Milo, she would only be reciting facts; with Bill she could progress to feelings.

"I'll have him call you as soon as he comes in, of course, but I haven't seen him since last night. I think he pulled an all-nighter with some other law students, something about a case..."

"Law or beer?" snapped Elizabeth.

"I just got home myself. My class is doing site work at some Indian mounds near here, and—well, don't get me started about that...Bill should turn up soon. If you give me your phone number, I'll have him call as soon as he comes in."

Elizabeth supplied the number, and a brief account of the situation. She thanked Milo and assured him that some other time she would very much like to hear about Indian mounds, and then she hung up, unreasonably annoyed with Bill for not being in. She reluctantly admitted to herself that she felt better. Milo was all right. Idly she wondered if he had brought home any more bones for the kitchen table. With a weary sigh, she prepared to join the mourners in the library.

To her relief, she found that only Captain Grandfather remained downstairs. He was sitting at the table, making sketches on a notepad.

"The others have gone to bed," he told her. "I have so much trouble sleeping that I have abandoned even the pretense tonight."

"Is there anything I can get you?" asked Elizabeth.

"No. More coffee will only make the improbable impossible. Have you eaten anything?"

"That's what I—no. I guess I will." She sat on the couch with a napkin in her lap, and helped herself to sandwiches.

"The sheriff called Robert a little while ago. Says they got the results of the autopsy."

"Oh? What was it? Heart failure?"

"They claim that Eileen was hit on the head, then thrown into that boat. It doesn't seem possible, does it? It isn't as if she were a stranger."

Elizabeth considered this. "I know what you mean," she said at last. "I always think of violent death as something that happens to people I don't know. How is—everybody?"

"I can't say that I took the trouble to find out. I let Robert handle them. He's a doctor; he's used to it."

"And Dr. Shepherd?"

"He went up to his room hours ago. The boys are all right. It's just Amanda."

Elizabeth nodded. It would be. "Is there anything I can do?" she asked.

"Not that I—oh yes, there is one thing. I promised Amanda hours ago that I'd let them know across the street." He inclined his head toward the castle. "It completely slipped my mind."

"Would you like me to tell them? I could go in a few minutes."

"Please. They're back now. Been to some flower show all day. You tell Alban that it's a murder case, and that the sheriff will be back in the morning questioning all of us."

Elizabeth nodded. "Captain Grandfather, do you think Eileen's fiancé killed her?"

Captain Grandfather snorted. "Him! It would surprise me if he had the guts to shuck an oyster, missy. And there's going to be enough turmoil in this house without you taking up detection as a hobby. Just stick to making sandwiches, that's my girl."

Elizabeth bristled. Make sandwiches, indeed! "I'll have you know I finished college," she snapped. "I wasn't the one who was planning to get married and be a housewife!"

Captain Grandfather eyed her speculatively. "No? Well, what are you planning to do?"

"I'm going to have a career, of course."

"I see. Well, as soon as you know what it is, let us all in on the secret."

"I already know!" said Elizabeth with great dignity. "I am going to be an archeologist!"

She tossed her napkin on the silver tray and left the room.

The night air was chilly, and Elizabeth wished she had brought a shawl or a sweater. Still, it wasn't far—just down the wide lawn and across the road. The quarter moon cast a gray light on the long grass and the live oaks lining the drive. Elizabeth was nearly halfway across the yard—silent, except for the sound of her feet in the grass—when she realized that there might be a murderer loose somewhere on the grounds. She should have waited for someone to come with her, she thought with sudden panic; or at least, she might have called to let Alban know she was coming. She found herself watching the shadows among the trees, looking for shapes that moved. It was too quiet.

The lights on the first floor of the castle twinkled from between the folds of heavy curtains. Safety was a hundred yards away. With a sob of terror, Elizabeth fixed her eyes on the steep front steps and began to run. As her feet pounded against the asphalt of the road, she imagined dark shapes gliding across the lawn in pursuit. At last she reached the great double doors, her breath coming in heaves, and her mind reeling with the sinister figures she had conjured from the darkness. There didn't seem to be a bell, and she took no time to search for one, pounding on the door as hard as she could.

After a few moments, the door opened to the dimly lit hallway, and there stood Alban, incongruous but safe-looking in his red sweatshirt and faded jeans.

"Elizabeth, what a pleasant— What's wrong? Are you crying?"

Without waiting for an answer, he shepherded her into his study and settled her onto the velvet loveseat. "Now, you just sit right there and take deep breaths," he advised her. "Don't talk!" He went to the sideboard, took out a cup and saucer, and began to arrange spoons and napkins on a tray.

"No coffee, please!" she called to him. "I've been drinking it all day!" Her voice broke as she finished.

"I am fixing you tea," said Alban, pouring water into a small china teapot. "You cannot drink and cry at the same time. Scientific fact. So you're going to drink. And then you'll tell me what this is all about."

He brought the tray over, and set it down on the marble-top table beside the loveseat.

Elizabeth took a few tentative sips of the tea. She settled back against the cushions and concentrated on untensing her muscles. Somewhat to her surprise, Alban was not hovering. Instead he poured himself some tea, then walked to his desk and returned his attention to the checkbook and bank statement in front of him. Elizabeth watched as he worked.

There was very little family resemblance among the Chandler cousins. The Chandler genes must be recessive, she thought. Their looks ranged from the tall, sandy blondness of Bill MacPherson to the Scotch-Irish look of Alban: a short, trim Celt, with dark hair against too-white skin and cold blue eyes. Eileen had been the middle ground: mousy. Elizabeth decided that she looked more like Alban and Geoffrey—the dark Celts of the family. The Highlanders of Clan MacPherson would approve, she thought to herself, and she smiled for the first time in several hours. Alban looked up just then and returned her smile. "Feeling any better, fair lady?"

"As much as I'm going to," Elizabeth replied. "I have some bad news, Alban."

He heard the urgency in her tone and stopped smiling. "Tell me. What's wrong?"

"Eileen is dead! They think it was murder, and the sheriff was here, and—"

"Stop. Right there. You're going off again. Take another sip of tea."

Elizabeth picked up her cup, and gulped a swallow of tea. After taking a deep breath to compose herself, she recounted the day's events, ending with Captain Grandfather's news of the sheriff's call to say that Eileen had been murdered.

"... which was just a little while ago, and then I came

over to tell you. It was dark outside, and I was about halfway here when I suddenly realized that the murderer might still be around. I just panicked. When you opened the door—I was never so glad to see anybody in my whole life!"

But Alban was not listening anymore. He stared down at the rug as if she were no longer there.

"Alban?" said Elizabeth, touching his shoulder. "Alban!"

"How do they know?" he murmured.

"Know what?"

"That she was—that somebody put her in the boat. How do they know?"

"Oh." He was looking at her again, but his attention was now on the events themselves, not on comforting her. Stifling a flicker of annoyance, Elizabeth answered, "The lab report said that she had been hit on the head. But they seem to think it was the snake that actually killed her. Do you think the killer knew that the snake was in the boat?"

Alban shook his head, uninterested in the question. "Poor Eileen. You know, every year, Miss Brunson from the high school brings her class up here when they're studying *Macbeth.*"

Elizabeth nodded, wondering what this had to do with Eileen.

"I give them a tour of this place—even though it has nothing at all to do with Scotland. And well, she even talked me into reading the Tomorrow soliloquy for them this year." He smiled, remembering himself at the top of the staircase quoting Shakespeare to thirty restless seniors. "I started with the line 'She should have died hereafter.' That's what this made me think of. That line— 'She should have died hereafter.'"

"I know."

"How are they taking it?" he asked.

Elizabeth frowned. "Oh, different ways, but they're putting up a good front."

"Is there anything I can do, do you think?"

"The sheriff will probably want to talk to you tomorrow. And you might try to keep Satisky occupied.

He's underfoot, nauseating everybody with quotes. In fact, when we found her body, he started spouting poetry. From *The Lady of Shalott* by Tennyson."

"Oh, you recognized it?"

"No. Geoffrey told me later. But I thought it was very insensitive of him. Oh, another thing you might do, Alban, is to tell your mother about this..."

"Tell me what?" Louisa, bundled in a lavender bathrobe, stood smiling in the doorway. "Oh, tea! Splendid!"

Alban brought her another cup, and she poured tea for herself. "Now what is this all about?" she demanded.

"I'm afraid it's bad news, Mother."

"Well—are you going to tell me or not?"

They told her, in rambling and what they believed to be diplomatic terms. Louisa, however, immediately pressed for details.

"Who do you suppose did it?" asked Louisa with lively interest. "Are the migrant workers here yet?"

"Mother!"

"Well, who else could it have been? That nervous young man she's engaged to? I don't see why he'd do it. It wasn't as if she had been unfaithful to him, like—"

"Mother, the sheriff will take care of the investigation!" said Alban sharply. "I think we should worry about what we can do to help Uncle Robert, don't you?"

"Yes, Alban," said Louisa in a more subdued tone. "It's such a shame. Eileen did so want to be happy. I don't think she would have been with that young man of hers, but I wish she had been given the chance anyway." She walked to the desk and began to rearrange the roses in a crystal vase. "Why is it that every time Amanda and I plan a wedding, something terrible happens? How is Amanda, by the way?"

"She went up to her room and we haven't seen her since," said Elizabeth.

"Just like her. Oh dear, Alban, do you think the white roses are past their prime? Or should we just go with the red?"

Elizabeth stood up. "I'd really better be getting back," she whispered to Alban.

"All right. I'll walk you to the door," said Alban, following her into the hall.

"Just to the door?"

"I'd better stay with Mother. Why? Are you so afraid?" Then he smiled and patted her shoulder. "Oh, you'll be safe, Cousin Elizabeth. As long as you stay off of boats. Now, do you want me to walk you back?"

"No," murmured Elizabeth. "I guess I don't."

With a hasty good night, she let herself out the front door, and hurried across the dark road.

By the time she remembered to worry about lurking murderers she had arrived at the front door of the Chandler house. The porch light had been left on for her, and the door was unlocked. She closed the front door as quietly as possible and tiptoed down the hall.

"Is that you, Elizabeth?" called a voice from the kitchen.

She peeped around the corner and saw that the kitchen light was on. "Geoffrey?" she called out in a stage whisper.

"No. It's me. Charles. I found some cookies. Want some?"

He was sitting at the kitchen table with a plate of chocolate chip cookies and a glass of milk.

"Well, maybe just one," said Elizabeth, taking the other chair. "Thank you for waiting up for me."

"Nah. Had to get up to answer the phone anyway. Your brother's roommate called. He said Bill wasn't back yet, and since it was getting so late, he'd have him call first thing in the morning. Want a glass of milk?"

"I guess so," sighed Elizabeth. If people keep comforting me with liquids, she thought, I'll have to carry a bedpan around with me.

He took a plastic milk jug from the refrigerator and filled another glass. "There you are."

"I guess everybody else has gone to bed."

"Yep."

"Couldn't you sleep?"

"No."

As conversations go, this one wasn't going far. Elizabeth cast about for a new topic.

"So Charles, what do you know about anthropology?"

Charles peered at her over the rim of his glass, which he had been about to drink from. "Anthropology?"

"Yes. Well, really, archeology. You know: digging for lost cities and all."

"Elizabeth, I'm a physicist."

"Well, of course, I know that." She coughed. "I—er—just thought that since it was science, you might know something about it."

Charles was puzzled. "But why would you think that?"

"I don't know. I just..."

His face lit up with mistaken comprehension. "I see! You mean because of the dating process!"

Elizabeth blushed. "Well, actually I haven't even met him—"

"Carbon-fourteen dating! Of course! It's practically indispensable in archeology. They use it to determine the age of their finds. Wonderful trick, really. Here, I'll explain how it works."

"But, Charles, I—"

"—heavy radioactive isotope of carbon, mass number fourteen, and—"

Elizabeth nodded politely through the explanation of half-life and radioactive traces. She reasoned that if she admitted her real interest in archeology—a misty image of herself and Milo discovering Atlantis together—she would sound much more foolish than she cared to. Sitting through Charles's lecture seemed to be the easiest way out. After several minutes of animated explanation, Charles wound down. Noticing a glass coffee pot on the stove, Elizabeth asked: "Were you planning to make coffee? The water's not on."

"Good Lord! I'd forgotten all about it. Thanks for reminding me! I'd better move it before somebody tries to make tea with it."

He moved the beaker of water from the stove to the countertop, in slow cautious movements.

Elizabeth watched him wide-eyed. "It won't explode, will it?"

"What, this? It's just salt and water."

"It looks clear to me," said Elizabeth. Like nitroglycerin.

"I supersaturated the water with salt while it was boiling. That's why you can't see it. That was hours ago. While we were waiting for the sheriff to call, and I didn't have anything to do."

"What is it?"

"Oh...just an experiment. Or maybe a statement. I dunno. Here, I'll show you. I boiled water in this glass container, and I dumped salt into the boiling water—lots of it. More than it would hold if it were room temperature. Got that?"

"Yeah. You wasted a box of salt. So?"

"Then I left it covered and waited a few hours for it to cool."

"Okay. And you want to see what will happen?"

Charles looked pained. "I know what will happen. Don't you?"

Elizabeth shook her head. "No."

He shook a few grains of salt into his hand. Carefully extracting a few grains from his palm, he blew the rest away. "Now. I have between my fingers a grain or so of salt. Watch."

He walked over to the glass pot on the countertop and lifted the lid. Elizabeth followed him, peering closely at the clear liquid inside. With a dramatic flourish, Charles dropped the salt grains into the liquid. As Elizabeth watched, the solution around the new grains began to thicken into a bog of oatmeal consistency, the reaction spreading outward from the grains second by second until the entire liquid had become a mass of soggy salt.

"Hey! I didn't even see any salt before!"

"I know. You want to know why I did this?"

Still watching the beaker, Elizabeth nodded.

"This wasn't an experiment. It was a prediction. I think that solution was like our family. There were a lot of things floating around, so to speak, but you couldn't see them. And Eileen's death is that little grain of salt I dropped into the pot, which makes everything crystallize."

He dumped the contents of the beaker into the sink and rinsed the pot. "Good night, Elizabeth," said Charles, strolling off toward the stairs.

Elizabeth stared after him, wondering for the first time if Charles might also be a poet.

CHAPTER ELEVEN

ELIZABETH SLEPT BADLY that night. Even though she locked her door and got up twice to make sure the bedroom window was fastened, she half waked at every creak the house made. A fitful early-morning dream about looking for an Indian village in the stacks of the university library abruptly changed into a funeral scene in which Aunt Amanda was nailing Eileen into a pine box. In her dream, Elizabeth suddenly became the one in the box, and she could feel the blows of the hammer vibrating against her upturned face. When she finally struggled to consciousness, she found that the pounding was coming from the bedroom door.

"Honey, you got a phone call!" Mildred was saying. "He says he's your brother."

Elizabeth shook her head and yawned. The clock on the nightstand said 7:15. In haste she grabbed the terry-cloth robe at the foot of her bed. She was still struggling to knot the cord around her waist when she reached the bottom of the stairs. The receiver was lying on the hall table, and Mildred was nowhere in sight.

"Hello...Bill?" said Elizabeth carefully. "Why are you calling at this hour? What do you mean you just got in? Did Milo tell you why I called? Oh, Bill, it's awful!"

"One thing I can't figure out, Wes," said Clay Taylor, reading the lab report. "If somebody threw her in that boat on the top of a snake, is that murder or just assault? I mean, the snake did the killing, if I'm reading this report right. Does that mean the person who hit her on the head isn't responsible, or do we just consider the snake an exotic murder weapon?"

Wesley Rountree sighed in exasperation. "I'll tell you what I consider it, Clay. I consider it the prosecutor's problem. All we got to worry about is finding him somebody to prosecute. Now let me alone a minute. I got to make up a list of things for Hill-Bear to do today." Rountree reared back in his swivel chair and considered his list.

Taylor put down the lab report and went over to check the electric percolator atop the filing cabinet. Its cord was loose, so that if he didn't keep jiggling it, the water never would get hot. "Don't forget the capias we got on Johnse Stillwell."

"Oh yeah. Another bad check. I'll put it on here. Anything else?"

"The Bryces went to the beach this week, and they wanted us to pay particular attention to the house while they're gone."

Rountree grunted. "Hope they remembered to stop the paper this time."

"The water's hot, Wes. Want some coffee?"

Rountree shook his head. "No. I'm meeting with Simmons this morning, and he doesn't use instant. I'll wait."

Taylor considered this as he poured his own cup of coffee and ladled sugar into it. "Chandler case, huh?"

"Yep. Consult the family lawyer."

Clay settled back at his own paperless desk. Months of neatness-by-example had failed to effect any change at all in Rountree's habits. "You know," he said thoughtfully, "this case could be tricky. I didn't come

144

up with any fingerprints on the easel and paintbox, except those of the deceased. We don't even know why she was killed."

"No, but we got a lot of whys to choose from," snapped the sheriff. "An inheritance, a reluctant groom, and let's not forget that damned picture that nobody can find."

Taylor smiled. "Aw, you don't think somebody killed her for a picture, do you, Wes?"

"Not to hang it in their dining room, no. But somebody sure wanted to get rid of it. And she was painting by the lake."

"I don't see what that has to do with it," said Clay, in a puzzled voice.

"Well, I don't either," Rountree admitted. "But you're going back out there right now, and check it out. Maybe you can come up with a few answers, instead of so many questions."

"Diving gear?" said Taylor hopefully. Since he had taken the scuba diving course the previous fall, he had been on the lookout for opportunities to use his skills in the line of duty, but so far there had been no drownings or aquatic emergencies. The Chandler pond would be the perfect excuse to test his newly learned diving prowess.

"No. Not diving gear," Rountree growled. "Whatever she was painting had to be visible to somebody standing on the shore. Just walk around and look on the banks and in the shallows. Report anything unusual that you find."

"I'm on my way."

Rountree deposited his note on Doris's desk. It was five minutes after eight; she should be arriving anytime in the next ten minutes without an excuse, or in the next half hour with one. "Meet me at Brenner's at eleven. I'll wait on Doris and Hill-Bear."

"Right."

"Oh, Clay! If you find a sunken treasure in that lake, call me at Simmons's office!"

Taylor closed the door to the sound of the sheriff's chuckle.

"Robert, I assure you that I am perfectly capable of carrying on," said Dr. Chandler's wife in a cold voice.

Amanda Chandler had come downstairs after breakfast, looking haggard, but without a sign of tears. Her stiff black dress was so severe and unfashionable that it could only have been used for mourning. Refusing all nourishment except a glass of grapefruit juice, she took her customary place in the den.

"Someone must see to these things," she informed her husband. "May I ask what arrangements have been made?"

"Arrangements? But, Amanda, there hasn't been time! It hasn't even been—"

She nodded triumphantly. "There. You see? No one has done a thing. I am not even allowed to mourn my child in peace, because I am the only practical soul in this house. So many people to be notified. Telegrams! Do they have black-bordered ones? And what does one do about gifts? Perhaps Louisa would know, since Alban's wedding was cancelled so abruptly."

Dr. Chandler blinked before the onslaught of such efficiency. "Must we do all this now, Amanda?"

"It is certainly my duty," said Amanda severely. "I'm sure you can cancel your rounds at the hospital, but you'll be of no help to me. You might send Elizabeth in, though. I would appreciate some assistance from her. I may also need Geoffrey. Please tell him not to make plans for today. I suppose Father Ashland has not been called?"

"Now, Amanda, you know he hates to be called 'father'—"

"Then he should have been a Baptist. As an Episcopalian, I assure you that my term is correct. Now, may we get back to my task, while I still have the strength?"

Chandler bowed his head. "All right."

"Thank you. Before anything can be planned, I need to know when we may put her to rest. Have you received word?"

He shook his head. "Not yet. But if you are going to

plan funeral arrangements, I'll ask Michael to come in and see you."

Amanda stared. "Robert, whatever for?" she demanded.

"Well, they were nearly married..."

"Nearly is immaterial. He is not family. His preferences in the matter do not interest me in the least. Now, please go and find Elizabeth."

Dr. Chandler opened his mouth to continue the conversation, thought better of it, and turned to go. "I'll be in my study if you need me."

When he had gone, Amanda settled back in her chair and studied the invitation list, making small pencil marks in front of the names of out-of-town guests. Those to be notified by telegram she underlined. This afternoon, Todd and O'Connor would have to be called and consulted about the final arrangements. A small funeral, perhaps, under the circumstances. Surely there would be no reporters or— she shuddered— television crews present? She must ask Azzie Todd about that, not that he was likely to know. Perhaps Father Ashland could help. She sighed. It would be up to her, in the end; it was always up to her. And, of course, Dad would know what to do.

Amanda Chandler had long ago amended her list of "advisors" to exclude her husband. Her feelings toward him had faded into a mixture of disappointment and maternal responsibility which she concealed in brisk efficiency. Robert Chandler's feelings and opinions had long since ceased to register with her; the truth was, at nearly fifty years of age, Amanda Chandler was "Daddy's girl."

When she tried to remember why she had married Robert, the answers were always vague. He was studying medicine, which had pleased her. His determination to become and remain a country doctor was something that she had discovered later. It had all seemed so romantic at the time. Second cousins falling in love— risking the taint of two-headed babies, or whatever that old superstition was. Perhaps she had insisted on the marriage as another show of spirit for her father's ben-

147

efit. She had expected him to fly into a paternal rage and forbid the marriage. He had done nothing of the sort. William Chandler had been polite and hearty to the prospective groom, and affectionately distant to her. It was as if he were backing away from her emotionally. Years later, when he retired from the navy, he came to live with them, and he still got on well with Robert and the children, but Amanda could not help feeling a silent reproach in his attitude toward her. She finally realized that he was disappointed in her: she had not become successful and independent; she had not even married a titan; and worst of all, she had not made either of them happy. Daddy's little girl was a failure.

Amanda tipped the reading glasses down to the end of her nose and squinted at the wall clock: 9:15 in the morning. Too early. But then, she *was* under an enormous strain, and she hadn't taken a sedative since the night before. She opened the cabinet and took a decanter of Old Grand-Dad from behind a stack of women's magazines.

It was a short walk from Wesley Rountree's office in a wing of the courthouse to the Main Street office of Bryce and Simmons. He took his time, because his appointment was set for 9:30, and he didn't want to be early. Doris had come in about eight-thirty while he was still reviewing the day's schedule with Hill-Bear, and he had ended up having coffee with them and telling them about the Chandler case.

Rountree frowned at a candy wrapper on the sidewalk. Clay always picked them up; said he couldn't abide litter, and Rountree would ask if he'd stop chasing a bank robber to pick up a beer can. Still, it was a civic-minded thing to do. Rountree sighed. No bank robbers in sight. Self-consciously, he bent down and picked up the wrapper, stuffing it in his pocket until he could get to a trash can.

"Morning, Wesley! I see you're on the job!"

Rountree straightened up. Marshall Pavlock, editor of *The Chandler Grove Scout*, had that eager look of one who has just discovered his lead story in time for paste-up. "You got a minute, Wes?" he asked politely.

Rountree sighed. It was bound to get out sooner or later, he reasoned, and Marshall might as well have it. He was usually pretty responsible; he had to be; all his potential newsmakers were also his neighbors. When Vance Wainwright was arrested for drunk and disorderly, Marshall could be trusted to leave out the details, like the pathetic notes he'd scrawl on the windows of his ex-wife's trailer. Most people in Chandler Grove already knew those kinds of details long before the paper came out anyway, and they agreed that such goings-on didn't belong in print. Marshall Pavlock saved his urge for detail for the place where it was appreciated: the society page. He not only told his readers what the bride and bridesmaids wore, but who made the dress, and who baked the wedding cake, not to mention who cut it, and who was there to eat it. He had been reserving half a page to do such a report on the Chandler-Satisky wedding, but now Eileen would be featured on another page.

"What can I do for you, Marsh?" Rountree grinned.

Marshall grinned back. "You should'a been a poker player, Sheriff. You know very well what you can do. Tell me about the Chandler girl!"

Rountree had long since given up trying to trace the origin of county news. It was enough to make a person believe in telepathy. In this case, though, he discarded ESP in favor of more obvious suspects: Doris, Jewel Murphy, and Mildred Webb. "You heard about that, huh?"

Marshall fished a notepad out of the pocket of his jacket. "I heard that ya'll took the body to the medical examiner yesterday, and that there's some question about cause of death. You wanna fill me in?"

Rountree glanced at his watch. "Well, I have an appointment in just a few minutes, so we'll have to make this fast."

"She didn't commit suicide, did she?"

"No, Marshall, I can promise you that. According to Mitchell Cambridge, death occurred sometime yesterday morning as a result of the bite of a poisonous snake—"

"Accident! Why, that poor—"

"—which she got when somebody hit her over the head and threw her on top of the snake," finished Rountree, noting with satisfaction that Marshall Pavlock was staring at him openmouthed. "In the obituary, you just put died 'suddenly,' like you always do. For the news story, I'll get back to you later. Just say the usual: Sheriff Wesley Rountree and his men are still investigating, blah, blah, blah."

"But—"

"I gotta go now, Marshall. 'Bye!"

Tommy Simmons did not usually work on Saturdays. It was one of the reasons he had become a lawyer, so that he could keep eating at dinner parties while his doctor friends were called away for emergency appendectomies. This Saturday was an exception; just as it was exceptional for one of his clients to be involved in a violent crime, even as the victim. Meetings with Rountree were fairly routine, but usually on lesser matters. Simmons heard the front door open and close.

"Open up in the name of the law!" called Rountree from the reception room.

Simmons swung open his office door with a grin. "You got a warrant, mister?"

The sheriff waved a packet of saccharin. "Nope! Just a prayer for coffee!"

"Well, get you some and come on in!"

When Rountree was settled in the captain's chair across from Simmons's desk, he opened the file in front of him and studied its contents.

"This is a sad business, Wes," the lawyer said in a sincere voice that might get him elected to something one day. "You know, I was only talking to her day before yesterday."

"That's what I heard," said Rountree. "What was that all about?"

Simmons looked wary. "I don't know how much I ought to reveal about a client's affairs—"

"Tom, I know that when I told you the girl was dead,

150

you assumed accident—or suicide maybe," he amended, reading Simmons's expression. "But now I can tell you that we're contending with a murder here."

"Oh," said Simmons faintly.

Rountree explained the circumstances of Eileen's death. "Now, I understand there's a will mixed up in this."

"Well, Wesley, there *was*," Simmons said, "but she doesn't get the money, because she didn't go through with the wedding." He explained the terms of Augusta's will.

Rountree considered this. "I guess somebody could have killed her for a shot at the inheritance money."

"It's about two hundred thousand dollars or so, before taxes," offered Simmons.

"So you were out there to discuss the inheritance with her?"

"Yes. But while I was there, she gave me a will of her own."

"We'll come to that in a minute. Who was the executor of this first will, the one leaving all that money?"

"That would be Captain William Chandler, the brother of the legator. The money is, of course, invested, and he—"

"Okay. Now if Eileen Chandler is no longer eligible to receive that money, who's got the next shot at it?"

Simmons blinked. "Well, nobody in particular. I mean—"

"You? Me?"

He smiled. "All right, Wes. I see what you mean. The possible legatees are: Alban Cobb, Charles Chandler, Geoffrey Chandler, Elizabeth MacPherson, and William D. MacPherson. The first of them to marry inherits."

Rountree ticked them off on his fingers. "Well, now we got five suspects."

"Four," Simmons corrected him. "I don't believe William MacPherson came down for the wedding."

"Four, then. How about the boyfriend? You said Eileen Chandler made a will. What if she specified that the money was to go to him?"

Simmons hesitated a moment before pulling out a handwritten document on stationery. "Well, it wouldn't matter, Wes. She couldn't leave that money to him unless it was legally hers first. I mean, I could leave you the Brooklyn Bridge, but unless I owned it..."

"Okay, I see. Is that her will?" Rountree held out his hand.

"Okay, Wes, I'll let you see it. But before you do, I'd better tell you that this will is the damnedest thing!" Shaking his head, he handed it across his desk to the sheriff. "The damnedest thing."

Geoffrey pulled back the curtain and peered at Alban's castle, white in the morning sunlight. "Did he say he was coming over?"

"I expect he'll be over later," said Elizabeth, "but he really didn't say. Would you like me to call him?"

Geoffrey shrugged. "I suppose not. He can't do anything. And I can always talk to you, can't I?"

Elizabeth was puzzled. "About what?"

Geoffrey waved vaguely. "Oh... about this rather theatrical situation we find ourselves in. It's sort of the reverse of *Hamlet*, isn't it? That line about 'the funeral-baked meats did coldly furnish forth the marriage tables.' Only the other way around."

"You're always going on about *Hamlet*," she observed. "I hope you're not planning to mention that to any reporters who happen to call. That allusion might be catchy enough to make headlines."

"No fear, Cousin," said Geoffrey grimly. "I have no desire to encourage sensationalism, or to gain immortality between the pages of a crime magazine. I just want to find out who did it."

"Even when you know, it probably won't make any sense," sighed Elizabeth. "It will probably be some drifter that we never even heard of, and even he won't know why he did it."

"That would be convenient, wouldn't it?" snapped Geoffrey.

"Would it be better to find out that it was someone we do know?"

152

"Just as long as we know. And I don't think it was just a senseless act of violence. A casual murder. Getting back to *Hamlet:* 'Yet there's method in it.'"

"More *Hamlet,*" muttered Elizabeth.

"It's called barding," Geoffrey informed her. "You should hear Sinclair doing it. He can bard through a whole conversation. It's marvelous!"

"I'm sure it is."

"I must call him today. The play will have to be put off. I think Mother would insist on six months. Or perhaps they could do a play without me in the meantime." He walked to the bookshelf and pulled out the large volume of quotations. Flipping to the *S*s, he ran his finger down the page and then intoned: "'Our wills and fates do so contrary run that our devices still are overthrown.'"

"I think it's cheating if you use the book," said Elizabeth.

"I just wanted to check to see what act it was in."

"*Hamlet,* of course?"

"Of course."

The duel was interrupted by the sound of the door chimes. "'The bell invites me,'" Elizabeth said, hurrying out. "'Hear it not, Duncan—'"

"You *would* quote *Macbeth!*" Geoffrey called after her.

A few moments later she came back to find Geoffrey still leafing through the *Dictionary of Quotations.* "That was Deputy Sheriff Taylor," she told him. "He wanted to let us know that he was doing more investigating at the scene of—at the lake."

Geoffrey nodded without looking up.

"I told him that it would be all right." She sat down again and picked up her book. She had found it on one of the shelves in the Chandler library: *Digging for Troy: The Romance of Archeology.*

"You know, it's unlucky to quote from *Macbeth,*" he remarked.

"Why? It's my favorite play."

"It would be. It's just terribly unlucky. All theater people are shy of it. Sinclair was telling me that the

153

boy actor who was to play the first Lady Macbeth took ill before the first performance, and the Bard himself had to play the part. The boy supposedly died while the play was going on."

"Coincidence," remarked Elizabeth.

"No, really. Two actors in the thirties took sick after having been given the title role, and when Olivier played it, the tip of his sword broke off and struck a member of the audience, who had a heart attack."

"Oh, dear!" said Elizabeth.

"Lots of actors won't even *say* the title, much less quote from it! They call it 'The Scottish Play.'"

"Alban was quoting from it last night. When I told him about Eileen, he said, 'She should have died hereafter.' I hope it won't bring him bad luck."

"One can never tell. Years from now he may be forced to sit through a bagpipe concert—"

Someone tapped on the library door. A moment later, Dr. Chandler opened the door with an apologetic smile. "Excuse me, Elizabeth. Could I possibly disturb you? Your Aunt Amanda is asking for you. She's downstairs in the den. I can't persuade her to rest. She keeps insisting that there's too much to be done. She's a brave woman, Elizabeth. Just don't let her exhaust herself."

"I'll try," murmured Elizabeth, wondering how anyone could be expected to prevent Amanda from doing something she'd set her mind to.

When she reached the pine-paneled den (or as Geoffrey termed it, "Mother's Lair"), Elizabeth saw that Amanda was making notations on the back of an envelope. With her auburn hair pinned in an untidy bun and her glasses balanced precariously on the tip of her nose, she looked like the classic picture of a schoolmarm.

"Here I am, Aunt Amanda."

"Elizabeth. Good. There is just so much to be done. Scads of things. You're very sweet to offer to help me." Elizabeth blinked at this, and Amanda continued, "I thought that we would just carry the burden ourselves and not disturb poor Michael with any of it. Don't you

154

agree?" Amanda patted the cushion of the couch next to her chair.

Elizabeth hurried to the couch and sat down.

"The first thing we must do is to compose a telegram to notify the invited guests from out-of-town. Oh, and I do wish you would call Todd and O'Connor. They're in the phone book, and...let's see..."

She leaned over to hand the scribbled envelope to Elizabeth. Without meaning to, Elizabeth pulled away. What was that smell? It took her a moment to place it, only because she would never have associated Aunt Amanda with whiskey. Elizabeth studied her aunt with a new interest. Amanda, mistaking this attention for dedication to the task, went on detailing the day's obligations.

What a strange reaction to Eileen's death, Elizabeth thought. I wonder if I ought to tell Uncle Robert. She forced her attention back to the problem of the funeral arrangements, and found that Amanda was repeating herself and rambling on about trivial details.

"...Todd and O'Connor. Did I tell you to call 'em? Silly-looking man, Azzie Todd. Like a stick with ears..." Amanda giggled.

"I'll call them, Aunt Amanda," said Elizabeth loudly.

Amanda nodded happily. "Flowers, of course. Got to send flowers to the out-of-town guests..."

Elizabeth sighed. This is impossible, she told herself. Telling a potted sophomore to go to bed and sleep it off is one thing, but one's bereaved aunt is quite another matter. There was a certain dignity to Amanda's condition, which made it sad. I can do the calling and the arranging, Elizabeth decided, but I cannot deal with this. With a murmured excuse, she fled.

Dr. Chandler was not in the living room or the library, both of which were empty. Elizabeth decided to check the morning room in case he had gone in for a midmorning cup of coffee. He was not there, but Carlsen Shepherd was, dividing his attention between French toast and the Atlanta newspaper.

"Where's Uncle Robert?" Elizabeth asked without preamble.

"He went to the community hospital; said he'd be back before noon. And good morning to you, too," said Shepherd.

Elizabeth flushed. "I'm sorry. I guess I got caught up in things. I just have to talk to Uncle Robert, because—" Her eyes widened. "Oh! You're a doctor, too!"

Shepherd put down the newspaper with a weary sigh. "Not me. I'm a shrink. I don't carry cold tablets, I don't prescribe Valium, and I don't know poison ivy from hives. Sorry."

"This is serious!" said Elizabeth, lowering her voice to an undertone. "I think my Aunt Amanda has been drinking!"

Shepherd speared another piece of French toast. "Umm-hmm."

"Is that normal?" she hissed.

"Well, it is for her, of course."

"To react to Eileen's death that way, you mean?"

"No. It's normal for her to drink. She's an alcoholic. Pretty close to the chronic stage, I'd say."

"I beg your pardon?" stammered Elizabeth.

"Yep. I only mention it because you came charging in here asking for Dr. Chandler, presumably to report all this to the poor guy. So I thought I'd head you off and save some embarrassment all the way around. Want some toast?"

Elizabeth sat down. "He knows?"

Shepherd nodded. "It's pretty obvious, don't you think? The psychological reasons are all there, of course: domineering woman married to a passive man; the daddy-fixation; perfectionist. Textbook stuff. The little signs that you seem to have missed. How she stays in her room after dinner and nobody sees her again until morning. That's drinking time. And the fact that she eats so little. Her moods..."

Elizabeth nodded absently. She was reviewing every detail of the past few days with Aunt Amanda. It made sense—now that someone had spelled it out for her.

"So, now that you know, I guess you can do like everybody else around here and ignore it. Pretend it's another family eccentricity, like theater or sailing ships." Shepherd's voice was heavy with sarcasm.

Elizabeth considered this. "Shouldn't she be getting help?"

"And your next words will be 'You're a psychiatrist,'" snapped Shepherd. "Look, her drinking problem has been going on for years, and it's not going to clear up in a ten-minute chat with me, the pope, or anybody else. She has to want help. At this stage, she wouldn't even admit to the problem."

"Oh."

"So I'm not going to offer her any advice, because she doesn't want it, and it would be an embarrassment to her and a waste of time for me. I'll give *you* some advice though. Okay?"

"Please."

"Go back in there and pretend that nothing is wrong. Do all the calling and writing and arranging that the poor woman wants you to do, and get it done as quickly as possible. Then tell her that you know she's devastated, or whatever, and send her up to her room to sleep it off. She should be all right by this evening."

"I guess I can do that. Just treat it as a form of grief?"

Shepherd nodded. "Well, it is. Only, she's been unhappy for a very long time."

Clay Taylor would never admit to being uneasy as he followed the footpath to the Chandlers' lake. In making as much noise as possible, brushing aside branches and trampling twigs, he attempted to be the picture of unconcern, complete with whistled accompaniment. The tune he had chosen was "Marching to Zion," and it was just as well that he did not dwell on its implications, because he was in fact more nervous than he cared to be. He had given up distracting himself with thoughts of the Tuesday night softball game or with attempts to compose a shopping list without paper. Finally he settled on picturing such outlandish dangers that he became entertained by the "movie in his mind," to the exclusion of more probable dangers. A large fin-footed swamp creature, twenty million years old, had awakened in the depths of Chandlers' pond, and...

As he arrived at the edge of the lake, the reverie was ending with himself in diving gear, having just harpooned the fish-creature, destroying monster eggs at the bottom of the lake. Clay looked out at the peaceful lake scene and grinned. He had not brought his crime kit with him this time because all the death scene procedures had been done the day before. His only assignment today was to look for unusual features about the lake and its surroundings. Something a painter might notice. He had brought a gunny sack to take back evidence. Did Wesley want him to photograph the stuff in place first? he wondered. Well, he hadn't brought the camera, so if he found anything, they'd just have to take his word for it. He reached the spot where the easel had been. There was a mark in the grass; he looked toward the forest. Trees... a lot of underbrush. Not too much visibility. Nothing out of the ordinary. He had read in some crime text about hikers finding a rag on a bramble bush that had turned out to be a piece from the shirt of a missing child whose body was found buried nearby. From his vantage point, he examined each bush within the range of sight. No rags signaled a forest grave. Taylor shrugged. The lake, then. Something floating in the lake? A bank bag, maybe? Showing where the loot from some holdup had been deposited in watertight containers? Except that nobody had robbed any banks around there since '52, and that money had been recovered. Taylor pictured Rountree shaking his head and saying, "Stop detecting, boy, and keep *looking*." Obedient to the phantom Rountree, he looked. Blue sky, pine trees, greenish brown lake, couple of dragonflies that had better watch out for bass, sun glinting on the water. He looked back, squinting, at a bright spot near the shore. Now what was that? He walked to the water's edge for a closer look. Just some brown glass in the shallows that had happened to catch the light. Taylor looked again. A *lot* of glass, he mused. Wonder what it is? He pulled out his handkerchief, because even if he didn't have to worry about fingerprints, there was broken glass to consider, and pulled out the shiny fragment. The label read "Old Grand-Dad." The deputy snorted. Some discovery! He was about to heave the glass into the center of the lake, when another thought occurred to him. There wasn't anything else, so maybe... With his mind busy on the implications of his find, Clay Taylor pulled the rest of the bottle out of the shallows. And another, and another, and another...

Half an hour later, Taylor was driving back toward town with a half-filled gunny sack of wet liquor bottles deposited in the back. Somebody was putting those bottles in the lake because they didn't want them to show up in the garbage can. Too many bottles. He glanced at the dashboard clock. He still had more than an hour before he was supposed to meet Rountree for lunch. Maybe he could find out something by then. Where do you buy that stuff if you don't want people to know that you drink it? Not in Chandler Grove, he thought, grinning. He stopped at the intersection of Hinty's Crossing. The road sign said: Chandler Grove 5, Milton's Forge 12, with arrows pointing in opposite directions. After a moment's consideration, Taylor turned left, toward Milton's Forge.

By the time he reached the Milton's Forge ABC store, Taylor had thought out his line of questioning. True, he had no jurisdiction in Milton's Forge, which was in the neighboring county, but he decided that it didn't take official status to ask a few polite questions of a clerk. It was only a hunch, after all; he'd just ask a couple of questions, which might not have anything to do with the case at all.

Entering the liquor store, Taylor straightened his holster and tried to look as official and serious as possible. He put the empty whiskey bottle—one of the unbroken ones—on the counter.

"We don't give refills, buddy," drawled the clerk.

Taylor's mouth twitched with annoyance. He pulled out his identification and handed it to the clerk. "I'd like to ask you a couple of questions," he said sternly.

"And we don't sell to minors, neither."

Taylor sighed. "Could I just *ask* my question?"

The clerk shrugged. "Might as well. Doubt if I can help, though."

"I need to know if you carry this brand."

The man smiled. "Third aisle to the right. Help yourself."

"I don't want to buy the stuff! Do you sell much of it?"

"So-so. Not as much as some. The one with the horse on it is our biggest seller."

"Okay, so if somebody bought a lot of this, you'd remember it, right?"

"I s'pose."

"Well, *does* anybody buy a lot of it?" Clay was beginning to wish he had brought a warrant. Or perhaps a judge.

The clerk thought it over. "You mean a lot at a time, or just reg'lar?"

"Either one. Anything you can remember about people liking this brand!"

"Oh. Well, Old Man Twiny from up around Barnard's Way picks up a bottle from time to time..."

"Anybody else?"

"And Delbert. Now, before he died, Delbert could—"

"Anybody else!"

The clerk blinked. "Oh, some woman comes in every couple of weeks for some. Says she's giving a party. Sure gives a lot of parties, that woman. Course, the way she dresses and with that car she drives, I reckon she can afford to."

"Any idea who she is?" asked Clay eagerly.

"Naw. Drives a big green car, though."

The Chandlers had a green car, Clay thought with satisfaction. The hunch was working. "What does she look like?"

The clerk frowned. "Like your fifth grade teacher," he said flatly. "You could just see her taking a ruler to your behind. Redheads have ferocious tempers anyway, and when they get older—"

According to the clock behind the clerk, Taylor had

half an hour to get back for his meeting with Rountree, so he thanked the man hastily, saying he might be back later. He didn't need anything else for a preliminary report to the sheriff: it was as good a description as he could think of for Amanda Chandler.

Brenner's Cafe, known for its reasonable prices and country-cooking rather than for its decor, was the favorite luncheon place for most of Chandler Grove. Those who lived too far from the office to eat at home could usually be found at a booth in Brenner's, socializing over a bowl of chili or the country ham plate special. Clay found the sheriff in his favorite booth, under the palomino-cowgirl calendar, with a can of diet cola in front of him.

"Thought I'd wait 'til you got here to order," Rountree grunted, as Clay slid opposite him in the booth. "I'm in no hurry."

Clay nodded. Today was Saturday, which meant that Rountree's lunch would consist of a salad and diet cola, a self-imposed regimen which the sheriff followed on days with a *u* in them. Taylor studied the menu board above the counter, wondering what he could order that would not annoy Wesley too much.

When they had both ordered salads, and the pony-tailed waitress had moved out of earshot, Clay leaned across the table and said: "I found out something."

Rountree sighed. "Figured you did. You been sitting there with a grin on your face like a wave on a slop bucket. Somebody confess?"

"Next best thing." Clay began to tell him about finding the liquor bottles in the lake, hardly stopping to chew forkfuls of salad when it arrived. He described his interview with the ABC store clerk in Milton's Forge, and concluded with his theory that the purchaser of the whiskey was Amanda Chandler, mother of the deceased. "What about that?" he ended happily.

Rountree listened to the entire story without interrupting. "The mother, huh?" he said. "That wasn't the way my ideas were going."

"I know. It's odd. I figure a society-minded woman

161

like that wouldn't want people to know she drank so much," said Clay, still delighted with his powers of deduction. "Aren't people funny? Picture Vance Wainwright killing somebody 'cause they found out he drank."

Rountree snorted. "Anybody that don't know Vance Wainwright drinks is already dead."

"What do we do now, Wes?" Taylor wondered if it would be necessary to go back to the office for the rifles.

"I reckon we'll go out and talk to the lady," sighed Rountree.

"So you agree that I'm right?"

"Well . . . I reckon you could be," said Rountree doubtfully.

Taylor grinned.

Rountree scooped up the check. "Even a stopped clock is right twice a day."

Elizabeth had managed to finish all the telephoning, ten letters, and the preparing of a lunch of sandwiches by the time Wesley Rountree interrupted their work session. Amanda, who had been composing the obituary for the *Scout* for the entire morning, was reading snatches of it aloud to Elizabeth while they ate in the den.

". . . devoted daughter and an accomplished expressionist painter. Ought I to say 'painteuse'? Elizabeth, what do you think?"

Rountree appeared rather uneasily in the doorway, twisting his white Stetson, while Deputy Taylor and Mildred hovered in the hall behind him. Elizabeth nodded slightly toward the door, and Amanda turned to look. She recognized the sheriff with a nod of satisfaction.

"Yes, officer? What is it?"

"Well, ma'am, we'd just like a word alone with you if we may," said Rountree in his politest tone. At all costs he wanted to avoid an outburst of hysterics, but the questioning had to be done.

Amanda regarded him carefully for a moment. "Just run along now and see how your grandfather is doing, dear, while I have a word with these gentlemen."

Elizabeth picked up the lunch tray and edged past the two officers. When the door had closed behind her, Wesley Rountree seated himself on the chintz couch, motioning Clay to a nearby chair. Unobtrusively, Clay took out his notepad and pen, and waited expectantly for the questioning to begin.

Murder suspect or not, Rountree was determined to remain courteous. It was force of habit as much as anything else; he had little liking for social lionesses. "Ma'am, you should know if we had anything to report about this unfortunate business."

"Yes. I should certainly think you've had time enough."

"Well, we've been working at it. First thing this morning we examined the lake, on account of the painting being missing and all. We wanted to see if we could find any hint as to what she might have been painting. And we have a theory."

Amanda was unimpressed. "May I know what this 'theory' of yours is?"

Rountree hedged. "Fact is, we figure that your daughter's death was an accident. Not a complete accident—I mean, a human-originated accident. Somebody did hit her over the head all right, but we don't believe that person was aiming to kill her. I think, under the circumstances, it wouldn't be right to push for first-degree murder. Why, it might even go to trial as manslaughter, provided the defendant cooperated."

Amanda's eyes narrowed. "And just why are you explaining all this to a grieving mother?"

The sheriff shifted uneasily. This part required careful handling, if hysterics were to be avoided. "Well, we figure that your daughter painted something that she wasn't supposed to, and that it had to do with the lake, since she always painted there. So this morning I sent Clay down there to see if he could find anything that somebody might not want in a painting." He looked at her encouragingly. It wasn't going to be easy, Rountree thought. "And sure enough he found something. You want to tell her about it, Clay?"

The deputy focused his eyes on the floor and said in

an apologetic tone: "In the shallows of the lake, closest to the house, I found a bunch of empty whiskey bottles. You could see them from the place where the easel stood. All the same brand, too. Old Grand-Dad."

"Good. That should enable you to find the tramp who did this. Look for a man who drinks that brand," said Amanda evenly.

"No, ma'am," Rountree replied. "First place, I don't know of any vagrants who could afford to drink that stuff. Now if we were talking eighty-nine-cent wine bottles, I'd say you had a point."

"Anyway, there were too many bottles to have been left at one time," said Clay. "Some were older than others. Anyway, I checked at the store in Milton's Forge, and I..." His voice trailed off.

Rountree nodded. Might as well tell her and get it over with. "We know that you bought them, ma'am. We could prove ownership with fingerprints, too, you know. Glass is good for prints." He looked sternly at the deputy as he said this, warning him not to mention the effects of immersion on prints.

Clay was obediently silent, as was Amanda, for several minutes. "I see," she said quietly. Nothing more.

"Now we don't think that—this person we're looking for meant for Eileen to die," said Rountree soothingly. "We think it was just a tragic...tragic accident. There she is, this young girl, probably not even knowing the significance of what she was painting. Meaning no harm. But somebody saw the painting and knew that a picture of all those bottles was going to let out a family secret. 'Course, alcoholism is just a disease, same as cancer, but some people don't see it like that." He hoped he was making it respectable enough for her to confess to. "So the plan was to stun the girl just long enough to steal the painting—maybe put her in the boat 'til she came to, not seeing the snake..."

Amanda watched him, her face a mask of calm. After a moment, Rountree continued, still watching the face of his audience of one.

"—And if it hadn't been for the snake, everything would have been all right, don't you reckon? The girl would have woke up with a headache, and the painting would be gone, but maybe even she would have wanted it that way, if she'd known the truth about what she'd painted, and how it would hurt ... somebody ..." He started to say more, then shook his head and was silent.

The woman in the chair said nothing.

Wesley Rountree tried again. "Mrs. Chandler, Mrs. Chandler ... come on now. We know you bought that whiskey. We know about your drinking—nothing to be ashamed of. Don't you want to tell us how it happened?"

Amanda's eyes widened. "Do I understand that you are suggesting I murdered my daughter?"

"Of course not!" Rountree assured her. "We know it was an accident. That you acted in a fright—"

Fixing him with a malevolent glare, Amanda Chandler leaned forward. "You stupid man!" she hissed. "So you think you've uncovered a great secret, do you?"

The two officers blinked at her.

"Do you really think my family doesn't know?" she demanded, her voice rising. "Well, ask them!" She waved toward the closed door. "Go on! Ask any of them! Oh, we don't discuss it. We pretend it doesn't exist, but I assure you, Mr. Rountree, that my family is perfectly aware of the situation. As was Eileen. And whatever it was in that painting, it was not liquor bottles! We are a family of standards, Sheriff, and I assure you that my daughter would never have painted that!"

"Yes, we all knew about it," Robert Chandler told the officers a few minutes later. He had received them in his book-lined study, where they had sought him out, with the explanation that certain points of his wife's statements required confirmation.

He sat hunched before his dented typewriter, his hand covering his eyes. "It is ... not a recent development. I tried to reason with her about it; she denies it, of course. Says that Mildred steals the whiskey, that kind of thing. And she has steadfastly refused counseling, so we have made up our minds to live with it as ... as quietly as possible." He smiled apologetically. "It isn't really bad, except occasionally, when she feels

165

anxious about something. I was afraid that the wedding would set her off—and now, this!"

Wesley Rountree nodded sympathetically. "Doctor, it was our theory that your daughter might have painted those liquor bottles into the picture. Then, of course, when your wife saw the picture, she'd have got het up and tried to knock her out, so she could steal the picture. We think the whole thing was an accident."

"No," said Robert Chandler. "My wife's form of panic is—drinking."

"But you realize that your daughter was probably killed on account of that painting—probably by somebody in the household—don't you, sir?"

Dr. Chandler sighed. "Since you tell me it is so, I suppose I must believe it."

"Well, it would sure help us out if you told us who you thought it might be," Rountree prompted.

"That would be of no use to you, Wesley. I could only tell you who I wanted it to be," said the doctor with a tight smile.

"I'd sure settle for that."

For a moment, Rountree thought that the doctor was going to confide in him, but after a long silence he merely said, "I'm afraid that would not be ethical."

Deciding that it would be useless to argue with him, Wesley Rountree thanked him for his cooperation and went off in search of another family member to question. They met Elizabeth in the hall. She was not immediate family, Wesley decided, and not a likely suspect. He'd talk to her later. "Excuse me," he said genially. "Can't seem to find anybody around here."

"Who are you looking for?" asked Elizabeth doubtfully.

Rountree picked one. "Charles Chandler," he said decisively.

"Oh. He's outside, I expect. He spends a lot of time sunning. Come on, I'll show you the way."

"Does he have a favorite rock?"

Elizabeth giggled. "Like a lizard, you mean? No. He uses a chair." Deciding that the conversational ice had

166

been broken, she ventured a question. "How are you coming along with the investigation?"

"Like a pregnant mule," Rountree declared. "I know what to do, but nothing seems to come of it."

"Mules are sterile," Clay explained to a bewildered Elizabeth.

"Oh." A thought occurred to her, and she brightened. "Tell me, Sheriff Rountree, how do you like being in law enforcement?"

"Being sheriff is a pretty good job. I like it. I'm the only law officer mentioned in the constitution, you know. They don't say beans about your chiefs of police or your highway patrol. But 'sheriff'—it's right there in black and white, from the founding fathers. And we have a nice quiet county, so things stay friendly, most of the time. You thinking about going into police work?"

Elizabeth considered it. "I don't know," she said. "I just got out of college..."

"Oh," said Rountree knowingly. "Well, I wish you luck. I was a sociology major, myself."

They found Charles sprawled in a lawnchair with his book. Elizabeth had pointed him out and slipped back toward the house, while Taylor and Rountree advanced on their next suspect. Charles, who heard them approach, hastily put down his book.

"My turn to be interviewed?" he asked, squinting up at them. "Can we stay right here while you do it? I came out here to get away from all of that in the house, and I'm in no hurry to get back."

With a grunt of annoyance, Clay Taylor took out his pen and notepad and settled himself on the grass near Charles's chair. Rountree continued to stand.

"You don't live here all the time, do you?" he asked.

"No. I suppose that's it. I'm not used to it."

"Where do you live, Mr. Chandler?"

Charles supplied the address. "It's a group of friends," he explained. "My family calls it a commune; seem to think I spend my time playing Indian. Actually, we are all scientists of one sort or another. My own interest is theoretical physics, though in fact I might be able to give you a pointer or two in forensics."

167

Rountree coughed. "Thank you. But we don't handle that. Use the state labs."

"Ah. Tell me, how are you coming along with the case?"

"Tolerable. I'm in the question-asking stage right now," said Rountree, with a meaningful look at Charles.

"Excuse me. Ask away," said Charles, settling back in the sunlight.

"Are you, by any chance, contemplating marriage?" asked Rountree.

Charles opened one eye. "You mean with a woman? You're not speaking metaphysically or anything like that?"

Rountree kept a straight face. "I never speak metaphysically," he drawled. "I mean regular old 'Til Death Do Us Part' type marriage."

"Then the answer is a definite no," said Charles. "There aren't even any contenders. Why ever do you ask?"

"Oh, I was just thinking of that interesting legacy in your family. The one that goes to the first one of y'all to get married."

"Oh, that," said Charles in a bored voice. "No, thank you. I am quite above bribery."

"Well...do you happen to know if anybody else has got wedding plans?"

"You'll have to ask them, Sheriff. I'm not really interested in that sort of thing. You might ask my brother Geoffrey. Knowing things about people always amuses him. Offhand, I'd say my cousin Elizabeth was the hausfrau type. Oh, and not to forget my cousin Bill. He's also eligible for the wedding sweepstakes, and I must say the MacPhersons need the money more than we do."

"Bill?"

"Elizabeth's older brother. But he's not here."

"Where is he?"

"Law school, they tell me. We're not pen pals," said Charles.

"And your other cousin—the one across the street. Alban?"

168

"Really, Sheriff. I have no idea. You might ask Elizabeth. She's been spending a lot of time with him. In fact, she was over there last night."

Rountree grunted. "I see that the society news is not your neck of the woods. Let's move on to something else. Did you ever see that picture your sister was painting?"

"No. She was quite a fanatic about the secret. I don't even know what she was painting—but we all assumed it was the lake, since she painted there."

Rountree considered this. "The lake. Anything particular about that lake that you know of?"

"No, Sheriff," said Charles with an indulgent smile. "It's just an ordinary little lake with mediocre fishing. No sunken Spanish galleons."

"No," said Rountree carefully. "Just a lot of sunken whiskey bottles. You know anything about that?"

Charles's smile faded. "I can't say that I do," he said after a moment's pause.

"Oh, I think you could. I guess you know who put the bottles there, too."

"Not I."

"No, not you. Your mother's drinking problem accounts for those bottles, don't you reckon?"

Charles regarded them steadily. "I don't know what you're talking about."

Wesley Rountree stared back into Charles's expressionless face for a few moments, and decided that he did indeed know what they were talking about. Rather than press the point, though, Rountree merely said, "Well, we won't talk anymore about it now. If you'll just give my deputy the name of somebody at your—er, where you live—to verify your statements, we won't trouble you anymore right now."

"Oh, all right," grumbled Charles. "I guess you would check anyway. Go and bother Roger Granville, then. That will give him something to do." Clay approached the lawnchair, notepad in hand. "Here give me that," said Charles. "I'll write down the phone number at our place."

Wesley Rountree picked up Charles's book. "More physics, huh?"

"Yes. Roger and I are working together on a little project. I'm just doing research."

"Which university are you with?"

Charles flushed. "People always ask me that! As a matter of fact, we're on our own just now, but we're thinking of applying for a grant."

"I bet you are!" said Rountree cheerfully. "Physics isn't cheap."

"That's another thing people are always saying!" snapped Charles. "But did you know that Einstein worked out his whole theory of relativity with just a pencil and paper?"

"And what are you working on?" asked Rountree, beaming with fascination.

"Uh...well, it's a bit technical, Sheriff."

"Is it wave particle duality? I always liked that! Or— not the unified field theory? You think there's anything to that?" There were times when even Wesley Rountree felt an urge to show off. He told himself that this approach might get more information out of Charles than his usual folksy manner, and besides, people who equated "drawl" with "dumb" annoyed him.

Charles blinked at the sheriff, wondering if *Reader's Digest* had included a physics article in its latest issue. Clay, whose duties included returning the sheriff's books to the county library, was less surprised; Wesley would read anything. Last month had been a biography of Einstein and a book on sea urchins.

"Well, actually, Sheriff, our project is so far ahead of conventional physics that we don't think any university will have the foresight to fund us. As a matter of fact, it does have to do with relativity. Time is relative, you know. We think that the high rotational energy of a body would enable us to cross the event horizon into the past, so to speak. Ideally, we would need a black hole—a collapsed star, you know, whose density will not even release light—but we think we can prove the hypothesis on a sub-atomic level, perhaps with a linear accelerator—"

"Now you're talking money!" Wesley put in.

"Uh—yes. We want to bombard a spinning electron with—"

"Guess you could use that inheritance of your great-aunt's, couldn't you?"

"Oh, it wouldn't buy one, Sheriff! Those things run into the millions. Oh, before you go, could I just have a piece of paper from your notepad to make a few calculations? You don't have an extra pencil, do you?"

Clay tore out a few sheets from the back of his notepad and fished the stub of a pencil from his pants pocket. As they walked away, Charles was already scribbling calculations.

"Did you understand that project of his, Wes?" asked Clay, when they were out of earshot.

"Generally speaking."

"Well, what is it?"

"A time machine."

Clay shook his head. "You think he'd kill his sister to finance that?"

Rountree shrugged. "Sure is turning into a scorcher out here today, isn't it? Reckon we can find somebody around with a water jug?"

Taylor nodded, mopping his forehead with his handkerchief. The midday sun glinted on the tin roof of the shed, casting short shadows in the grass. "I'm surprised there's not a garden out back here, aren't you, Wes? It looks like the sort of place that would have one."

"Well, I think there was one once," Rountree replied. "Back when they kept a pony in the shed. But the gardener in the family seems to be the castle-lady—Mrs. Cobb. She sure does grow beautiful roses."

"Yeah. I don't think Mrs. Chandler gets much pleasure from gardening."

"Might be better if she did," grunted Rountree. "Who do we talk to next?"

Clay consulted his notebook. "Well, you haven't talked to the other son yet."

* * *

They found Geoffrey Chandler in the sunny break-fast room, sipping coffee at the glass-topped table as he read the morning paper.

"No, you're not disturbing my breakfast," he assured them.

When they had settled themselves, with glasses of ice water supplied by the kitchen, Rountree explained that they were in the process of questioning all the family members, and that it was now his turn to be interviewed.

"Am I the last one?" asked Geoffrey. "I don't know why, but people seem to dread talking to me. Perhaps I have no small talk. Do you think that's it?"

"I couldn't say," said Rountree with a slight cough. He studied Geoffrey's morning attire: tight white trousers, red tank top, and sandals. "I see you're not observing mourning."

"In my heart," said Geoffrey, placing his hand in the appropriate place. "Is the absence of black taken as a sign of guilt?"

Sheriff Rountree refused to be drawn into this discussion. With a frown of distaste, he continued the interview.

"You are Geoffrey Thomas Chandler—"

"Of the home," finished Geoffrey in funereal tones.

"And what do you do?"

"Do?" He looked quizzically from Rountree to Taylor. "I am at a loss."

"For a living," Taylor prompted, his pencil poised.

"Ah! I toil not, neither do I spin. I am, however, working on a play which I hope will spark the renaissance of the American theater—"

Clay wrote down "unemployed." Further particulars concerning Geoffrey's age and education were given in much the same style. When these had been recorded, more prosaically than they were given, Rountree said, "Now, I expect you already know that we think your sister was murdered."

Geoffrey inclined his head, indicating that this was so.

"Well, is there anybody that you know of who would profit by her death?"

Geoffrey sighed. *"Are* you talking about that will of Great-Aunt Augusta? You seem to be under the impression that this is some matrimonial sweepstakes. Somebody or other once said not to marry for money because it is cheaper to borrow it from a bank. Most of us here subscribe to that theory—except perhaps the bereaved groom."

"You saying he was marrying her for the money?" Rountree barked.

"That thought did occur to me," murmured Geoffrey vaguely.

Rountree considered this. "Well... you know, if that's a fact, it clears him of suspicion in the case. After all, her dying before the wedding eliminates him from the sweepstakes, as you put it."

Clay Taylor, who had just scribbled down "Thinks Satisky was marrying for $," looked up to catch Geoffrey's reaction to this remark, but there was none.

"Then there's that painting she was working on to consider," the sheriff continued thoughtfully. "Sure would help if we knew what was in it. Did you happen to get a look at it?"

"No."

"We thought it might have shown all those whiskey bottles in the lake," Taylor suggested.

Geoffrey favored the deputy with a cold stare. "As I was about to say, she did not show the painting to anyone, but once I asked her how it was coming along, and she remarked that she had a difficult time doing portraits—or faces. Something to that effect."

"Faces!" echoed Rountree. "Well! That is interesting!"

"I thought you might find it so," commented Geoffrey.

"Was anybody posing for her?"

"Not that I am aware of."

Rountree thought for a moment. "Charles sure does spend a lot of time out of the house, don't you think?"

Geoffrey smiled. "Really, Sheriff. A portrait of Charles

173

would make a rather peculiar wedding gift for one's betrothed, would it not?"

Rountree was still puzzling over the implications of this bit of information when Elizabeth came in from the hall. She glanced at him nervously, appealing for permission to interrupt, so he gave her a nod.

"Excuse me, but Aunt Amanda sent me to get Geoffrey, if...if he's able to come, that is."

Geoffrey held up both hands. "No manacles as yet adorn my wrists!" he announced. "Sheriff, may I go to my grieving mother?"

"Please do," said Rountree politely.

"And while I am gone...let's see...what can you amuse yourselves with? The family album? I know! Cousin Elizabeth, why don't you stay and tell them about the last time you sat for a portrait?"

He swept majestically out of the room, leaving Elizabeth stammering at the two officers who were inexplicably interested in that subject.

"My portrait?" she was saying. "Well...do you count my graduation picture? What's the matter? Why are you both staring at me?"

June 12

Dear Bill,

Get me out of here. (And bring your alibi when you come.) First I had to address wedding invitations; now I'm having to write to people about the funeral. I feel like an apprentice monk. If somebody doesn't rescue me, I'll be here in December doing illuminated Christmas card lists!

Actually, I couldn't leave even if you came down to get me—which I know you too well to expect. Technically, we are all suspects. I've been questioned by the sheriff twice! That wasn't so bad, but everyone else here is getting on my nerves. Geoffrey has gone from manic to depressive; Michael Satisky is terrified that we'll find a way to pin the murder on him; and Aunt Amanda turned out to be an alcoholic. I don't mean that she took up drinking out of grief—it's been going on for years, according to Dr. Shepherd. Don't be smug and say you knew it all along, because I know perfectly well you didn't. By the way, could you check up on Dr. Shepherd at the med school? He seems like a very nice person, but when he first arrived, Eileen took one look at him and ran. It *might* just have been her nerves, but it was unusual for her to be so dramatic. I can't help wondering if there was something strange about their doctor-patient relationship. (Yes, I'm keeping my door locked.)

Thanks for returning my call this morning—although you *would* do it so early in the morning that I was incoherent. I'm trying to remember what I haven't told you. I hope you've remembered to notify Mother and Dad. The main purpose of this letter is to remind you to do so, and to warn you not to lay on the horrors with them. I am perfectly fine. In fact, I wish I were more upset. Eileen was such a mousy little creature that I can't even claim to miss her, which makes me feel terrible. I catch myself not being sad at all, thinking that I'd like to meet Milo (do *not* broadcast that!), and then being angry with myself for not missing her more. I'm not even terribly interested in knowing who did it, because it might turn out to be someone very nice like Dr. Shepherd, which would only compound the tragedy. I'm sure *you're* dying to know who did it, though, so when the sheriff solves the case, I'll notify you. Heaven knows when they'll let me leave.

If you think of anything to cheer me up (such as Milo mentioning that he found me fascinating), write me at once, or better yet, call—collect!

The Prisoner of Chandler,

Elizabeth

CHAPTER TWELVE

DESPITE GEOFFREY'S GLOOMY supposition, he was not the last family member to be interviewed. That honor was reserved for Captain Grandfather, whom they found in Robert Chandler's study in front of a black-and-white portable television.

"*Silent Service* reruns," he said gruffly, turning down the volume. "Not very accurate, but good drama. Those were the days! You wanted a word with me, I suppose?"

Rountree perched on the side of the doctor's paper-strewn desk. "Sorry to come barging in like this, but we're talking with everybody in the family."

"To find out if we know who did it? *I* wouldn't, you know. My granddaughter...I knew her as a child, Sheriff. She liked ponies, and coffee ice cream, and a song called 'Froggy Went A-Courtin''; but when children grow up, you lose track of their real selves. Eileen, now, I can tell you her bloodline down to the last cousin, but I have no idea who she was inside."

"*Which of us is not forever a stranger and alone?*" said Clay.

Rountree closed his eyes. "If we could just get back to this case..." He always dreaded the second phase of grief. When the shock had worn off a little, the deceased became preserved in memory as a wax figure without flaws or feelings. A few more days and Eileen Chandler would turn into a fairy-tale princess who had never made a mistake in her life.

The old man watched a submarine churn beneath the waters of the North Atlantic. "Was there anything in particular you wanted to ask me?"

"You're an early-riser, aren't you, sir?"

Captain Grandfather nodded. "Always have been. Stood me in good stead in the service."

"I expect it did," said Rountree. "Reason I asked is: you must have been the last person we know of to see Eileen on the day she died. Am I right?"

"As far as I know, Sheriff, nobody saw her that day. I came downstairs at a little past seven—I'd been up late reading the night before. Anyway, I came into the breakfast room, and there was a used cereal bowl on the table, which I took to be Eileen's. But I didn't see her, no."

"Well, it was a thought," sighed Rountree. "I had hopes of finding someone who'd seen her. Well, what can you tell me about her state of mind?"

"Next to nothing. Eileen was always nervous. Didn't get enough exercise, if you ask me."

Clay looked up from his notepad. "What does that have to do with—"

"Well, let's get on to motive," said Rountree hastily. "Tell me about this inheritance she was due to get."

Captain Grandfather told him, in no uncertain terms and with considerable scorn expressed for his sister's life-style, judgment, and malice aforethought in making such a will. "—And the little witch, knowing full well how I would feel about such a piece of foolishness, had the unmitigated, unsurpassed, sheer feline gall to name me as executor of the damned thing!"

Rountree coughed. "So they tell me, Captain."

"Can you imagine? Expecting me to take an interest in the wedding plans of a bunch of children who would probably get on a good deal better in life without Augusta's money! Do them good! They'd grow some backbone!"

"They might do better in character without it, but it might not stop some of 'em from wanting it," the sheriff pointed out.

William Chandler laughed bitterly. "No argument there! That much money would solve every trifling problem the bunch has!"

"Problems?"

"It would buy Charles a reactor, or whatever thing it is he and his crowd seem to think is standing between them and a Nobel prize. It would set Margaret's son Bill up in law practice in pretty good style, or buy Elizabeth some time to chart the course of her life—archeology, last I heard" —he snorted— "and Geoffrey— God knows what he'd do with it! Something arty, I expect, like try to start a Shakespeare festival in Chandler Grove!"

"What about Alban?"

"Perfect example! You see what Walter's money has done for him! Took his castle in the air and built it for him! What ambition has he got?"

"Maybe he doesn't need to be ambitious," Clay suggested.

Captain Grandfather sighed. "I've nothing against being eccentric," he said at last. "Or being well-off. If it buys you independence, that's fine—but—since Eileen died, I keep thinking that it didn't do her any good. The money was almost hers, you know, and it didn't make her happy. It wasn't going to, either. She wanted that young man, and there was no use trying to tell her any different, but...some things you ought not to try to buy."

"Do you think he killed her?" asked Rountree.

"No. I've seen his type in the service many a time. He's weak and selfish—don't trust his loyalty in a pinch, and don't put him in charge of the canteen on the lifeboat—but to call him a killer would be overestimating him."

"There's something else I'd like to talk to you about,"

said Rountree cautiously. "It might be a touchy subject, but it's got to be dealt with." He explained the finding of the whiskey bottles in the lake and their theory that Amanda Chandler had accidentally killed her daughter while trying to steal the painting.

"That's hogwash!" snapped the old man. "Amanda may have her problems, but she's not a coward! A picture wouldn't scare her like that. If she didn't like it, she'd have bullied the girl until it was changed. And it would be changed, I promise you that. Amanda runs a tight ship." He shook his head and sighed. "I doubt that the painting was like that, anyway."

Rountree straightened up. "Did you see it?"

"No. Why? Is it important?"

"Yeah. Because we can't find it. That bothers me. But if we knew for sure what she was painting, it would be a load off my mind. Did that lake mean anything special to her?"

Captain Grandfather rested his head in his hand. "Did it?" he muttered. "That sounds familiar...I think. Right at the time of her breakdown, there *was* something about the lake, or water, or something. Can't recall what. My son-in-law might know."

"If anybody knows anything around here, they're not telling!" snapped Rountree. "I'm beginning to wonder if there's some reason folks might not want this case solved. Are you afraid one of the young people killed Eileen to get a shot at the inheritance?"

"No, Sheriff. I'm afraid of not knowing them well enough to be sure; but then, the captain is always the last to know of a mutiny." He watched the two officers leave the study, and with a placid smile, he turned again to his television.

Closing the door behind him, Rountree muttered, "Make a note for me to interview the lawyer again, Clay. If the old gentleman is so against any of them getting that money, I just want to make sure it's still there to be gotten! After all, he is the executor."

"But I didn't think an executor could touch money in trust, Wes."

"I aim to find out."

"Excuse me, Sheriff!" Michael Satisky was waiting for them in the hall. He was leaning up against the wall, clutching the small Chandler Grove telephone book. "Could I speak to you for just a moment?"

Rountree frowned. "Talk? I reckon. How about the library?" He opened the door and peered in. "Okay, nobody's in there. You go on in and have a seat. Listen—do I have to read you your rights or anything? Clay, got your notebook out?"

Satisky sank down in the armchair with a strangled cry. "My *rights!*"

Rountree shrugged. "You know. For confessions. We have to warn people first about their rights, so the court won't throw it out. I have the card in my billfold someplace." He reached for his hip pocket.

"I am *not* confessing!" Satisky said shrilly. "I have *nothing* to confess!

"Well, it was a thought," sighed Rountree. "What did you want to say?"

"I wanted to know if I could leave," snapped Satisky.

The sheriff raised an eyebrow. "And miss the funeral of your loved one?" he drawled.

Satisky opened his mouth and closed it again.

Rountree nodded. "Actually, I do understand," he said in a softer tone. "This place makes you kinda nervous, doesn't it?"

"Well, it does," Satisky admitted. "These people are all strangers, and I know they all think I did it. Is there any necessity for me to stay?"

Rountree chewed on this thought for a minute. "Have you been asked to leave?"

Satisky blinked. "Well...no."

"Then stay put."

"I have to stay?" Satisky persisted.

Rountree thought about it. "Well, no," he admitted, and Satisky brightened at once. "You don't have to stay exactly here, but while the investigation is going on, you can't leave the county. We haven't even had the inquest yet. But so long as you are somewhere nearby— why, I've no objections to you making a change of venue, as we say in legal terms."

Taylor changed his laugh into a discreet cough, and began to study his notepad.

"In fact," Rountree was saying, "I may even be able to make a suggestion. Say, Clay, doesn't Doris's mother still rent out rooms over at her place? You'd have to share a bathroom with the kids, of course, but I bet it wouldn't set you back more than forty bucks a week. Meals are extra, of course, but Brenner's Cafe makes a real good cheeseburger. Right, Clay?"

"Uh—uh—sure, Wes."

Rountree leaned toward the phone. "If you want, I can even give Doris's mom a call and put in a word for you. The place might fill up with reporters, you never know. Now what was her number?"

"No! Don't call!" Satisky said hurriedly. "I mean—well..."

He nearly reached for his own hip pocket to count his money, but it wasn't necessary. In his mind, he could see a ten, two fives, and three ones: the price of pride was, as usual, beyond his means. The thought of an inheritance from Eileen flickered through his mind. He was afraid to ask about it, though. It would shout a motive for murder to those for whom he was already a favorite suspect, or so he imagined. Besides, he was in no particular hurry to hear news that would almost certainly be bad. Eileen had died before they were married; therefore, the inheritance could not be claimed.

Wesley Rountree's bland smile suggested that he required no explanation from the young man, but as he was not vindictive toward the technically innocent, he merely said, "I understand. You don't want to risk hurting these good people's feelings by refusing hospitality."

Satisky stammered that this was the case and was left feeling like an utter fool as Rountree and the deputy left. He was still brooding over the awkwardness of the interview a few minutes later when Geoffrey sauntered in. Satisky, whose natural inclination was to flee from Geoffrey, rose to leave.

"Please!" said Geoffrey. "Don't get up. I feel that I must have interrupted you. No doubt you are ferreting out a few appropriate quotations to drop at the funeral."

182

Satisky looked away. "It isn't like that," he mumbled. "I just find it hard to express my feelings. I'm not very verbal, I guess."

"Not very," Geoffrey agreed. He had pulled out the drawer of the desk and was leafing through the leather address book, occasionally making notes on a piece of paper.

After a few moments of heavy silence, Satisky ventured another remark. "Have the funeral arrangements been made?"

Geoffrey paused and laid down his pen. "They have, actually. It will be on Tuesday. I hope that's convenient for you. Oh, perhaps we should have consulted you."

"Well—"

"In case you wanted to read one of your own poems at the service."

Satisky flushed. "I tried to leave. The sheriff says I have to stay until after the inquest."

"Just in case," remarked Geoffrey, flipping pages in the address book.

"You think I did it, don't you?" Satisky's voice quivered with rage, as he approached the desk with more decision than usual.

"One can but hope," murmured Geoffrey without looking up.

"Why would I kill her?" Satisky demanded. "I could have just broken off the engagement if I wanted to. And if it was the money I was after, don't you think I would have waited until we were married so that I would inherit it? As it is, I don't get anything."

Geoffrey fixed him with a frosty stare. "That, dear Michael, is the one point in your favor—and to me, the only consolation."

"But you admit that I am very unlikely as a suspect?"

"Wishing will not make it so," Geoffrey conceded. "The only crime of which I can be sure of your guilt is the petty larceny of my sister's affections. *If* you will excuse me!" Conscious of a good exit line, he swept out.

Even after Geoffrey had gone, Satisky was unable to think of a suitable retort. Geoffrey was really quite odious, Satisky thought. He could certainly divulge a thing or two. Especially about Geoffrey, who deserved to be made uncomfortable.

He peered out the front window. Rountree and the deputy were standing in the driveway talking. He could approach them if he chose. Still smarting from his last bout with Geoffrey, Satisky considered his moral stance. After all, one had a civic duty to assist the police, which meant telling what one knew. Certainly the truth could harm no one. Eileen's death must be avenged, and it was his duty to her memory to shed all the light he could on the inquiry. His personal feelings for Geoffrey were of no consideration: this was above petty revenge. Duty must be done.

Thus fortified with nobility of purpose, Satisky hurried to the front door, pausing only long enough to ensure that he was not seen, and called: "Sheriff! I must speak to you!"

Wesley pushed his Stetson back from his forehead and sighed. "Wonder what he wants now?"

"Police protection, probably," snorted Clay. "And the way that family feels about him..."

Satisky began to run down the driveway toward them, occasionally glancing over his shoulder at the front windows. He stumbled into a hedge during one of these backward glances, nearly falling into the gravel, while Rountree and Taylor waited by the squad car with solemn expressions.

"I have something very important to tell you," gasped Satisky, still breathless from his dash down the driveway. "You may want to take notes," Satisky informed Clay.

Glancing at Rountree for confirmation, Clay obligingly extracted his notepad from his hip pocket and scratched Satisky's name at the top of a clean page.

"You wanna go ahead?" drawled Wesley.

Satisky drew a dramatic breath. "I haven't told you this before because I did not wish my motives to be misinterpreted. Those with petty minds might conclude that I am telling you this information out of spite, but I wish to see justice served."

Rountree frowned. "Is that a quote?"

Satisky's eyes widened. "Er—no."

"Oh. Just checking. I was going to guess Benedict Arnold. My mistake. Go ahead."

Satisky peered at the sheriff, wondering if he were being ridiculed, but the sheriff looked perfectly serious. Reassured on that point, he continued: "Am I correct in assuming that it would assist you to know the last person who saw my fiancée alive?"

"Since that would be the murderer..."

"Oh! Well, I can't go that far! I mean, I didn't see anything. But I was out walking that morning on the path near the lake."

"Why?" asked Rountree.

"I wanted to talk to Eileen. I was going down to the lake to find her, when I heard angry voices. There was an argument going on by the lake, and it sounded quite vociferous. Naturally I—"

"Just a minute," said Clay.

"Yes?"

"Is that *i-r-o-u-s?*"

"What?"

"Vociferous."

"No. It's an *e*. Now shut up, Clay, and let him get on with it."

"Well, as I said, there seemed to be quite a scene going on, but since it was a family matter, I felt that the polite thing to do would be to leave. I didn't want to embarrass them—"

"Embarrass who?" demanded the sheriff. "You remind me of one of those old movies where the witness talks around and around a thing until somebody shoots him before he can ever say it."

"It was Geoffrey," Satisky said promptly. "Geoffrey was shouting at Eileen. He sounded quite hysterical, if you ask me."

"Did he now?"

"Yes. Has he told you about the incident?"

"No," said Clay. Rountree shot him a warning glare.

Satisky smiled. "I thought not. That is the reason I felt that I could not shirk my responsibility."

"Well? What were they arguing about? You?"

"Unfortunately, I cannot help you there. In order to get close enough to hear the words distinctly, I would have had to get close enough to be seen. It was broad daylight."

"And you didn't want to be seen by Geoffrey," offered the sheriff.

Satisky hesitated. "It would have been unpleasant. I had no desire to intrude."

"I understand. I also understand why you didn't tell us before. Admitting that you overheard the fracas also means admitting that you were out by the lake that morning, too. Who's to say that the fight wasn't about you? Maybe that fellow convinced his sister not to marry you after all, and you snuck back later on when she was alone, argued about it, and killed her."

"Of course I didn't!" Satisky blurted out. "I wanted to call it off myself! That's what I went out there..." His voice trailed off, as he realized what he was saying.

Rountree smiled grimly. "Well, so much for your grief. Now, as to the subject of the argument, I guess we'd better discuss that with ol' Geoffrey."

Satisky glanced at Clay's scribbled notes. "Do you want me to sign that?"

"No," said Clay. "You have to be able to read what you're signing. Doris will have to type it up."

"I'll be seeing you by and by, Mr. Satisky," Wesley assured him. "And thank you for coming to me with this." He patted Satisky's shoulder.

Michael basked in official approval. "Well, I'm glad to help *y'all*, Sheriff."

"You know, Northerners always make that mistake," Wesley told him seriously. "Y'all is not used when talking to one person. It's second person plural, like *vos* in Latin."

"Oh...er, yes, of course."

"You'll get the hang of it. 'Bye now." Rountree turned away.

Satisky hurried back to the house, attempting to reassess his image of the county sheriff, and wondering what explanation he would give in case anyone had seen him talking to Rountree and Taylor. Of course, if Rountree questioned Geoffrey about it, it would all come out soon, anyway. He'd better go up to his room and pack, just in case.

"Wasn't that interesting?" asked Wesley, when Satisky had gone. "Geoffrey had a fight with his sister at the death scene."

"I'm surprised that guy came to us about it," said Clay. "I'd expect him to blackmail Geoffrey with it, instead."

"Well, he is hard up for money," Rountree said. "We established that in our boardinghouse talk. But if Geoffrey is the murderer, that would be a good way to share double billing with the original deceased. Satisky may have just enough brains to have figured that out. But my guess is that he doesn't have the nerve to approach Geoffrey for blackmail or anything else. This business of sneaking behind his back is more in Satisky's line of country. I'll bet he enjoyed getting Geoffrey in trouble, don't you?"

"I think it settled a few scores between them," said Clay. "I take it we're going to discuss this with Geoffrey now?"

"Oh, yes. Yes, indeed we are."

They walked back to the front door, where Mildred presently appeared and informed them that Geoffrey had gone out for a walk about twenty minutes earlier.

"What do you want to bet he's gone down to that lake?" asked Rountree. "Morbid so-and-so."

"We've finished up there, haven't we? I mean, he can't destroy evidence now."

"Not unless you missed something. We didn't find the murder weapon, but I bet that's in the lake. Mitch says it was a piece of wood, like a branch."

"Oh, I looked all right. It's not around the lake. Let's go."

Geoffrey had not gone to the lake, however. When they finally found him, nearly half an hour later, he was sitting under an apple tree with his script of *The Duchess of Malfi*.

"Eagles commonly fly alone; they are crows, daws, and starlings that flock together. Look, what's that follows me?" He looked up in mock surprise. "Oh, hello, Sheriff. Just learning my lines."

"Learning your lines?" Wesley repeated.

"Yes. For the community theater production. We're doing *The Duchess of Malfi*. Do say you'll come and see it, Sheriff. I shall be so honored."

"I read that in English class!" said Clay eagerly. "It's about a guy who has his sister killed because he's in love with her!" He faltered, as he realized the implications of this.

Rountree brightened. "No! Is that the truth?"

"Somewhat oversimplified," Geoffrey retorted. "It has to do with the honor of a noble family."

"I'd say your family is a pretty noble one around here." Rountree sank gingerly to the grass beside Geoffrey, and motioned for Clay to follow.

"If you are under the impression that I am conducting an al fresco seminar on medieval drama, you are misinformed," snapped Geoffrey, closing the book.

"Fact is, we came to talk about your sister's murder. Or rather, an incident that happened shortly before."

"And what is that, pray?"

"You tell us. You were there. What did you and your sister argue about on the day she died?"

Geoffrey raised his eyebrows. "What makes you ask?"

"You were overheard. We're just giving you a chance to tell your side of it." Rountree held up a restraining hand. "But don't start yet. Just let me read you your rights. I'm not charging you with anything—yet. I just want to make sure you know where you stand before you say anything."

Geoffrey stared off into space while Rountree fished out his "rights" card, and read it in the cheerful tones of a radio announcer. When he finished, he put it back in his wallet and beamed expectantly at Geoffrey. There was a minute of silence.

"Well?" prompted Rountree encouragingly.

Geoffrey sighed and shook his head. Finally, he said,

"All right, Rountree. We'll have our little talk, on certain conditions..."

"Now, plea-bargaining is strictly the province of the district attorney," Rountree began warningly.

"It's not that. I am about to discuss personal family matters which, I might add, have no bearing on this case. I don't want my statement to be discussed at the diner. I don't want it mentioned to my family. And I don't want Doris Guthrie to type up my statement, because she has the biggest mouth in the state of Georgia."

"Police matters are always confidential—" Clay began.

"Type it up yourself, Clay. He's right about Doris. Okay, Mr. Chandler. You have my word on it. This interview will be confidential insofar as it can be. You know, confessions of murder—even accidental killings—can't be our little secrets. But why don't you just tell me what happened that day, and let's take it from there, shall we?"

"If I thought I could refuse to answer you without being charged with murder, I would certainly do so," Geoffrey sighed. "And my only objection to that would be that it would deter you from finding the real killer. I would not deny him his rightful place in the penitentiary, I assure you. Very well—my discussion with Eileen. Who told you about it, by the way?"

"We can't discuss that," said Rountree.

"I believe I can guess," offered Geoffrey.

"Now, what time Friday morning did you go to the lake?"

"About eight o'clock." He acknowledged their look of surprise with a slight nod. "Yes, such an admission would shock my family, because I've trained them not to expect to see me before ten in the morning, but nevertheless it is true. In fact, I even changed back into my dressing gown for breakfast later so as not to impair my reputation for sloth."

"And you found your sister painting by the lake?"

"Yes. And I know what you are thinking. I must

189

have seen the painting. I wish I had. It was my intention to do so."

"That's why you went down there? Just to see the painting?"

Geoffrey sighed. "I know my sister very well, Sheriff. Better than any of the rest of the family. And there was some reason for her not showing us that picture. Some reason other than the one she gave."

"Uh-huh," mused Rountree, who had come to the same conclusion. "And what was that reason?"

"I don't know. But I was worried. She had been acting very distraught the day before, and I knew she was afraid of something. She broke a mirror in the upstairs hall, and made a scene in front of Dr. Shepherd, which is not like my sister at all."

"We've discussed your sister's medical history with Dr. Shepherd."

"Yes. Well, in the early days of her illness, she used to say that she saw things—things that weren't there. And she couldn't stand mirrors. So…when she broke the mirror Thursday night, I began to be afraid that she was getting sick again."

"Did you discuss that possibility with Dr. Shepherd?"

"Of course not! I didn't want him to know!"

"Why not?"

Geoffrey gestured impatiently. "Because they'd lock her up again! And Eileen doesn't—didn't—need to be put away. She needed to feel safe and happy away from this house! At first I thought that she might be able to do that with Satisky, but it didn't seem to be working. She had him, and the symptoms were still coming back! I was so afraid for her. She was going to blow it, and get sent away again."

"And you told her this?"

"Yes—eventually. Not the way I'd planned. When she saw me at the lake that morning, she put the painting away immediately. And I asked her if I could see it. She said no; something about being sensitive to criticism. I told her to come off it. I knew her symptoms as well as she did. I told her that she'd been acting strangely, and that if she turned up the day before the

190

wedding with a painting of purple-eyed demons, then she could find the wedding cancelled right out from under her."

"I don't imagine she took kindly to that."

"She started to cry. Said that Michael loved her and nothing could stop them."

"And what did you say?"

"I'm afraid I lost my temper. I told her that if she didn't control herself better, she would ruin things all by herself."

"You wanted her to be able to go through with the wedding?"

Geoffrey rested his chin against his knees. "Well, Sheriff," he said, "it's like the fairy tale Snow White—to put things on your level: I wanted her to get away from the Wicked Queen and her magic mirror, even if she had to live in the woods with seven little men to be able to do it."

Rountree paused for a moment, phrasing his question carefully. "Geoffrey...did you, in this quarrel with your sister, get madder than you intended? Did you hit her or knock her down? Not on purpose! Did she fall on a rock, for instance, and get knocked out? And maybe you panicked and tossed her into the boat?"

"No, Rountree. The brave man uses a sword. I did it with a bitter look."

Rountree and Taylor looked at each other and shrugged. Another quote. Finally the sheriff said, "I take it that means you didn't cause her death, accidental or otherwise."

"Right, Sheriff. I did not cause her death."

"What would you say her state of mind was when you left her?"

Geoffrey looked away. "She told me to go away. That there was nothing the matter with her. And she accused me of trying to break up her romance with Satisky. She said..." His voice trembled.

"Yes?" prompted Rountree softly.

"She said: 'Which one of us are you jealous of?'"

• • •

"What did you think of that?" asked Clay.

Rountree shrugged. "I stopped trying to spot killers a long time ago."

"I didn't mean that, Wes. It seems kind of strange, though, that he's taking it so hard. And you notice he didn't volunteer that information about the fight they had. How do we know it went like that?"

The sheriff snorted. "I guess you want that man from Atlanta to come up here with his lie detector, so you can plug everybody in and see what's what."

Taylor knew he was being laughed at, but he couldn't see why. It did seem like a pretty good idea, at that. "I guess we'd have to charge him first."

"Just keep taking notes, Clay, and stop trying to think up TV tricks to improve law enforcement." Taylor reddened and gave a quick nod. "Besides, you wouldn't learn a lot. Lie detectors can be beat."

"Oh, sure, I've heard that," mumbled Clay.

"I did it myself," said Wesley complacently.

The Chandler house loomed in front of them. but Wesley didn't seem to want to go back in. He circled around the garage and headed for the front driveway. Taylor followed along, wondering if they were through for the day. If they finished before three, he could usually get Doris to type up his notes.

"How'd you beat the lie detector, Wes?"

The sheriff grinned. "Well, it was while I was in the M.P.s. We had one of those things laying around, so we got an expert in to give us a course in it. He asked for volunteers to demonstrate how the thing worked, and I went up there and let him strap me in and ask me questions. The thing works on your breathing and movements—on the notion that it makes you nervous to lie, I reckon. So I lied up a storm, and it never registered, because my mind wasn't on the questions."

"Yeah?"

"S'right. He'd ask me if my name was Henry, and I'd say 'yes,' just as calm as cow dung, 'cause all the while I'm naming off the parts of my rifle in my head, trying to get them in the order you break it down. So I'm answering the questions without really thinking about them, because in my head I'm saying: 'Pin, charging handle, bolt, stock...' And, you know, I never trusted one of those things since, 'cause I figure that if an honest fellow like me can get past that machine, think what a real liar could do! How are we doing with those interviews, anyway?"

Taylor ticked off the names in his notebook. "That seems to be everybody. You want to interview anybody else today?"

"Yeah," said Rountree thoughtfully. "I think I want to talk to the Emperor."

"Oh. Yeah. I hope he's home. I'd sort of like to look inside that place myself."

The sheriff smiled. "Now, try not to be impressed."

"Oh, it's *immoral*, of course," said Taylor hastily. "I certainly don't think anybody should live in a place like that while so many people are doing without electricity and indoor plumbing, but from an aesthetic point of view...well, as long as he's built it, I might as well look at it."

"Might as well, Clay. Only try to keep your mind on the investigation while you're taking inventory, okay?"

They crossed the road and approached the castle.

"Sure is a lot of steps," Rountree remarked, looking up at the front door a flight above them. He took the steps at a leisurely pace, while Clay bounded to the top and began to thud on the brass dragon door-knocker. Rountree joined him just as the door opened, and a short frowning woman peered out at them.

"This ain't no museum," she warned.

"Hello, Mrs. Murphy," said Clay. "Remember me?"

The door opened wider. "Clay Taylor! How in the world are you?"

"Doing fine. Here on business, though. Sheriff, this is Willie Murphy's mother. You working here now, ma'am?"

"Three days a week," she sighed. "And you couldn't hardly call that enough. I don't know how those people managed without electric floor-polishers in them days." She pointed to the gleaming marble staircase, and the squat machine on the first landing.

"I beg your pardon for disturbing the work," said Rountree, "but we need to see Mr. Cobb if he's around."

"He's upstairs. I'll get him for you. Who do you want me to say is looking for him?"

"The sheriff," said Wesley. With a trace of a smile, he added: "Of Nottingham."

Alban was still laughing when he came downstairs to meet them. He escorted them into his study and installed them on the velvet sofa. Clay reached for his notepad.

"You, I suppose, are Robin Hood," Alban said grinning. "Actually, Sheriff, you have mistaken your castle. This one is not twelfth-century English. It's nineteenth-century German."

"Very impressive," said Wesley politely.

"Look, I know you didn't come here on the Garden Club tour. What can I do for you? Can I get you some coffee?" He sank down in the wing chair and put his head in his hands.

"None for me, thanks," said Wesley. "But you look like you could use some. Anything wrong?"

Alban looked up in amazement. "Quite a lot is wrong, don't you think? I'm afraid I have a rather bad headache. Probably stress. But please don't think I'm trying to put you off. I believe I will get some coffee, so you just go right ahead and talk."

Wesley watched as Alban poured coffee into a beer stein with a stag painted on it. "This is just routine," he remarked, settling back against the curve of the sofa. "We've interviewed everybody across the way, and we thought you might be able to give us some information about your cousin."

"Could you tell me first—what has happened? I'd like to sort out all the tales I've heard about maurauding tramps and—er—houseguests. Is there a suspect?"

"A whole raft of them. All I'm prepared to say for sure is that Miss Eileen was supposed to be painting a picture down by that lake. Everybody says it was a wedding gift for her fiancé. Did you happen to get a look at it?"

"Judging from the other samples of her work, I'd have expected an abstract, Sheriff."

"Can you think of a reason for someone to kill her because of an abstract?"

Alban smiled ruefully. "I'm afraid Eileen's work was not so promising."

"Well, whatever it was, it's gone. From what we can make of it, she was painting early that morning by the lake, and someone sneaked up behind her and hit her."

"You haven't found the weapon that killed her?"

"The weapon that *hit* her, no," Wesley corrected him. "I may have to drag that damn lake yet. What killed her is another thing. According to the coroner's report, death was caused by snake venom. She was thrown into an old rowboat pushed up in the weeds, and there was a water moccasin in the bottom. Must have been a big one. He got her in the jugular vein, and a full load of undiluted venom hit her heart about a minute later. That did it. We haven't found the snake, either," he added drily.

Alban sighed. "My poor cousin's death was certainly more dramatic than her life."

"This is about the most unusual case I've ever come across," Wesley remarked. "Where were you on the day of Miss Chandler's death, by the way?"

"Escorting my mother to a flower show in Milton's Forge."

"And you left when?"

"Around nine, I should think."

"Had you had any conversations with Miss Chandler about her forthcoming marriage?"

"Only to wish her well. My conversations with Eileen consisted mainly of pleasantries. We were not close. She has been away so long that we scarcely knew what to say."

"How about the groom? What do you think of him?"

Alban shrugged. "He's rather quiet. The family attitude seemed to be polite tolerance, so I followed their example."

"Ummm. How about the rest of the family? Did she have problems with any of them?"

"Eileen wasn't a fighter, Sheriff. She faded. When my charming Aunt Amanda became overbearing, Eileen just wasn't there; physically if she could manage it, mentally if not. In any family skirmish she was definitely neutral. Even Geoffrey exempted her from his verbal barbs. Eileen kept to herself."

"Well, she must have been in somebody's way."

"I'm afraid I'm not much help. I really think in this case a trespasser might actually be the answer to the problem."

Rountree puffed his cheeks and let off a sigh of exasperation. "Vagrants don't have art collections, Mr. Cobb."

"It always comes back to the painting, doesn't it?"

"Yep. And you have no idea what could have been in that painting?"

"Well, a couple of nights ago, Eileen was late for dinner, and I happened to be a guest of the Chandlers myself, so I volunteered to go and get her. Aunt Amanda is a stickler about meals. When I got down to the lake, she was just packing up her painting gear. I just got a glimpse of it, not even worth mentioning—the light was going and I was quite a distance away. But my impression is that it was the lake—though perhaps in abstract."

"The lake. That's what everybody figures. And it gets us nowhere. Why should anybody take a painting of the lake? Any ideas?"

"Dozens of them," said Alban grinning. "All ridiculous. Would you like a few examples? Well, I thought that perhaps Cousin Charles had a marijuana plantation around the lake, and that Eileen had painted the leaf fronds too accurately. Or the Governor might have some secret ship model that he's testing for the government, and Eileen put it in the painting. Shall I go on?"

Rountree stood up. "We'll just muddle along by ourselves, if it's all the same to you. That's quite an imagination you've got there!"

Alban looked around him. "I thought you might have guessed that already, Sheriff."

"Um. I see what you mean. We'll be going now, Mr. Cobb. If you can think of anything else, please call me. Hope your headache gets better."

"Thank you, Sheriff. Perhaps I can persuade my cousin Elizabeth to go riding with me. That used to relax me considerably."

When they were outside, Rountree, who had been pondering this last remark, said, "I haven't seen any horses around here, have you?"

Taylor shrugged. "Maybe they're in the guest room."

CHAPTER THIRTEEN

ALTHOUGH SUNDAY proved to be a day of respite from the inquiries of the law, to Elizabeth it was the most tedious day of all. The shock of Eileen's death had begun to wear off, leaving raw nerves among personalities already too inclined toward drama. Funeral arrangements and notifications had been completed, so that the tragedy could no longer be obstructed through routine tasks; it loomed large in the empty day. Breakfast had been a tense and silent meal, presided over by Amanda, who was a fierce antithesis to her former hostess-self. She seemed to begrudge every mouthful to those who were callous enough to eat in the presence of her sorrow. She herself sipped coffee and shredded a piece of dry toast on her plate.

After breakfast, while everyone was scrambling for sections of the Atlanta newspaper, Amanda appeared at the door in a black linen suit and gloves, informing them that church services began in one hour.

Satisky mumbled something about "keeping the Sabbath staying at home," and Geoffrey, recognizing the reference, snapped, "Oughtn't you to be celebrating it in a garden in Amherst, Massachusetts, then?"

As the Chandlers regretfully surrendered their newspaper sections and prepared to go upstairs and dress, Carlsen Shepherd remarked that there was an interesting old Baptist Church he'd seen in Milton's Forge on the way in, if anyone would care to join him in visiting it. Since he was looking at Elizabeth as he said this, she accepted the invitation at once.

Half an hour later, the two of them were in Shepherd's car on the road to Milton's Forge—Shepherd looking more presentable than usual in a navy three-piece suit.

"I didn't know you were interested in old churches," Elizabeth remarked.

"I'm not. I just thought the two of us could use some time off."

"It's getting to you, too?" asked Elizabeth, incredulous.

"Sure. And please don't say 'But you're a psychiatrist.' Give me a break. I treat patients; I don't move in with them."

Elizabeth nodded. "It's like waiting for a storm, isn't it? Sometimes I wish that Aunt Amanda would have her hysterics and get it over with."

Shepherd nodded. "Maybe she'll do it while we are gone. By the way, I mentioned that we might not be back in time for lunch. Is that all right with you?"

"Yes! With Aunt Amanda glaring at us during breakfast, I could hardly swallow!"

"It's a difficult time to be an outsider. I wonder when the sheriff will settle all this so that we can leave."

"Do you think we'll have to stay until he finds the murderer?" asked Elizabeth, considering that unpleasant possibility for the first time.

Shepherd shook his head. "I don't know. They asked me what I thought about it, but it's hard to guess why she was killed when we don't know much about her family situation."

"I thought you did."

"Now, remember, I've only been seeing her as a patient for a year. Dr. Kimble did most of the therapy. I was just someone to talk to if she had adjustment problems. We didn't go into great detail about her childhood or anything like that."

"Well, since you're a psychiatrist, can't you just sort of look at the crime and figure out who would have done something like that?"

Shepherd grinned. "You mean relate the snake to Oedipal impulses, and stuff like that?"

"Well—I guess so."

"But you can't rule out coincidence. Maybe the murderer didn't even know the snake was in the boat. Or maybe it was just a businesslike murder for money, and the killer took advantage of a handy time and place. Sorry—I think the sheriff is going to have to solve this one on his own."

"Psychiatry sounds pretty interesting. Aside from the crime element, I mean. Do you like it?"

Elizabeth's consideration of psychiatry as a potential career continued until they arrived at the church and was resumed after the service over a platter of fried chicken in Brody's Roadside Inn.

"It's nearly one-thirty," Shepherd told Elizabeth, when they had finished their meal. "Should we start back?"

"What's the alternative?" asked Elizabeth.

"Well, there's a little historical museum in Milton's Forge; we could visit that. You know: quilt exhibits and potters. I should do some sight-seeing while I'm down here."

"What tourist attraction could compare with the one in the front yard?"

"Maybe he'll offer a tour."

"I shouldn't joke about it," said Elizabeth with a guilty look. "He said I was his favorite cousin, and here I am making fun of him. I told my brother Bill that, and he said that Alban's taste in cousins is consistent with his taste in architecture."

"Your brother sounds like one of the family, all right."

"It's a zoo. I wonder why you let yourself in for it. Why *did* you come?"

201

Shepherd looked uncomfortable. "You know, I wondered if anybody would ask me that. I don't go to all my patients' weddings. I guess you could say I had a hunch about this one."

Elizabeth stared. "You mean...you *knew*—"

"Oh, no! Not about the murder. I'm perceptive, but not psychic. I just thought this wedding might not come off. From what I'd seen of Satisky and what I'd heard of the family, I just thought—well, there could be trouble. I thought I'd come down as a friendly neutral, in case I was needed. And if the worst did happen—no wedding—I figured Eileen would need me for sure."

"That was very nice of you," murmured Elizabeth.

"Professional ethics," said Shepherd, getting up. "How about a museum?"

After several hours of admiring colonial handicrafts, Shepherd and Elizabeth returned to find no one at home but Mildred, who informed them that the family had gone to Todd & O'Connor's Funeral Home to view the body. The coroner had authorized the transfer of Eileen's body to the local funeral home sometime that afternoon.

"Do you suppose we ought to drive out there?" asked Elizabeth in hushed tones.

"Do you want to?" asked Shepherd.

"No." She shivered, picturing the emotional storm breaking in the funeral home.

"Then don't. There's always tomorrow. I think I saw a chess set in the library. That doesn't seem like a frivolous game, does it? Even in a house of mourning. Come on. It'll take your mind off all of this."

They played until after nine o'clock, when the flash of headlights in the driveway sent them scurrying tactfully to their rooms.

The next morning, Dr. Shepherd accepted an invitation from Robert Chandler to tour the county hospital and to meet some of the local physicians. Elizabeth passed most of the day reading in her room. Dinner loomed ominously in her thoughts: another opportunity for family melodrama. She considered skipping the meal altogether, but after some reflection decided that her presence would exert a calming influence. If it would avert a nasty scene, she'd better go.

When she came downstairs at a quarter past five, Geoffrey was in the hall, about to go into the dining room. "Ah, there you are, Elizabeth! You have been quite the hermit today, haven't you? Very wise! Who knows who'll be next?"

Elizabeth frowned disapprovingly. "Not funny. It's just that I don't have your tolerance for drama in everyday life."

"Then you will be distressed to hear that this evening's floor show will consist of a performance by Tommy Simmons in his legal capacity, followed by Sheriff Rountree's feats of mental marvels."

"They're coming to dinner?"

"Mercifully not. But they will be expecting us to convene in the drawing room at seven. Try not to think about it; it might curdle your Hollandaise sauce. Stress is fatal to digestion."

"What does Rountree want now?"

Geoffrey struck a pose. "I applied for the job of Watson, but the offer was not well received." Then, in a serious voice: "Surely you don't expect me to know? Something trivial, I expect."

"I suppose so. He has already talked to all of us."

They went into the dining room, where Amanda and Captain Grandfather, already seated, were talking together in low voices. Elizabeth made her way to the other end of the table, where Charles and Dr. Shepherd were sitting. Geoffrey started to follow her, but then he seemed to remember something and hurried back out into the hall.

A moment later he was back, waving a blue and white envelope. "I nearly forgot, Elizabeth! This Mailgram came for you today. Perhaps an offer from one of those supermarket newspapers to tell your side of the crime!"

He handed her the envelope, and everyone stopped and looked at her while she opened it. Elizabeth read the message twice, and slid the paper back into the envelope.

"From Margaret?" asked Amanda.

"No," murmured Elizabeth. "From Bill."

"No doubt he is informing you of when they will be down for the funeral."

"Well...they're not sure yet."

Alban appeared at the door. "At dinner already! Oh dear. Shall I go away?"

The question was addressed to Amanda, but Captain Grandfather answered it. "You might as well stay, Alban. I just had a call from Wesley Rountree and he's coming back out to talk to us this evening. Tommy Simmons has asked for a conference with us, and Wes will be sitting in on that as well."

"Stay to dinner?" asked Dr. Chandler.

"If it's no trouble. Shall I call Mother and let her know about the meeting?" He sauntered toward Elizabeth's end of the table.

"Yes, please, Alban," said Amanda. "I spoke to her about the Simmons meeting earlier today, but she may need to be reminded. She said she wasn't feeling well."

"No. She's hardly been out of her room today."

"Perhaps I'd better step across and see her," said Captain Grandfather quietly.

Amanda's jaw tightened. "Of course, if anyone ought to be taking this in seclusion, it is I. None of you can possibly understand the strain that all this has been..."

"Can't we have just this one meal in peace?" snapped her husband.

"Robert, I *will* express my grief! And my concern that my daughter's murderer be—"

"Do you want him caught?" thundered Captain Grandfather. "Damned if *I* do!"

The bickering leveled out to a series of strident tones, which washed over Michael Satisky, leaving no meaning to soak into his consciousness. He was trying to think about Eileen. There should be grief somewhere in his mind. He was sure that if he could burrow through the tension of the enforced stay as a houseguest, and his terror that the police might obligingly arrest "everybody's favorite suspect," he would feel some sorrow for Eileen herself. Each time he tried to find her in his mind, he encountered a wave of relief that he was freed from an awkward relationship. The temptation of so much money had finally been removed, so that he could go back to being the sincere and unworldly person he was sure he was. Poverty dragons were much easier to slay than the monsters Eileen had presented him with. He was glad to be released from the commitment, but it bothered him that he could not grieve for the sad little princess he had loved. He was sure that beneath his personal anxieties he was devastated. Of course he was! A person of his perception and sensitivity might take years to get over such a tragedy. A slim book of verse perhaps... "The Lady of the Lake and Other Poems" by Michael Satisky... His thoughts drifted lazily toward similes and imagery.

"Hello, Elizabeth, I haven't seen much of you lately," said Alban, taking a seat beside her.

"Well, Carlsen and I went to church yesterday, and then we visited a museum." She was surprised to feel herself blushing.

"I see," said Alban quietly. Without another word he began to eat his salad.

Elizabeth looked down at her plate and tried to think of something to say. Her mind was not blank—that was just the problem. It abounded with possible topics of conversation. "Are you jealous that I was out with Dr. Shepherd?" "When is the inquest?" "Do we have to attend?" "Do you think one of us is a murderer?" Since none of those subjects seemed likely to produce peaceful dinner conversation, she was trying to clear her mind of them and find something more neutral to talk about. She was worried about Geoffrey. Despite his breezy repartee in the hall, he had been unusually quiet since they sat down to dinner. This might be a sign of tactfulness—perhaps he had foresworn a natural urge to torment certain of his table partners—but she thought the odds were against Geoffrey doing anything from altruistic motives. At the moment, his face was a courteous blank; she wished she knew the state of the mind behind it.

Charles looked up suddenly from his squash and rice casserole and remarked to no one in particular, "Actually, I find it comforting to think of death as the great benefactor of mankind. Death has made possible natural selection, which allowed for genetic improvement. Reproduction by mitosis merely duplicates the existing organism."

Geoffrey sent his fork clattering into the center of his plate and ran from the room.

"Don't go after him!" said Shepherd, as Elizabeth rose from her chair. "He works so hard at that brittle façade of his. He won't thank you for seeing him without it."

"He's been so quiet. I wondered what he was thinking."

"I think he feels it very much," Shepherd told her. "Just from casual observation, I'd say that like most defensively witty people, Geoffrey is awed by real—how shall I put it—innocence. He seemed very protective of his sister."

"Did she ever say anything about him?" asked Elizabeth.

Shepherd smiled. "You really mustn't ask."

"He's right, though," said Alban. "Geoffrey was always quite human with Eileen."

"Which is more than he is with anyone else," snapped Satisky.

"He shows his feelings, yes," offered Shepherd. "I find it commendable that he has any to show."

Satisky smiled maliciously. "Or else he finds it necessary to put on a show—for other reasons!"

Alban set down his coffee cup with a clatter. "Enough! Just stop all this talk about the murder! If you just let it alone, time will fix it—"

"Time—is—relative!" chanted Charles, pointing a fork at Alban.

Alban seemed about to roar back across the table, but suddenly he checked himself. "I'm very sorry," he mumbled. "All of this is getting on my nerves, I'm afraid.

I don't like scenes, you know. Never have. I think people ought to be well-bred about things. I hate it when people go raking things up."

Elizabeth stared. Raking things up? So Alban's attitude about Eileen's death had come down to "least said, soonest mended." She wondered if he would be so forgiving if one of his precious antiques had been smashed—but then Eileen hadn't been worth much, had she? Just a colorless young woman, not even pretty enough to interest the crime magazines.

Setting her napkin beside her plate, Elizabeth stood up. "Excuse me, please."

It took her half an hour to find Geoffrey. She had checked his room, Eileen's room, and the fields near the house before she thought of the attic that used to serve as a playroom when they were children. She remembered it as she was walking back to the house from the apple orchard, when she caught sight of the round window beneath the eaves. They used to pretend it was the porthole of the *Nautilus*. The other end of the attic had been converted into a kitchen-sized laboratory for Charles, although he rarely used it anymore, but the part of the attic that had been the *Nautilus* (and Richmond and Valhalla) had not been changed. She wondered if Geoffrey had thought of it.

Elizabeth hurried up the narrow stairs which led to the eaves. The door was unlocked. Afternoon light filtering in through the circular windows enabled her to see the dressing-up trunks and cast-off toys which furnished the attic. When her eyes grew more accustomed to the dimness, she saw Geoffrey, hunched up against the far wall with his arm clasping his knees. He did not look up.

Elizabeth hesitated for a moment. Comforting did not come easily to her, particularly when it was a grief whose magnitude she could not share. At such times there was an awkwardness to her conversation, and she could make no move without consciously planning it. I may be worse than nothing, she thought. Somehow, though, it was better here than in the dining room.

Geoffrey's grief made her uneasy, but the attitude of the others had disgusted her. If there had been anyone else to comfort Geoffrey, she would have left them to it, but there was not.

Brushing aside an old bride doll, she sat down on the floor beside him. "I thought you might come to Valhalla," she murmured.

"I was Frey and you were Brunhilda, the Valkyrie. Did we get that from Alban, do you suppose? We should have played Greek gods, Elizabeth. There was no death on Olympus."

"I'm sorry about what they said downstairs. I left, too."

"Well, you won't find me very good company this evening. My supply of wit to fling in the face of adversity is depleted. I should be back in form soon, never fear, but...not...just...now." His voice had a brittle lightness, and Elizabeth was terrified that he would cry.

"What are you thinking about?" she asked finally.

Geoffrey sighed. "Nothing. Everything at once. I find it helps to think of a lot of different things at the same time, so as not to dwell on any one long enough to feel it." He fingered the yellow bride doll lying facedown on the floor. "That was Princess Grace. Eileen used to play royal wedding by the hour. Once she caught Hans, the old tomcat, and dressed him up in doll clothes to be the prince. He escaped, of course. We chased him all around the house, but we never caught him. I wonder if Eileen was afraid that her prince would escape."

"I think so," said Elizabeth, wondering if she should say more.

"I think so, too. And I think she blamed us for it."

"You? Why?"

"Oh, because...It wasn't until he came here that he began to have doubts about it, I guess, and—"

"You weren't very kind to him, you know."

"I'm not very kind to anybody. But he alternately cringed and fawned. Eileen wanted St. Michael the Archangel to slay her dragon, and he was afraid of his own shadow. St. Michael, indeed!"

208

"Do you think he killed her? Oh, I guess you don't want to talk about it."

"No to both. It isn't murder I'm trying to come to terms with yet. It's death. And the fact that nobody seems to mind."

"Your mother..."

"Mother! Yes! She's giving a convincing portrayal of a bereaved mother, isn't she? Actually, I think Mother is relieved. After all these years, she finally has a good reason for being unhappy. A legitimate sorrow to drown. And everyone else is being correctly solemn."

"Perhaps they don't show their feelings. *You* don't show yours."

He laughed bitterly. "Don't I?"

"You were very close to Eileen, weren't you?" Elizabeth struggled to understand this new side of Geoffrey. How would she feel if Bill had died? Angry...She couldn't get past that to see what would come after it.

Geoffrey was looking beyond her at the scattered toys. "Yes. I was close to her. Eileen was kind. She was the one really kind person I have ever known. It wasn't just an act to make people like her. I suppose it surprises you that I would value that, since people who like me are attracted by my viciousness. I get by on being clever. But I was always a little awed by my sister's kindness. She always seemed to know what to say to people. I haven't the foggiest myself. If they don't care for repartee, I manage to be civil until they go away. Eileen knew more about the damned maid than I know about Charles!"

Elizabeth realized that she was trying to sort out the difference between gentleness and unintellectual naïveté, but she pushed the ungracious thought away. Kindness, she thought. Well, whatever it is, I haven't got it either.

"I keep thinking about her dying. It should have been me. You realize that, don't you? One day I should have uttered one quip too many and been bashed over the head by an inarticulate bridge club member! Damn it! She's dead, and all I can do is analyze it!"

"You have to feel it in your own way," said Elizabeth gently.

"I wish I could be sure that I *was* feeling it! Part of me is standing off a little way watching me grieve and checking my utterances for clichés! Eileen wasn't like that. If I were dead, she would cry for me!"

"It won't help to feel guilty about it."

"Not now, it won't. It's ironic that Alban should trot out that *Macbeth* line: 'She should have died hereafter.' I can't even say that. I don't think she was ever going to be happy. I just wish she'd had a better time while she was alive. I could have been more understanding. I could have stopped bringing out the worst in that sniveling beast she brought home."

"Why do you hate him so much?"

Geoffrey looked at her. "If I tell you, you won't understand. Even she didn't understand."

"Tell me anyway," prompted Elizabeth.

"Because he was wasteful! Oh, that's the wrong word, but it's as close as I çan come. Just—there are so few good, *real* people in the world, that they should be cherished for the miracle they are. And he couldn't see how special she was. He thought she was a shy crazed girl that he was doing a favor by marrying! A favor! She built him a soul. Eileen saw a wonderful prince charming in a piece of shit!"

Elizabeth thought about this for a moment. She agreed that Eileen's vision of Michael did not appear to tally with reality, but she wondered why that misconception bothered Geoffrey so much.

"Maybe he only saw a reflection of himself," Eileen said slowly. "Or what he wanted to see. He wanted to think he was doing her a favor..."

Geoffrey nodded. "And I wanted to see someone who would love me even when I wasn't being clever. Tell me, Elizabeth—how did *you* see Eileen?"

Elizabeth shook her head. "I don't think I saw her at all."

Tommy Simmons, somberly attired in his charcoal gray wool, felt that he presented the proper attitude of dignified efficiency. Black would have been overstating the case. He modulated his voice to hushed reverence and endeavored to convey an air of "money is not important at a time like this, but the formalities must be observed." A professor of his had once said that all attorneys were actors manqué. Fortunately this was not difficult, since his audience was intent upon maintaining the same façade. He ruffled his papers, glancing up at the Chandlers who were sitting pale and erect, waiting for him to begin. He had been forced to delay the meeting for a few minutes until Geoffrey and the scatty cousin had arrived. His audience was now complete and properly attentive, and he decided that it would be appropriate to begin. He hoped things went smoothly; Tommy's fondness for acting did not extend to melodrama.

"As you know, I am here to discuss the estate—if we can call it that—of Miss Eileen Chandler." He paused, clearing his throat before taking the first hurdle. "I—er—hope that no one will object to the presence of Sheriff Rountree and Deputy Taylor in the family conference. As an attorney, I might venture to say—"

"We just thought we'd save Mr. Simmons the trouble of going through it twice," said Rountree from the doorway. "That is, if nobody minds."

Dr. Chandler summoned a pale smile. "Come in, Wes," he said softly.

They eased into the room, with Taylor looking as if he wanted to tiptoe across the thick blue carpet. The silver coffee service had been set up on the table next to the window, and Dr. Chandler motioned them toward it. With the help of Dr. Shepherd, they assembled extra cups and napkins from a sideboard and fixed their own coffee. Amanda Chandler sat motionless on the sofa, oblivious to it all.

When the officers had poured their coffee and found empty chairs, Tommy Simmons began again. "Now this is a purely unofficial discussion of finances, concerning"—he glanced at the papers in front of him —"concerning the immediate family." Simmons paused tentatively.

"Then I shall excuse myself," said Elizabeth quickly. She hurried to the door before anyone could think of a reason to detain her.

Alban, who had started to get up when Elizabeth spoke, turned to Dr. Shepherd. "I think they can spare us, too, Doctor. Why don't we go out for a walk?"

Shepherd glanced at the tense faces around him and nodded to Alban. As they rose to leave, Wesley Rountree leaned over to Dr. Chandler and said: "Robert, let me just get this in real quick. We're going to have to drag that lake in the morning. Can I get your okay on that?"

"Of course, Wesley," whispered Chandler. He gave an encouraging nod to Simmons, who looked inquiringly at the sheriff. Wesley smiled and nodded. As the door closed behind Shepherd and Alban, Simmons began, "I always feel that in awkward situations it's best for the parties involved to sit down and talk things out—"

Amanda's head jerked up. She seemed to notice him for the first time. "I have yet to learn that my daughter's death is an awkward situation!" she snapped.

Simmons looked pained. "I was speaking *legally*."

"And are you about to render a dramatic reading of the will?" Geoffrey inquired.

"It is an unusual will. She wrote it herself, you see, and—"

"All the women in this family write silly wills!" snapped Captain Grandfather. "Look at Augusta's piece of nonsense. Reminds me, where's Louisa?"

"She called and said she isn't feeling well," said Charles.

"Her presence is not necessary. She isn't mentioned," said Simmons.

Michael Satisky flushed. He felt them all looking at him, but he did not raise his eyes to see whether they were or not. He wondered if he should request permission to leave, but that would only draw more attention to himself.

"I think I'll just go ahead and read this," said Simmons. He held up the piece of stationery. He glanced

212

up nervously at the expectant faces, then plunged into the narrative.

"This is the last will and testament of me, Eileen Amanda Chandler, being of sound mind, despite opinions to the contrary. I think of a will as being an expression of consolation from the dead person to those who will miss her. To Captain Grandfather I leave the wooden ship he carved for me when I was a little girl with my thanks. Captain Grandfather—'may there be no moaning of the bar, when I put out to sea.' To Daddy, I leave my paintings, because he said he liked them. To Charles, I leave my picture—in case he has forgotten me already. To Geoffrey I leave my stuffed animals, because they often comforted me when I needed them. I want Mother to have the dressmaker's dummy in the sewing room and all my clothes; that way she may never notice I'm gone. And to Michael Satisky, my husband-to-be, I leave Great-Aunt Augusta's money and my copy of *Sonnets from the Portuguese,* with all my love. Signed: Eileen Amanda Chandler." Simmons looked up to indicate that he was finished.

Amanda Chandler was already on her feet. "Is this your idea of a joke?" she hissed. "My daughter would never have written such a spiteful thing to her mother!"

Simmons held out the sheet of paper. "It's handwritten. You are all welcome to examine it." He turned to Satisky, who was staring at the floor with a dazed expression. "Of course, the legacy from her Great-Aunt was not hers to give, since your marriage did not take place."

"She knew," murmured Satisky, without looking up.

"Robert, what did she mean by that?" his wife demanded. "Dressmaker's dummy! I was a good mother to her!" Her voice rose, and she pitched forward, steadying herself on the arm of the sofa. "Ungrateful little—"

Captain Grandfather and Dr. Chandler sprang up, one on each side of her. "Amanda! That's enough!"

"It isn't decent for her to leave a thing like that!" she screeched at Simmons.

"Amanda! Hush!" Dr. Chandler attempted to get her

213

to sit down on the sofa, but she lurched away from him and continued to shout at the lawyer.

"Excuse her," said Captain Grandfather. "She's overwrought."

"I quite understand," said Simmons, who had smelled the bourbon fumes from several feet away. He wrinkled his nose distastefully.

"Let's get her upstairs," said Captain Grandfather briskly.

Throughout the disturbance Michael and the young Chandlers looked embarrassed, while the sheriff and his deputy sat still and tried to look as if nothing were happening. It was a family situation, Wesley reasoned. He had unobtrusively motioned Clay to remain seated; the less notice they took of it, the easier it would be on the family's feelings.

Simmons put the letter in his briefcase, taking an inordinate amount of time on the locks and untying the folder string. He, too, felt that such an exhibition should not be witnessed by outsiders.

"She was laughing at me! She always blamed me when we sent her away, Robert! Never you! Oh, no!" Amanda grew steadily louder and less coherent. Finally the two of them half carried her to the door.

Unable to restrain his curiosity, Clay Taylor stole a glance at Geoffrey, who returned his gaze levelly. Clay turned away quickly. "Want to get out of here, Wes?" he whispered.

"Can't do it," said Wesley softly. "I still need to talk to the doctor about that lake. I sure do hate to bother him, though. As if he hasn't got enough troubles."

Clay nodded. "That's for sure."

Elizabeth stood in front of the wall of books opposite the fireplace, running the tip of one finger over the book titles. Wedged among leather-bound classics and tattered paperback war novels, she found a set of encyclopedias. Her hand hesitated at the volume marked "L," but instead she continued to examine the rest of the bookcase. A few more minutes of searching turned up nothing more helpful. There were books on ships, dec-

214

orating, and many medical volumes, but not many histories or biographies. She reached for the encyclopedia; it was better than nothing.

When she had settled in the wing chair with the book in her lap, Elizabeth reached into her skirt pocket and drew out the Mailgram.

"If this is a joke, I'll kill him."

Through the closed door, Elizabeth heard faint sounds of upraised voices, which made her wonder what Eileen had written in her mysterious will, but since it had evidently created a scene, she was just as glad that she had not stayed to hear it. She would ask Geoffrey later what the fuss had been about, but just now Bill's message intrigued her more than the distribution of Eileen's possessions.

She read the Mailgram again.

"READ UP ON LUDWIG/TELL SHERIFF/BUTT OUT. BILL."

Now what was that supposed to mean? At first she had suspected that it was a satirical puzzle to tell her when the family would arrive for the funeral, or an attempt to goad her into delusions of detection. Bill's sense of humor occasionally approached Geoffrey's in appreciation of the bizarre, but the more she considered these possibilities, the less likely they seemed. Bill had not been in a joking mood on the telephone when she told him about Eileen's murder; he had been very serious indeed. "TELL SHERIFF/BUTT OUT." It sounded unusually urgent coming from Bill. That phrase "Butt out" reminded her of the time the hearth rug at home had caught fire. She and Bill had both dived for it at the same time, but he had pushed her away. "Butt out!" She ran to the kitchen for a pitcher of water, but by the time she got back with it, he had beaten out the flames. His hands had stayed bandaged for a week. Elizabeth smiled, remembering their father's comment on the incident: "You should trade in some of your courage as a down payment on judgment."

She looked at the message again and sighed, wondering if it would be worth it to call the apartment manager again and ask him to rout Bill out of his apartment so that she could demand an explanation. On second thought, that seemed like more bother than following the instructions in the message. Tell the sheriff what? A history lecture from an encyclopedia? What did that have to do with anything? She had been meaning to read up on Ludwig, anyway, though, in case Alban dredged up any more unpleasantries about the Bonnie Prince. Shaking her head in resignation, she opened volume ten and turned to the article on Ludwig II of Bavaria.

The entry on Ludwig took only half a page, and was accompanied by a small photograph of a weak-chinned young man in an elaborate military uniform. He looked like a dreamer, Elizabeth decided; the sort who today read science fiction and play role-games in which they are wizards or paladins. She wondered what he had done besides building fairy-tale castles in his insignificant kingdom. She read the article twice, the second time slowly, her finger tracing out each word in the last paragraph. That must be the connection, but its significance escaped her. Perhaps the sheriff would know what Bill was getting at. Elizabeth slid the Mailgram into the book to mark her place and left the room.

Clay Taylor, who was sitting nearest the door, heard the tapping. Shoving his pencil behind his ear, he signaled for the others to remain seated, and got up to see who it was. Dr. Chandler and the old man had not come back downstairs yet, so Wesley had decided to go ahead with the order to drag the lake. He was on the phone now making the arrangements.

"Well, where *is* Hill-Bear, Doris? I need to talk to him!" Wesley was shouting into the phone.

Clay hastened to open the door. "Oh, hi!" he said, brightening at the sight of Elizabeth. "Do you want to come back in?"

"I need to talk to the Sheriff," she said, looking past the deputy into the parlor. She could see Rountree hunched over an end table talking excitedly into an extension phone. His conversation drowned out the murmur of voices from the corner of the room, where

Tommy Simmons was talking with Geoffrey and Charles. Satisky had picked up a decorating magazine from the coffee table and was leafing through it with no indication of interest.

"Wes is on the phone. He's trying to get the number of the rescue squad people from Doris. He had to get permission from Dr. Chandler so that we could drag the pond. At least, I expect we could have done it anyway, since this is a homicide, but Wesley says, 'Never stomp when you can tiptoe.' So we asked first. They agreed, of course. So he's setting that up now for tomorrow morning." He paused for breath, noticing that she hadn't seemed to be listening. "Is there something I can help you with?"

"I don't know," said Elizabeth. "I was supposed to tell the sheriff, but...where's Dr. Shepherd?"

"He left just after you did. He and Alban—Mr. Cobb, that is—said something about going for a walk by the lake. Guess they knew that this meeting would—"

Elizabeth thrust the book at him. "Look, I can't wait! Just see that he reads this as soon as he gets off the phone. There's a Mailgram in there, too. I'll be at the lake!"

"But you haven't—" Taylor shrugged. She was gone. He leaned against the door and began to flip through the book.

CHAPTER FOURTEEN

ALBAN AND CARLSEN SHEPHERD had slipped out the back door of the house, taking the footpath that led to the lake.

"I'm glad we got out of there," Shepherd confided.

Alban nodded, eyeing the doctor's baggy khakis and faded tee shirt. "I thought you might prefer it out here."

"I was sure there was going to be a scene. It's been building up to one. Professionally, I have to take this sort of thing in stride, but personally, I'd rather not watch."

It was early evening. In the shadowy parts of the path, the trees were becoming less distinct, blending into gray shapes beyond the bushes that lined the path. Behind them, the shade trees on the lawn cast long shadows in the fading sunlight. The house stood black against the bright sky, but as they entered the untended woods that surrounded the lake, the twilight deepened.

Shepherd was thinking how little   of landscape. Although the path was d wet ground around him—from the underground stream that fed the lake, he supposed. Short dogwoods and matted underbrush of shrubs he did not recognize made it difficult to see much beyond the path itself. The tangle of bushes choked the land around the tall pines and hardwoods, making him feel closed in. He eyed the spider webs stretched between tree branches, imagining the cotton stickiness on his face if he should stumble into one stretched across the path. He had been watching the ground as much as possible, expecting every branch to coil and strike at him.

"Is it far to the lake?" he asked when he could stand it no longer.

"No. Less than a mile. We ought to be there before dark. It's pretty country, isn't it?"

Shepherd grunted.

They walked on for a few more minutes in silence. Alban seemed to be deep in thought, and while Shepherd would have welcomed any conversation that would distract him from the unpleasant terrain, he found himself unable to think of any topic that would not lead back to the death of Eileen Chandler.

"Do you suppose we should have stayed to hear what the sheriff had to say?" he ventured.

Alban shrugged.

"Maybe they've set a date for the inquest. I'd like to know when I can plan on leaving. I expect they'll want to drag the lake first, though."

Alban turned and stared at him. "Drag the lake?"

"Sure. In case whatever she got hit with was thrown into the lake. And maybe the painting was thrown in. The sheriff has to be able to say he tried all the possibilities." Now that Shepherd had begun to talk about the case, he seemed unable to stop. His thoughts poured out in a rush of words, requiring no responses for priming. "I've been thinking about the psychological implications of this case, trying to come up with a pattern. The actions of every mind arrange themselves into some kind of order, which, if you study it carefully, should ⸻ you something about the personality of the indi⸻ There's not much to go on in this case, though, and of course everything could have six different meanings. Depends on whose subconscious you're looking at. Take the snake for example. Now, is that a coincidence or a phallic symbol, or what?"

Alban had thrust his hands in his pockets and walked a few feet ahead. "I'm sorry," he said absently. "What did you say?"

It was obvious that he had not heard a word of Shepherd's unburdening, which was just as well, Shepherd decided. Perhaps the sound of his own voice had been so soothing in itself that the sense of the words had been unnecessary. He certainly felt better for having voiced his thoughts, even if they went unheard.

A small tendril of honeysuckle draping over the path brushed Alban's cheek. He shrank back, flailing at the white flowers with a startled cry before he recognized them. With a grunt of anger, he snapped off the branch and ground it into the dirt.

Shepherd watched him thoughtfully. "This has been very upsetting for you, hasn't it?" he said at last.

Alban nodded, turning away. "That was childish," he muttered. "I'm jumpy, I guess."

"Very understandable," said Shepherd encouragingly. "I've seen about ten snakes so far myself, but they all turned out to be sticks."

"I haven't been able to sleep," Alban said softly. "Did I tell you about my headaches?"

"No. Bad ones?"

"Yes. Just lately. I never got them before." Alban reached out and patted an oak tree near the path. "Isn't this a wonderful old tree?"

"Tell me more about your headaches, Alban."

"It's as if there were a noise inside my head. I keep thinking there's something I ought to be concentrating on, but the noise gets in the way. Do you think it's serious?"

Shepherd blinked. "Well, it's hard to say. It might be a reaction to stress. Wouldn't hurt to have it checked out, though."

"Nonsense! I am perfectly well, and I am sure Lutz is aware of it."

Shepherd blinked. "Lutz? Is he your doctor?"

Alban pointed straight ahead. Between the branches the sky shone lighter, a luminous gray indicating a break in the trees. "We have almost arrived. Just around that bend in the path, you will be able to see Starnberg Lake."

"Starnberg? The lake has a name? How long has it been called that?"

Alban regarded him with a calm stare. "But it has always been called that, Dr. Gudden."

Elizabeth did not know why she was afraid. She was nearly running, although the path to the lake was almost dark beneath the trees. There was no sound of voices on the path ahead of her. They must be far ahead—perhaps they had already reached the lake.

It didn't make any sense. The Mailgram telling her to read about Ludwig...Alban going for a walk beside the lake with Eileen's psychiatrist...and the curious coincidence. It had to be a coincidence, didn't it? Because if it weren't...Not far to the lake now. Elizabeth slowed to a walk. She mustn't make too much noise. She should have waited for the sheriff, but they would have lost valuable time in explanations and argument. Or she might have left a note with the book. Saying what?

Like someone mouthing a foreign language, she turned the encyclopedia article over in her mind.

"Ludwig II...mad king of Bavaria...attempted to be an absolute monarch in the style of Louis XIV, but several centuries too late....Because of his financial excesses and eccentric behavior, Ludwig was deposed in June 1886, and confined as a private mental patient in Berg Castle. A few days later, Ludwig and his psychiatrist were found drowned in a lake on the grounds of the estate. It is generally believed that Ludwig killed the doctor in an attempt to escape, and subsequently died of a heart attack while attempting to swim to freedom...."

And now Alban and Dr. Shepherd were walking by the lake, but—so what? Alban wasn't a prisoner. And what did it have to do with Eileen? Nothing. Eileen was dead. The reality of that had been eclipsed by other concerns: the sheriff's lumbering attempts at finding a suspect; Bill's attempts at detection; Amanda's exchange of one social event for another; and Michael's mixture of relief and fear for his own safety. Except as a puzzle to solve, no one seemed to mind that Eileen's life had ended. But everyone seemed to care who killed her. Elizabeth didn't see why it mattered so much. The person who had thrown Eileen into the boat had certainly killed her, but she had been fading out of existence for such a long time before that that the actual termination of her life seemed little more than a formality. Was that the reason that Eileen had broken the mirror? Because people had ceased to see her except as a reflection of their own needs? The family was missing an audience, a dressmaker's doll, a possession—but the personality of Eileen had slipped away long before. Elizabeth decided that she didn't want to play detective; she didn't much care about getting the right answer in the murder game; but she hurried on toward the lake because she felt that the danger was still present. Preventing a murder mattered more than solving one.

As she came to the last bend in the path, Elizabeth could hear the murmur of voices. Instinctively, she left the path and eased her way through the underbrush until she could see them clearly through a thicket of honeysuckle a few yards from the lake. To her right lay the boat dock and the grassy verge where Eileen had set her easel; about five yards to her left she could see Alban and Dr. Shepherd standing on a small spit of land in the clearing where the path ended. Beyond them the trees and the underbrush made dark patterns in the deepening twilight.

Elizabeth could just make out Alban's expression in the gray light. His eyes were narrowed, and his head was thrown back in a posture of arrogance or anger. His voice sounded different. She strained to catch fragments of the conversation.

"You are working for Lutz, aren't you?" he said harshly. "You'll tell them I'm not fit to be king!"

Carlsen Shepherd, who stood with his back to Elizabeth, spread out his arms in a cosmic shrug.

"You are part of the conspiracy! Admit it!"

Shepherd sighed wearily. "Look, Alban, are you putting me on? Because if so, I'm not laughing."

"Did you laugh when they brought me to Berg, Dr. Gudden? When they took my kingdom? And what has become of my letters to Bismarck? Did you have them destroyed?"

Shepherd took a tentative step backward. "Uh—Bismarck. Wait a minute. Letters to Bismarck, huh? Something about your kingdom? Why don't we go back to the house and talk about this, Alb—er, Ludwig?"

The false heartiness of Shepherd's reply had made Alban even angrier. He stamped his foot and shouted something, while Shepherd continued to edge away. Should she run to the house and get the sheriff? Elizabeth wondered. It would take a little over ten minutes to get there and back, not counting the time it might take to explain it all to Wesley Rountree. She had left the encyclopedia for him, though. Perhaps it would make him curious enough to follow her. She had to gamble on the fact that he'd come, because if she left, there would be no one to help Carlsen Shepherd. But if she stayed, what could she do? Elizabeth looked about her for a rock or a stick.

"I'm not going back there," Alban was saying. "So you can tell them I'm mad. I'm going to escape and get help from Bismarck or Maximilian! I will have my kingdom back!"

Shepherd looked at him. After a moment's hesitation, he began to walk toward Alban with his hands outstretched. "I don't mean you any harm," he said gently. "I think you're probably right about those guys plotting against you. I just need to ask you a few questions, though."

Alban blinked. "Questions? What questions?"

"Did you ever get mad at any young girls?"

Alban looked puzzled. "Are you speaking of Sophie?"

"Who?"

"The youngest daughter of Maximilian. We were en-

224

gaged once, but she never understood me. Still, I felt no bitterness."

"You didn't hit her over the head or anything?" prompted Shepherd.

Alban drew himself up proudly. "I am a king," he hissed. "Not a drunken peasant! If I take a life it is my divine right to do so." He bowed. "I regret that such a step has now become necessary, Herr Doctor. I am going to swim that lake to freedom, and you must be prevented from stopping me."

Elizabeth saw him lunge forward, choking off Shepherd's reply in mid-sentence. She had begun to twist at the stem of a honeysuckle branch, thinking that it might distract Alban even if it were too small to be considered a weapon. Between the two of them, they might be able to subdue him. As she tugged at the branch, she noticed a movement in the clump of bushes to the left of the lake.

"Ludwig!"

Elizabeth stared into the darkness to see who had spoken, but the woods beyond Alban were black. She could see that his hands were wrapped around Shepherd's throat, and the two of them had sunk to their knees in their struggle.

"Ludwig!" said the voice, more loudly this time.

Alban stiffened, and turned his head in the direction of the voice. Elizabeth thought he had loosened his hold on Shepherd for the moment. Now she could make out a dark shape standing against an outgrowth of shrubbery. The voice was masculine, but not familiar to her.

"Well, Ludwig, I see you are back at Schloss Berg. Will you not come to Villa Pellet?"

"Pellet?" murmured Alban. He stood up straight, releasing his hold on the doctor, who fell to the ground at the water's edge and lay still.

"Yes—to Pellet! Have you forgotten?"

"Pellet," said Alban again. He took a step toward the dark figure.

"Surely my Wotan has not forgotten his Siegfried?"

Alban put his hands to his temples as if to shut out

the voice—or the unseen noises obstructing it. "Wagner?" he said hoarsely. "Is it you, then?"

The shadow chuckled. "Of course, Your Majesty. It is I. And you have promised to listen to my plans for the new play tonight, remember?"

Alban put his face in his hands. "No! Wait! There's something..." He looked back at Shepherd's body. "Wait..."

"Your Majesty gave me his word," the voice chided.

He continued to speak in a coaxing tone while Elizabeth edged forward, wondering what she should do and trying to make sense of the scene before her.

"Come along with me now," the soothing voice urged. "Come now; come closer. It's quite chilly here by the lake."

Alban actually began to walk toward the woods. The figure, about twenty feet away from him, motioned him forward, gently encouraging him to come closer. Elizabeth was bracing herself to make a dash for Shepherd, while Alban was distracted, when she heard shouts up the path.

"Cobb! Elizabeth MacPherson! What is going on around here? Yo! Answer me somebody!"

The spell was broken. Alban's head snapped in the direction of the voice. He looked back at Shepherd's body a few feet away, and then straight at Elizabeth, who had come out of hiding in preparation for a dash to pull Shepherd to safety. Their eyes met, but in the darkness Elizabeth could not tell if he had known who she was. For an instant he stood perfectly still on the edge of the lake, and then he was gone.

"Sheriff!" she yelled. "I'm here! Hurry up!" She ran to Shepherd and knelt by his body, trying to turn him over. She glanced up at the churning water a few yards from shore and caught a glimpse of Alban's arms flailing as he made for the tangle of weeds in the middle of the lake. "Sheriff!" she wailed.

A sound from the bushes made her turn. She suddenly remembered the strange voice who had been speaking to Alban. It was still only a shadow but it was coming closer.

"Now look, Whoever-You-Are...you are *not* Richard Wagner...The sheriff will be here any second and if you come any closer he'll blow you away..."

Two more figures came snapping through the thicket. "I'm going after that son-of-a-bitch," said one of them. "See what you can do for that guy, Milo."

Elizabeth watched a tall, thin shadow dive into the lake. She sank down beside Shepherd. "Oh, shit," she murmured. "It's Bill."

The man who had emerged from the thicket with Bill was wearing a sheriff's department uniform, but it was not Rountree or his deputy; he was big enough to be both of them put together, she thought. He hurried to Shepherd and began to apply mouth-to-mouth resuscitation. The Wagner imposter took her arm and led her away.

"Are you all right?" he asked.

Elizabeth stared at him. He looked about Bill's age, with clever brown eyes and good cheekbones. "Are you Milo?" she said finally.

"Of course." He glanced back at the lake. "If you're okay, I think I'll go back and help Bill."

She heard him hit the water as the sheriff and Clay burst into the clearing. Rountree took in the scene, and walked toward her. "Are you all right?" he demanded.

"Yes."

"Then you want to tell me what's going on down here?"

Elizabeth stared out at the lake. She could just make out two swimmers circling in midlake. Two swimmers; not three.

"Alban did it," she said softly.

"Well, I knew that," drawled Rountree. "I just want to know what this stunt was all about. And what is Hill-Bear doing here? Will somebody tell me that?"

Elizabeth shook her head. She felt dizzy.

Rountree steadied her arm. "Easy, now. Clay, get

her back up to the house and call for an ambulance. I'll stay here and give these fellas a hand."

Elizabeth saw Dr. Shepherd's legs move a little, and the uniformed man bent down to say something to him; then she turned and followed Clay back to the house.

CHAPTER FIFTEEN

ELIZABETH DID NOT SEE them again until much
later, after the ambulance had come and gone, and Taylor in diving gear had retrieved the body of Alban and
a sackful of bones from the lake. Bill and Milo had
stayed in the library for over an hour talking to Rountree, Dr. Chandler, and Captain Grandfather, while
Elizabeth and Mildred had done what they could to
comfort the rest of the family.

It was nearly midnight before the meeting ended.
Dr. Chandler announced that he was going to the hospital to look in on Shepherd, and left by the front door
as Elizabeth was coming back downstairs. She saw Bill
in the hall saying good night to Wesley Rountree, and
she slipped into the kitchen to get coffee and sandwiches
to offer in exchange for an explanation of the night's
events.

A few minutes later, she brought the silver tray into
the library, where Milo was sitting at the desk making
sketches on a sheet of typing paper and Bill was looking

out the window at Alban's castle, just visible in the light of a quarter moon.

Elizabeth set down the tray on the coffee table and settled on the couch beside him. "I brought you some coffee and sandwiches," she said, talking to Milo. "Come and eat."

Milo made a few more notes before coming over to join them. Bill said nothing. His forehead, under a thatch of blond hair, was wrinkled, the way it was when he was tense or deep in concentration.

Elizabeth tried again. "I called the hospital," she announced. "Carlsen is all right, but they're keeping him overnight. I'm going to see him tomorrow. What—what did the sheriff say?"

"That we were damn fools," said Milo, smiling.

"It's over," snapped Bill. "Case closed."

"But what made you come here? How did you know?"

Bill poured himself a cup of coffee. "It was all there in your letters, Elizabeth."

"How could it have been in my letters when *I* didn't know?" Elizabeth demanded.

"I mean all the information was there; that, plus what you told me on the phone the morning after Eileen was killed. I had to put it together, though."

Elizabeth stared at him in disbelief. She turned to Milo, expecting to see the knowing grin of a fellow practical joker, but he merely nodded in agreement.

"Look," said Bill impatiently. "You told me that Eileen's painting was missing, and that she had been painting by the lake, and I wondered if the lake had any significance. With Eileen dead, the only person likely to know if the lake meant anything special to her was the psychiatrist you mentioned: Nancy Kimble. So I asked her."

"But she's in Vienna!"

"Yeah. I got her address from the med school and sent her a telegram." He fished a crumpled yellow envelope out of the pocket of his jeans and handed it to Elizabeth.

She unfolded it and read aloud. "Early in treatment, patient occasionally mentioned woman's face in lake.

Please explain query. Nancy Kimble." Elizabeth looked up. "How did you get her to tell you this?"

Milo coughed. "I believe she got the impression that we were colleagues of hers."

"You said you were doctors?" Another thought occurred to her. "But, Bill, Eileen was seeing everything in those days! Demons, visions, who knows what? How did you know this wasn't another hallucination?"

"Because Eileen was dead."

"If somebody stole the painting of the lake, and Eileen had been seeing a face in the lake, then we figured there had to have been a face in the lake for her to see," Milo explained.

"But whose?"

"Alban's fiancée, Merrileigh Williams. The one you told us had disappeared shortly before their wedding was to have taken place. I wondered if that had been arranged. Maybe she was out to marry the boss's son, and Alban changed his mind, or maybe she had been fooling around with some other man. I don't know. We found her bones, but they won't tell us why she was killed."

"A skeleton also won't tell you who it was!" snapped Elizabeth.

"Oh, yes, it will," said Milo, leaning forward eagerly. "I study that kind of thing, you know. Forensic anthropology. Mostly burial mounds and things like that, but the principle's the same. We were lucky to have recovered the entire skeleton. He wrapped her in a sack when he dumped her, which prevented the bones from scattering. That would have been tough! Anyway, the sagittal sutures indicated that we were dealing with a person approximately twenty-two years of age. Definitely female; we found the pelvic bone; and the dentition indicated—"

"Okay, okay, I believe you. You identified her from the bones."

"Well, we didn't, actually," Milo admitted. "You said a skeleton couldn't tell you who it was, so I thought I'd explain it to you. We could have done it that way, but the fact is, Dr. Chandler identified her from Eileen's painting."

"You found that, too?" gasped Elizabeth.

"Oh, sure. In the lake. In a sack with some bricks. The deputy found it close to the other sack. Apparently, Alban threw it in some time after he'd killed Eileen."

He nodded toward an object covered with a cloth on the table by the window. Elizabeth went to look at the painting. It was still damp to the touch, but because it was done in oils the colors had not run.

Eileen had painted the lake at twilight—drab green water shadowed by the gray trees surrounding the lake. In the foreground, the shallows, a woman's face floated just below the surface of the water. Her eyes were closed, and her hair streamed out in the water like weeds.

"She must have pictured it over and over in her mind to get so good a likeness," said Bill softly.

Elizabeth shivered.

"We think she must have actually seen the face in the water six years ago, when Alban first dumped the body there. He had probably gone back for the sack and something to weight it down. It's a miracle he didn't catch her then."

"But why didn't she say anything about it?"

"Who'd believe her? She was already beginning to lose touch with reality. She really did have schizophrenia, you know. Even if she told somebody, they would have written it off as another delusion. Later, when she began to get well, she didn't even believe it herself. In fact, I think she had succeeded in forgetting about it completely, until she started that painting down by the lake. Staring at the lake hour after hour began to revive the memory of the face in the water. She painted it because she saw it—in her mind."

"Is that the reason she wouldn't show anyone the picture?"

"Sure. Do you blame her? One year out of a mental institution, still in analysis—how's she going to tell anybody she sees a dead face in the lake? She was terrified that she'd be locked up again. And even more terrified that she deserved to be."

"And of losing Michael," Elizabeth murmured.

"Yes, that, too," agreed Bill.

"Where is Michael, anyway?" asked Elizabeth, noticing his absence for the first time.

Milo grinned. "When he found out the case was over, he got Deputy Melkerson to take him to the bus station in the squad car. I think that other deputy loaned him five bucks for the ticket."

"Why did she paint it, though?" asked Elizabeth. "Why didn't she just paint over the face and show everyone a nice landscape?"

"I don't know," said Bill. "Milo thinks she was trying to exorcise her own demon by putting it on canvas, but I think that deep down she knew that it had been real, and she was trying to let somebody know about it. Unfortunately, the one who caught sight of it was Alban. Do you know when?"

"I think so," Elizabeth said. "He went down to the lake to get her once when she was late for dinner. He must have got a glimpse of it before she packed it up."

"And he thought she knew. Of course! If that painting ever went on display at the wedding, people would recognize Merrileigh's face. They might get curious enough to drag the lake," said Milo.

Elizabeth considered this. "I don't know," she said. "I think they may have suspected. Captain Grandfather kept saying that he didn't want the murderer caught. And I remember hearing that Aunt Louisa had wanted to hire a detective to find Merrileigh when she first disappeared, and then she suddenly stopped insisting on it."

"But they didn't know for sure," said Bill. "Didn't want to know. This painting would have forced them to face the unpleasant facts."

"Did he mean to kill her?"

"I don't know. I think so. She might have described the painting to someone. Or painted it all over again. And he couldn't afford to have people getting interested in the lake. It was either the shock of this second murder or the fear of discovery that sent him over the edge."

"But he'd already committed a murder. He must have been afraid of discovery."

"Sure," said Milo. "Six years ago. But he got away with it. Merrileigh was hardly missed; nobody suspected him; and gradually it got pushed to the back of his mind. It wasn't relevant anymore. He'd gone on with his life, built his dream house, and suddenly—when he'd almost forgotten it—the terror of discovery hits him when he isn't prepared for it. And he couldn't deal with it."

"You sound sorry for him," said Elizabeth wonderingly.

"Well, I am for that part," Milo admitted. "It wouldn't be so bad to get arrested for murder while you're still standing there holding the gun, so to speak. You're expecting it then. But to go on with your life, to let years pass, until you can't even remember the emotions that caused you to do it, and *then* to get caught for it, and have your life wrecked—that's a nightmare."

"He seemed so normal."

"I think he worked at it," said Bill. "He even made that castle sound plausible, didn't he?"

"Where does Ludwig fit into all this?"

"He always admired Ludwig, even before, and I think it was a retreat for him. When he discovered that he might be a murder suspect, he decided to be somebody else. I got suspicious when you told me on the phone that you were his favorite cousin, since we hardly knew him."

"Not flattering," said Elizabeth, wrinkling her nose.

"I was right, though. When I looked up Ludwig, the book said that his favorite relative was his cousin, the Empress Elizabeth of Austria."

"And did she have a brother named Bill?"

"No. Theodore. But when I read that Ludwig had died in a lake after strangling a psychiatrist, and then you told me that a psychiatrist was staying here, I thought I'd better come down."

"Couldn't you have called the sheriff?" asked Elizabeth drily.

Bill smiled. "Actually, we did stop by the office on

the way in. Rountree wasn't there, but one of his deputies—some guy named Hill-Bear Melkerson—agreed to come along with us in case there was trouble. Milo and I had worked out that Wagner thing in case he tried to reenact the death scene by the lake."

"And the deputy went along with it?"

"A lot easier than Rountree would've," said Milo.

"Turns out Rountree had the painting business figured out, and he was going to wait until he'd dragged the lake for the evidence to make an arrest. Of course, he didn't know that he had Ludwig of Bavaria to contend with, so it was a good thing we staked out the lake."

"You could have stopped by the house first."

"I thought I'd better guard the lake. And besides, that explanation might have been too much for Rountree. I figured him for a backwoods country sheriff, and I thought he might have locked *me* up!"

"Did you really think you could talk Alban out of a murder by posing as Richard Wagner?"

Milo blushed. "Not exactly. But I did have Bill and the deputy in the bushes in case there was trouble. I thought we could listen long enough to get the evidence we needed, and then distract him with the Wagner impersonation so that Bill and Melkerson could tackle him."

"It would've worked, too, if you all hadn't come charging in. It was the Mailgram, I guess. But you were beginning to sound too interested in Alban, so I had to take the chance and warn you, before *you* started taking strolls by the lake."

Elizabeth shook her head. "You're both crazy."

"Though this be madness, yet there's method in it," said Geoffrey from the doorway.

Bill stiffened in his chair, without turning around. "Hello, Geoffrey," he said evenly.

"'Hail fellow, well-met, All dirty and wet!'—Swift. But I see you've dried out now. Are you staying for further melodrama? I'm afraid there may be reporters on the way."

Bill got up slowly and stared into Geoffrey's mocking

235

face. Finally he said: "'Go hang yourselves all. You are idle shallow things. I am not of your element.'—*Twelfth Night*."

Geoffrey bowed. "I am silenced."

ABOUT THE AUTHOR

SHARYN McCRUMB is an award-winning crime novelist and short story writer. Her first mystery featuring Elizabeth MacPherson was SICK OF SHADOWS; that novel was followed by LOVELY IN HER BONES (named "the outstanding work of fiction for 1985" by the Appalachian Writers Association); HIGHLAND LADDIE GONE; PAYING THE PIPER; and THE WINDSOR KNOT. Ms. McCrumb also wrote the Edgar Award-winning comic whodunit, BIMBOS OF THE DEATH SUN. Her short fiction has been published in *Crescent Review, Appalachian Heritage, Central Appalachian Review, Harvest from the Hills, Ellery Queen's Mystery Magazine,* and the Ballantine Books anthology, MR. PRESIDENT, PRIVATE EYE.